D0829439

**Love Me
If You Must**

Love Me If You Must

A PATRICIA AMBLE MYSTERY

Nicole Young

Revell

Grand Rapids, Michigan

Published by Fleming H. Revell
a division of Baker Publishing Group
P.O. Box 6287, Grand Rapids, MI 49516-6287
www.revellbooks.com

Printed in the United States of America

Library of Congress Cataloging-in-Publication Data
Young, Nicole, 1967–
    Love me if you must / Nicole Young.
        p.   cm. — (Patricia Amble mystery ; bk. 1)
    ISBN 10: 0-8007-3157-3 (pbk.)
    ISBN 978-0-8007-3157-1 (pbk.)
    1. Title
    PS3625.0968L68 2007
    813'.6—dc22   2006037465

Published in association with the literary agency of Janet Kobobel Grant, Books & Such, 4788 Carissa Ave., Santa Rosa, CA 95405.

In memory of:

Anne C. O'Donnell, Best Friends Forever

and

Doug Fix, Escanaba High School Creative Writing
Teacher, who asked in the margin of my 11th grade
journal, "Do you really believe that?" and set in
motion a spiritual journey that continues today.

1

Old and ugly. And that was being kind. The sprawling Victorian looked like something straight out of a gothic thriller, creepy and broken, looming on the corner of Main and Railroad. Leave it to me to move into the one house in town that could pass for haunted.

The wraparound porch had lost chunks of fieldstone, the balcony above had a distinct sag, and the ancient cupola was ready to lose more than just a few pieces of wood siding. A gnarled catalpa tree, sans leaves, lurked in the side yard, adding to the spookhouse effect. And to think it was only three o'clock in the afternoon.

I paused at the curb, hoping I hadn't made a colossal mistake.

"Patricia Louise Amble," I said aloud to myself, mimicking the voice of my grandmother. "If you're smart, you'll charge admission when the trick-or-treaters come around next week."

Heaven knew I'd have to come up with something to offset the expense of fixing this place, at least until I could sell it.

Looking at the vacant windows and peeling paint was like looking in a mirror. Turmoil inside. Neglect outside. Doctors would have some fancy label to explain the whole warped line of thinking that led up to the purchase of the Victorian. Post-traumatic delirium, or some such thing.

But there's hope. Always hope. If not for me, then for the building I'd taken on as my latest Bring It Back to Life project.

I ran my fingers through hair long overdue for a cut and color and started up the crumbling sidewalk toward skewed front steps. Beginning today, the inhospitable abode would be home for one, maybe two years, depending on how stubborn the once proud painted lady decided to be.

I balanced the bag of munchies I'd bought on the way into town on one hip and reached for the storm door. The hinges let out a squeal that set my teeth on edge. Its '70s metal scrollwork confirmed that a human being had actually cared for this home sometime in the previous century, at least enough to add some weather protection.

Of course, that hadn't been the only improvement or I would never have considered the property. When I looked through it in July, the prior owners had already gotten a good start toward renovation, beginning with repairs to a leaky foundation and the addition of a second bathroom upstairs. Then a bitter divorce stopped their progress cold.

I dug around in the pocket of my denim jacket for the house key. I couldn't help but shake my head at the memory of the seller's attorney changing the closing date yet again.

"Sorry, my client's wife can't be located to sign over her half."

Probably in Mexico spending the last of the joint savings account, I figured, when the man had appeared alone at the closing, with quitclaim deed in hand.

I found the key, inserted it, and gave a half twist. The tumblers screeched. I pushed open the heavy oak door and breathed in the scent of my new home—a light, spicy odor of wood rot combined with half-starved carpet mites.

I had to smile at the thought of all the six-legged microscopic critters writhing in protest as they took their last magic carpet ride out the front door. Every stitch of polyester and olefin fiber would be replaced with good old-fashioned, hypoallergenic hardwood flooring. Today's buyers loved the open, clean look of real wood. They'd even pay extra for it.

Yep. This place would take a lot of hard work and a good chunk of change to bring up to snuff, but I guessed by the time I was finished, I'd pocket close to double my investment at the sale. Everything I'd read supported my theory of Rawlings, Michigan, becoming the newest fashionable Detroit suburb. It was the next stop along I-75 past Clarkston, and look what had happened to *that* burg. Homeowners were commanding top dollar for their properties, with nowhere for the prosperity to head but north.

"Let's get you into a new millennium, old gal." I patted the doorframe, sure the lady wouldn't disappoint.

I stepped over the threshold into gloom and silence. The storm door slammed behind me, shaking the four-by-four entryway with its clattering crash. I jumped, nearly donating my turkey croissant and side salad to the ever-greedy rug bugs. I clenched the paper bag containing my only calories 'til morning to my chest and took a few deep breaths to steady my heart. If I were going to survive alone in this creepy place, I'd have to change my reading material from gothic nightmare à la the Brontë sisters, to something a little less terrifying.

"Hello," came a deep voice from behind me.

I whirled and screamed at the sight of a man's face pressed close to the glass of the storm door. My supper went flying, landing in a heap against the baseboard.

I flung a hand to my chest. Good grief, I had nearly pelted my first visitor with chunks of lettuce. After a moment, the pounding of my heart calmed to a dull thud in my ears. For lack of words, I bent down to retrieve the salad greens and salvage what remained of my sandwich.

"Sorry. Could I help?" the man asked.

A British accent. How quaint.

I blew the bangs out of my eyes and looked up through the murky glass. If I lived closer to Detroit, there was no way I'd let a stranger in the door. But this was Rawlings. Even through the buildup of water spots and dirt, I could see he looked nice enough. Handsome, too, with a proud, straight nose and squarish jaw. Judging by his clothes, he was only here to drop off an end-of-the-world tract, anyway.

Besides, I'd learned a thing or two about self-defense

10

in my thirty-two years. He'd never get past the inner door of the vestibule without a fight.

"Sure. Come on in." I resumed my task.

The storm door squeaked and his oxfords came into view, bringing with them the smell of new leather. His long-fingered hands fumbled along with mine at the tiny pieces of carrot and cucumber embedded in the inch-high shag.

He grabbed for the cherry tomato at the same time I did. Our skin touched, and I felt my face flush as red as the fruit caught between us. I heard a high-pitched teen-aged titter.

Was that me? I gasped and stood up, banging my forehead against his in my rush to put a safe distance between us—an impossible task in the tiny entry.

"I am so sorry." Somehow, my hand ended up in his light brown hair, rubbing his scalp like he was a three-year-old with a boo-boo.

Oh, my. I jerked back and stuck my fingers in my own protein-deprived disaster.

Get a grip, Tish. Tish was the name my mother had called me. I'd always preferred it to the usual variations of my name.

"Do you always greet the neighbors with a pat on the head?" the stranger asked, rising. His blue eyes smiled at me, and suddenly I felt less like a complete idiot.

"Neighbor?" The gloom of my two-year sentence in Rawlings lifted.

"David Ramsey. Two doors over in the Greek Revival."

His house was my favorite in Rawlings. The thing had been restored to its former grandeur. It stuck out in the

11

neighborhood like a diamond among lumps of coal. From my perspective as an investor, the renovation had gone over and beyond what Mr. Ramsey would ever recover upon sale. The rest of the homes in the area just didn't support the extravagance of the project. But once my Victorian jumped on the restoration bandwagon, every home in a three-block stretch would gain value.

I weighed the idea of asking David Ramsey in beyond the vestibule. It would be neighborly of me, and it couldn't hurt to get off to a good start. The guy didn't have fangs, after all.

"Would you like to come in a minute?" The words rushed out before I could stop them.

He gave a nod. "I haven't been inside this house for some time. I'm curious to know what you have planned for the place."

That accent again. I refused to swoon.

I opened the inner door and led him through the parlor, past the tiger-oak fireplace. I couldn't wait to take a bottle of wood restorer to its carved pillars. The front stairs twirling off to one side would get the same treatment.

I trekked through the dining room, doing my best to be hospitable. "I'd offer you something to eat, but I'm afraid you'd remember where it's been. And the only thing to drink is water from the faucet. Are you up for a little arsenic poisoning?"

I set the paper bag on the kitchen counter and turned to face my guest.

"You're thinking of the township wells," he said, leaning against the refrigerator as if he belonged there. "The village water tests pretty good, actually."

"I'm not taking any chances. I think I'll stick to my Evian."

I pulled a bottle out of the bag and twisted off the cap. I'd already ordered the oversize jugs of water and accompanying dispenser that would help cut down on throwaways. I didn't splurge too many places, but fresh water was nonnegotiable.

I offered my guest the first sip.

"No, no. Really. I just came over to introduce myself."

His accent had me captivated. As did his khaki slacks and burgundy sweater. I wondered if the cashmere was as soft as it looked. My palm itched, but I controlled the urge to find out.

I sighed. Here was the kind of distinguished guy I'd pegged for myself lo those many years ago when life had been ahead of me instead of down the drain. The kind of guy I'd hoped to meet in college and one day marry.

"Don't tell me," I ventured, "you're an engineer."

He smiled and scratched the back of his head, seemingly shy. "Close. Computers, actually."

I set my water on the counter and reached for his hand. "Tish Amble."

"Nice to meet you." He glanced around. "Will your moving van be arriving soon?"

"Moving van? No. I always rent my furniture. Never made sense to buy a set and then not have it match the next house."

At his look of puzzlement, I explained. "Houses are my living. I fix them up and sell them. There's usually enough money left after I pay off the contractors to put

13

a little food on the table, then do the whole thing over again."

His eyes roved the kitchen. I followed his gaze to the bank of floor-to-ceiling cupboards against one wall. The built-ins were one of my favorite features, though they made the room too small for today's families.

"So, what are your plans?" David asked, turning to look at me.

I forced myself not to stare at the fullness of those British lips. "Well, I'd like to put a rec room in the basement, I'm thinking about bumping this wall out to make more space in the kitchen, I want to link the library and drawing room to make a master bedroom suite, and upstairs there's just a whole lot of ugly that needs a facelift."

He broke into a charming grin. "Well, watch you don't disturb the ghosts."

Ghosts? Was he serious?

I'd hoped to get a good night's sleep after my grueling day, and probably would have before he mentioned ghosts.

I chewed my lip. I couldn't blame any loss of sleep on David. I'd always known it was only a matter of time before the ghouls that lay in wait came to do their haunting.

2

There are no such things as ghosts, I singsonged in my mind a little while later as I climbed the back stairs from the kitchen to the second story. The dashing David had stayed only a few minutes, but his off-the-cuff comment had stuck to my brain like ectoplasmic slime. Only the British could talk about ghosts as casually as they would a visiting relative.

I paused under the light of a dim bulb to assess the work ahead. The narrow staircase would need fresh wallpaper in a neutral design. The foil-flower look had to go. And the creaking steps could use a few more screws to hold down the noise. After I stripped the old finish and gave the wood a good sanding, I'd add a fresh coat of polyurethane and the passage would be good as new.

I reached the top and faced the long run of hallway that made a left-hand turn up ahead, then emptied onto the front stairs. Each open doorway looked suspiciously like a jack-in-the-box, with a surprise waiting to pounce out of the blackness beyond the threshold.

I gave a quick look down the back stairs to be sure no one followed, then launched ahead, disgusted with myself for feeling so afraid when I knew I was alone in the house. And, please, if someone had followed me up the back stairs, wouldn't I have heard every creaking step?

Unless that person was a ghost.

"Tish, stop it!" I growled at myself in the silence. "No such thing as ghosts. No such thing as ghosts."

I pressed my back against the uneven plaster of the hallway, praying for calm even as my racing blood threatened to burst vessels.

"Please take away my fear," I whispered. It wasn't too much to ask, was it, that after all these years I quit expecting the ghost of my grandmother to reach through the wall and choke the breath from me?

At the thought, I leapt across the hallway, hands to my throat. I looked back at the place I had just stood. No ghostly arms. No stranglehold. Only dust from a crack drifting to the floor where I had disturbed the air with my display of faithlessness.

I dropped to my knees on the worn carpet runner and buried my head in my arms, hoping to blot out the guilt. I took a deep breath to calm myself and ended up hacking on dust mites.

With a sniffle, I lifted my head and called out to the ceiling, "I won't go back there."

I wiped the tears defiantly from my cheeks and stood up. If I couldn't hold it together better than this, I'd better sell the place now before I went stark-raving mad.

Maybe I should have taken some time to relax in Cancun, like Jan Hershel, the unaccounted-for wife of the previous owner, surely was. I could be soaking in rays of sunshine right now instead of inhaling dirt and fending off nonexistent spooks.

One week would do the trick.

I pulled at my hair to get the temptation out of my mind.

I couldn't abandon my goal even for a moment. How long would this house stay standing without my loving touch? Who else would spend the time and money to restore it to its former youth and beauty?

Besides, I'd forked over a generous down payment, with just enough set aside to live on while I made improvements. I couldn't afford to be afraid.

I squared my shoulders and poked my head into the rear bedroom. Paint, updated flooring, and new windows were pretty much all it would need. Satisfied, I continued my tour. I pulled out a pocket notebook and a golf pencil I'd found in a parking lot to note minor details along the way.

Sometime later, I caught myself squinting to see the pad and realized the day's halfhearted sunshine had faded to dusk. Task complete, I flicked a switch to light up the front stairs and made my way back to the kitchen.

Hunger hit at the smell of room-temperature salad that had managed to permeate the air during my two-hour foray upstairs. In my freak-out over the Brit's mention of ghosts, I had forgotten to put my supper in the fridge. I ran to the bag sitting on the counter and stuck in my nose. A fly, annoyed with my intrusion on its private feast, buzzed past my cheek toward the light over the sink. My stomach gave a gurgle of complaint. I crumpled the bag.

Well, it wouldn't be my first night going to bed hungry.

Thinking of bed reminded me that I had yet to bring in my suitcase, cot, and sleeping bag. One quick trip to the car should do it.

I bounded out the front door and down the steps. I slowed at the feel of the uneven sidewalk beneath me, and picked my way carefully across the shadows. The streetlight directly in front of the house sent a pale glow over the hardtop of my inherited classic auto—a teal '66 Buick Electra 225 Coupe that had been Grandma's pride and joy.

The chill of the October night raised goose bumps on my arms. I glanced up to enjoy the sight of a quarter moon shining through the uppermost branches of the maple across the street. I sent a silent chorus of thanksgiving heavenward, grateful for the celestial night-light. I thought back to the years I'd endured with no glimpse of the moon at all. But that time was past. I'd regained my right to moon-gaze if I wanted.

A movement caught my eye. I squinted toward the white-sided house hidden beneath the maple. A downstairs curtain fell back into place.

The Neighborhood Watch must be on duty. Every small town could boast of those nosy, yet essential, residents. It seemed in Rawlings at least, my watchdog was located directly across the street. I hoped the person wasn't *too* curious. I intended only to do my work, then move on. There was no time to answer questions, head off rumors, or get involved in neighborhood affairs.

At the corner, a pair of headlights bounced across

the railroad tracks that split the sleepy village down the middle. The vehicle narrowly missed the back end of Granny's "Deucey," as she'd fondly called her beloved Electra.

I gulped. One scratch on Deucey, and Grandma was sure to haunt me to the grave. Wisdom dictated that I pull the vehicle around back.

I sank into the cold vinyl of the front seat and dreamed of the day I'd be brave enough to trade this lowrider in for an SUV. I wheeled down the driveway I shared with the house next door and parked in front of my very own two-car detached garage. I'd check tomorrow to see if a garage door opener had been installed or if I'd have to add that major perk to my list of must-haves.

The slam of my car door echoed through the stillness. I headed around to Deucey's cavernous trunk and started to unload the essentials. In the distance came the pleasant sound of a train whistle.

I sighed in contentment. Certainly I'd made the right decision moving to Rawlings. I broke into a song, keeping the volume beneath my usual bellow, so as not to become a plague to the neighbors.

Things couldn't be more perfect. I could almost smell the ink on the bank check . . . almost see the smile on the nice thirty-something mommy's face as I congratulated her on a charming new home.

Then I'd take that week in Cancun. Or maybe a month.

A rustle of leaves sounded in the blackness beyond the garage.

"Who's there?" I called, tensing.

19

"Your neighbor in the yellow house around the corner. Hi." The sound of the gentle masculine voice helped me locate its owner among the shadows near the picket fence marking my rear property line.

The neighbors sure were friendly around here. This was my second greeting of the day. The last town I'd lived in, only the children had a smile for me. The grown-ups all looked the other way when they saw me coming. News of my past had somehow made the circuit even before I'd moved in. Must have been that prying realtor who'd somehow managed to finagle every detail out of me, all while selling me the wreck she'd called "an absolute *doll*house." Of course, I had forgiven the gossip-hound the moment I'd pocketed the fifty thousand from the sale of that property.

"Hi there." I prodded my way through crunching leaves toward the form.

"Careful. The ground's uneven."

And such *caring* neighbors. If these people got any more polite, I might actually consider settling down here.

At the fence, I held out my hand to the stranger. "If you're the neighbor in the yellow house, then I'm the one in the haunted house."

I liked how the man's face got all crinkly when he smiled, the creases deepened from shadows cast by far-off streetlights. He seemed to be a few years older than me, thirty-five to forty-ish, in my estimation. Not hand-some really, just easy to look at.

He took my hand in return. At the warmth of his skin, I realized I'd been shivering. I pulled my fingers away and rubbed my upper arms.

"Cold tonight," I said.

"Here, put my coat on." Without waiting for my consent, he took off his jacket and leaned over the fence to wrap it around my shoulders. His body heat still emanated from the fabric as I pulled it close.

The chill disappeared immediately. I meant to thank him, but a noise, growing louder by the moment, held me in frozen bewilderment. The approaching rumble shook the earth under my feet. Even the fence vibrated. Suddenly a head-splitting shriek cut through the air.

Wooooo! Woo-woo! Wooooooo!

The blast of the train whistle sent my hands flying to cover my ears. I stared across the yard in horror as three engines and at least a million freight cars vibrated their way through my once-quiet neighborhood.

My stupidity was drilled into me with each deafening lurch of metal grinding metal. I hadn't dared ask the real estate agent if the train tracks were still active. What if she'd said yes? Then I would have had to walk away from the deal of the century. But, come on, did they even use trains anymore?

"Welcome to Rawlings," my new neighbor shouted over the din.

I gave him a weak smile. No sense trying to answer until the calamity passed. A flashing light marked the last car. I watched as it disappeared from sight.

"Tell me that only happens once a month," I said, wrapping the leather of his jacket more tightly about my shoulders now that both hands were free again.

"I wish I could say the thing only came through once a day, but—" he sighed—"once an hour is more accurate."

21

I straightened, indignant. "Once an hour! I've been here since three p.m. and this is the first I knew that Rawlings had trains!"

"It all averages out," he said with a shrug. "By the way"—he reached over the fence and touched my hand again—"I'm Brad Walters. Officer Brad, the kids call me."

My hand turned clammy in his. "Officer? As in police officer?"

"That's right. One dedicated boy in blue at your service."

I was sure his smile was meant to charm, but I could only see the leers that had spread viciously across the faces of other wearers of blue. Officer Brad's gentle voice, asking me if I'd like some tomatoes he'd gleaned from the garden before the freeze, was masked by the cruel memory of clubs raking across bars.

I pulled away from him and mumbled a good night as I headed toward the back porch.

"Wait!" came his voice from behind me.

I stopped, breathing deeply to collect myself.

I turned to face him.

"My jacket," he said, smiling. "I need it for my shift."

I wore his uniform. I whipped the leather off my shoulders and carried it back to him, dangling it between two fingers like used facial tissue.

The officer's hand wrapped my wrist as he collected his pilfered coat.

"You never told me your name." He said it softly, like a guy might say, "Have I ever told you how much I love you?"

I could only stare at him, asking myself why I was still

standing there by the fence, letting him touch me . . .
asking myself what it might be like if he leaned over and
kissed me with those lips that weren't all that handsome
but housed the kindest voice.

"I've got to run." I sprinted toward my house, glad to
have escaped before I blurted out my name, giving the
officer the two words that, when entered into his police
computer, would once again make me the outcast of the
neighborhood.

I double-bolted the kitchen door, then leaned against the
scorched countertop and put my head in my hands.

He had no right to my past. I wasn't a sex offender with
an obligation to announce my crime to the community
every time I moved. My past was private.

And I intended that it stay that way.

3

Daylight poured through the windows of the six-sided drawing room, the one I'd chosen for the new master suite. I groaned and rolled to my elbow on the narrow cot. My travel clock said nearly nine. I could kick myself for thinking that sleeping in was possible without blackout shades to cover the array of double-hungs.

I rubbed the sleep from my eyes, though I could swear I hadn't gotten a wink. After reading past midnight, I'd fallen into a fitful slumber punctuated by train whistles that seemed to blend into one all-night-long peal.

At the thought of the train, my meeting with Officer Brad splashed over my mind like a bucket of cold water, bringing me to immediate wakefulness.

I sat up. I hadn't wanted to start out with stares of accusation right off the bat. I'd rather enjoyed my encounter with David Ramsey and had hoped to keep a low profile, at least until I found out if David was available. I hadn't been in a relationship since college. I figured I could handle one by now. And David Ramsey, with his ring finger bare of gold, made a possible candidate. But one wrong word from Brad Walters could put the kibosh on that in a hurry.

I tweaked my split ends. What chance did I stand with a hunk like David anyway? I'd have more luck with the boy in blue, even with my record. But honestly, Brad Walters could be available 'til the moon turned to cheese. I wasn't about to get involved with a police officer. I had run for my life to escape his prying last night, only to sneak back outside later to retrieve my forgotten gear. The last thing I needed was a table for two at the local restaurant, with Sherlock Holmes in the seat across from me.

I faced facts. Whether I liked it or not, my love life would remain as barren in Rawlings as it had in Walled Lake, Pontiac, and Rochester. But that didn't give me permission to lie around and get depressed.

I jumped up and did my morning stretches, giving the neighborhood watchdog quite a show in my T-shirt and spandex shorts. The woman was in her front yard, bundled in one of those fat, quilted coats. She appeared to be minding her own business as she cut back her rosebushes for the season. Yet, every so often, she'd toss her gray hair in my direction.

Spy.

Let her have her thrills. I reached toward the ceiling, then touched the floor. I wasn't about to start caring what the neighbors thought—except for one.

Five minutes later, I gave a final stretch. I checked out my reflection in one of the far windows. Tall, slim, and toned.

Mm-hmm. I still had it.

I took a few cleansing breaths. The contractors would be here at ten, and I still needed to shower and find some food to stuff into the hole that had formed in the lining of my stomach.

I rifled through my backpack and picked out my supplies: two-in-one shampoo, a bar of Dial, and a razor. The double-bladed Daisy with lubricating strip was a privilege I didn't take lightly. I probably had the smoothest legs in the state.

I headed to the bath off the kitchen. Twenty minutes later, I ran a brush through my snarls, then pulled on blue jeans and a turtleneck. I tied my sneakers, flung on my denim coat, and covered my still-wet hairdo with a floppy knit hat that Grandma had given me when I'd been a freshman in college. I'd hated the flashy pink thing back then and had pitched it in the back of my closet. But now, I treasured it. Grandma had made it with her own hands.

I locked the front door and started up the street toward the quaint business district that made Rawlings seem like the set from a '20s mobster movie. The crisp morning air was invigorating. All the phantoms from the previous night disappeared into cool autumn sunshine. I paused at the railroad tracks, determined not to let one of the numerous Midnight Specials that had flown past last night flatten me this morning.

All clear.

I angled kitty-corner over to Independence Alley and the Whistle Stop Coffee Shop. I'd seen the local coffeehouse on my first trip to town and spent many an hour plotting leisurely morning walks over to its irresistible row of carafes marked Hazelnut, Vanilla Nut, Amaretto, Irish Cream, Chocolate Raspberry . . . Its convenient locale was probably the determining factor for the purchase of my big old haunted mansion.

I smiled at the server behind the cash register, a girl of about eighteen whose hair matched the mahogany of the counter.

I consciously avoided staring at all the face jewelry. "I'd like a tall café mocha with extra whipped cream, please."

The girl looked at me over her nose pearl, with a long, sweeping gaze that had my dream of a quick cup of java melting like a marshmallow in boiling water. I tried not to breathe any more of the robust coffee scent than absolutely necessary. A caffeine headache already prodded my temples, no doubt aggravated by the delay.

The teen's eyebrow ring gave a tilt. "You totally look like someone who used to live around here."

Yeah, that's me. Generic face.

"I just moved in," I said. "Maybe it's the hat that's familiar." I gave the brim a jaunty slant. "It's me, Ilsa Lund."

The girl's lip curled in ignorance.

"From *Casablanca*," I said.

The clerk's eyes glazed.

"It's an old movie." That was one thing I had been grateful for over the years. I'd gotten to see the classics, something of which the younger generation was obviously deprived.

I waved it off. "Never mind. I think I'll have a cinnamon roll too. That big one in front will be perfect."

I pointed through the glass of the display case. The

girl wrapped the pastry in paper and handed it to me, then got busy at the coffee machine.

While I waited, I looked out the window and took a bite of the aromatic roll. The sugar melted on my tongue, nearly sending my mouth into spasms from the sudden onset of food.

Rawlings was about as perfect a town as I could imagine. Cobblestones paved the one-block length of Independence Alley. Near the corner, the stones made a Liberty Bell pattern with the numbers 1776 beneath, welcoming visitors to the one-way street. Across from the coffee shop was Clothing Junction. Sweaters with Halloween designs hung like scarecrows in the window. Next to it was Heavenly Scents, then Fashion Depot and Victoria's Sweet Shop. Pumpkins, bales of straw, and stalks of corn decorated the street all the way to the door of the historic Rawlings Hotel at the far end.

"Here's your coffee." The tapping of fingernails on wood accompanied the words.

I turned and gave the girl my biggest smile. "Thanks. Have a great day." I left a big tip, hoping that my next visit would merit top-notch service.

As I walked down Main Street, I could see a burgundy truck pulling into my driveway, the words LLOYD & SONS etched in white on the side.

I quickened my pace, shoveling down bits of roll in between sips of coffee. I loved a contractor who was early. The project had a chance of getting done on schedule if the pattern held.

"Here I am," I called, waving as I cut across both street and tracks. I'd just landed my foot on the corner of my lawn when the high-pitched squeal of a police siren sounded behind me.

I froze. The cinnamon roll and coffee I'd been savoring suddenly lodged in my throat.

Bleep. Bleep. The siren persisted.

I turned slowly, crushing my eyes shut, not wanting to believe it possible I could be detained for jaywalking.

I opened them.

A silver and blue police cruiser angled to a stop against the curb. The driver's side door opened. Officer Brad got out and flicked me a wave over the top of the vehicle. I tried to shrink inside myself. My eyes dropped to the sidewalk at his approach.

Never look a uniform in the eye. Be submissive. Don't smart off. The lessons that had served me well over the years were second nature to me now. I dropped my hands to my sides. The coffee cup dangled between two fingers. The last bite of cinnamon roll plunked to the ground.

"Hello, Miss Amble." In front of me, shiny leather boots glinted in the morning sunshine.

My nostrils flared and I diverted my gaze to a patch of grass growing over the concrete.

So. He'd already looked me up in the computer. Already knew my name. My crime. The number of days I'd served penance.

My jaw clenched. I held back the smart comments begging to burst out.

He leaned toward me as if trying to catch my eye. I gave him a broader view of my cheek and ear instead.

He cleared his throat. "I enjoyed talking to you last

night, and I wondered if you might be interested in grabbing a bite to eat with me after work. You know, a welcome-to-the-neighborhood kind of thing."

The wind kicked up a swirl of leaves. A curly gold one settled on my crosstrainer. I tipped my foot and shook it off.

"How about the Rawlings Hotel?" he said. "The beef Wellington is tremendous."

I looked sideways at the bare branches of the maple standing between me and the tracks. As much as I would love to taste the cuisine at the gourmet restaurant, Officer Brad was probably just hoping to use me for the subject of some evening-class dissertation. I could hear the questions now. "So, Miss Amble, why did you do it? What was going through your head while you administered the lethal dose? What, if anything, did you learn from your rehabilitation? How can you live with yourself today, knowing what you've done?"

My adrenaline had soared with the first blare of the police siren. Now, I was too keyed up to rein in my anger. I met his eyes and jabbed one finger toward his shirt.

"Listen, Officer Brad"—I spat his name—"if you come near me again, I'll have a restraining order slapped on you so fast your hat will spin. And if you breathe one word of my past to anyone—ANYONE—you'll find yourself in a civil suit that'll last 'til Judgment Day. Are we clear about that?"

"Perfectly." His lip twitched. "So if you don't want to do dinner tonight, how about church on Sunday?"

My jaw locked open. How dare he mock me? I wasn't

about to parade my list of sins in front of good, God-fearing people.

He tipped his cap. "Well, if you change your mind, I'll be at the one up on Rawlings Road. Service is at ten."

He walked back to the cruiser.

I started to turn toward my house, but stopped as my gaze landed on the neighborhood spy. The woman stood beside an island of leaves in a sea of grass. She held my stare, rake pointed skyward. I bristled. The woman didn't even try to pretend she hadn't witnessed the scene with Officer Brad. I could only pray the words had disappeared in the breeze.

A melancholy crept through my mind, turning high hopes into black goo. I clenched my fist. The lid popped off the Styrofoam coffee cup and blew away. I supposed I'd get ticketed for littering next.

So what. Let Brad Walters gossip to the world. With any luck, I'd finish this project and shake the dust of Rawlings off my feet by spring.

4

The pungent odor of a thriving mildew colony met me as I led the contractor and his two assistants into the basement.

"Careful. These things were made for a size 5 shoe," I said, turning sideways on the steps to keep my footing.

Bare bulbs, scattered about the seven-foot-high ceiling, cast a dim glow on stone walls. The cement floor, a novelty in a turn-of-the-century home, had mostly turned to dirt over the years. Only a narrow slash of concrete around the perimeter shone a bright white, the results of a recent attempt at waterproofing. The way the realtor explained it, workers jackhammered a twelve-inch-wide ditch around the edges, buried porous drain pipes, and tied the whole thing into a sump pump. Any water trying to seep into the basement from the water table below would be safely diverted.

I unfurled the floor plan I had sketched, and hunkered under a lightbulb with Lloyd. His two cronies wandered over to the area containing the furnace and hot water heater. I pointed at the drawing with one

32

hand and gestured with the other as I described my intentions.

"We'll make that section the mechanical room, with a door at one end. Next to it, we'll put a smaller room for storage. The rest will be open. Just drywall, a barely dropped ceiling, and yards of carpet."

I turned toward the staircase and frowned. In a corner behind the steps, a half circle of fieldstone rose almost five feet from the floor, forming a cistern. In the old days, it had been a reservoir for collecting rainwater. But I had no use for the thing in my new rec room.

I walked over to it and put one hand on the cool stone. "How do you plan to get rid of this baby?"

Lloyd scratched his pure white head of hair and hunched his six-foot-something frame over to the cistern. He kicked at it with his bulky work boot. The reinforced steel toe made a hollow *thunk* against the stone. A pebble-sized piece of grout bounced to the floor.

He shook his head and looked around the cellar. "You're already asking for a miracle." One enormous hand grabbed at the rock outcropping that formed the top edge of the structure. "What you've got here is a wall a foot thick. There probably isn't much of a floor behind there, so you're looking at having to pour a new one. I'm betting you'll have to add a bunch of dirt to make it level." He whistled through his teeth. "You're looking at five, maybe six thousand dollars between the demo and finish. And all you've gained is about eighty square feet. I say just leave it there and cover it with drywall."

I gave a half smile. "What would I do with a leftover

nine-by-nine corner behind the stairs? The design only works if the cistern's gone. I need the full space."

"I'm just saying you'd be better off walling the thing up and putting folding doors over the rest of the back end. Make it more storage. People can always use storage."

I could feel a stubbornness settle in the little dip at the front of my neck. My star contractor was quickly becoming a no-man. I only worked with yes-men. I'd hired him because he was already familiar with the house. He'd done the work on the second bathroom and had spearheaded the waterproofing project. Lloyd & Sons had also gotten stellar reviews from owners of other historic properties in the area.

He was the best. I couldn't afford to lose him. I'd simply have to help him change his mind.

With a breath to boost my self-control, I plastered on a smile. "If we turned it into a closet, we'd be blocking a light source. But I'm sure we could use that window's handy location to remove the stones once we knocked them all down."

Lloyd gave me a look. He folded up his reading glasses and tucked them in the pocket of his flannel shirt. "There's no way these stones're going through that little window. You'll have to haul them out by hand."

I turned at the brush of air behind me. Tweedledum and Tweedledee stood with hands tucked in the pockets of their tight blue jeans. They stared slack-jawed at the cistern.

"I'm not carrying that thing out of here," the youngest said, a look of disbelief sending his myriad of freckles into disarray. "Come on, Dad. You're only paying minimum wage. I'll end up on my back and miss finals. No way."

"Can it," Lloyd said with a slash of his hand. I could have sworn sparks flew out of his eyes as he looked at his carrot-topped son. Lloyd moved his gaze, softer now, back to me. "It'll take a permit, but what you need to do is separate the cistern from the rest of the foundation, so you don't damage any supporting walls when you knock the thing down. You might be able to dump some of the stones in the center and just level out the floor with concrete. A quick look should tell you."

Lloyd dug into his utility belt and pulled out a flashlight. He turned it on and shone it into the cistern, then stuck his head in after it.

"Well, well. Would you look at that?" Lloyd gave another whistle.

"What?" I could hardly stand it. The look on Lloyd's face told me he'd found something very interesting.

"Take a look," he said.

I threw my arms across the ledge and scrambled up the stones, scraping my elbow raw and knocking my knee hard against the sharp corner of a rock. I pulled myself up for a full view of the inside.

The beam of the flashlight bounced around and it took me a minute to figure out what I was looking at.

I gasped.

A faint ringing sounded in my ears and the acute pain in my knee throbbed in time with my racing heart. My fingers, frozen in curious horror, clutched the edge.

Someone had already filled the bottom of the cistern with cement. And lying beneath it, with a silent scream etched in stone, was the outline of a body. Splayed fingers pressed frantically alongside the face, as if a living person had been trapped under ice and now tried in vain to smash through. A ridge of toes formed one foot, the rounded tip of a shoe, the other.

I couldn't rip my gaze away. An uncontrollable shiver coursed through me. I ground my fingers into the ledge, but nothing could stop the scream from coming. The piercing noise bounced against rock and concrete as I gave voice to the stifled cries of the body so long forgotten.

The scream came to a stop. I felt the blood drain from my head. I loosened my death grip and slid slowly down the rock wall. My cheek scraped along, soaking in whatever coolness it could gather from the stones as I fought back the darkness.

5

I crouched against the wall of the cistern in a near fetal position.

"You okay?" Lloyd shook my shoulder. My temple bounced against the same sharp rock that had nailed my knee.

I swatted at his hand. "How can I be okay? There's a corpse in my cistern."

I breathed. In. Out. In. Out.

Why *my* basement? Why couldn't they have buried the body in somebody else's basement? No wonder I'd gotten such a deal on the home. I was living on top of a cemetery.

Lloyd scratched his head. "I kind of figured you bumped your knee when you let out that scream. I didn't realize you'd hit your head." He turned to the gaping men beside him. "Dial 9-1-1, Josh. I think she's got a concussion."

His red-haired assistant flipped open his phone and dialed.

I lifted my arm to wave off the call, but the kid was already giving the address.

"I don't have a concussion," I said. "Just tell them to bring a jackhammer and a body bag."

I leaned my forehead against the knee that wasn't throbbing. Like I really needed to start my life in Rawlings exhuming someone's cast-off relative from the nether regions of my home. If wind of this got around, I'd have a devil of a time trying to sell the place.

Whiner, I chastised. Go ahead and fling a body at me. I'd handle it, and even make it to my advantage somehow.

I looked up. The kid had ended the call. The trio stared down at me. The looks on their faces reflected the same shock and outrage that I'd felt moments earlier. As well they should. Rick Hershel had a bunch of explaining to do. How dare he not mention the body on the seller's disclosure?

I slapped a hand to my mouth. "Oh, my word."

The men lunged back as if afraid I'd vomit.

Could the body be Jan's? Would Rick have buried his own wife in the basement? Jan hadn't been available for the closing, after all. And the concrete at the bottom of the cistern was of fairly recent vintage. Probably poured when the rest of the waterproofing had been done a year ago, or maybe even after. Who knew how long Jan had been missing?

Rick had certainly had the opportunity.

I hated to think about it. The guy had seemed scruffy, but nice. And so lost without his wife. The split had definitely been her idea, not his.

Perhaps theirs had been, like Heathcliff and Cathy's, a case of obsessive love. That would qualify as a com-

38

mon enough motive for murder, even in this modern day and age.

I dusted grime from the floor off my hands. You just couldn't tell by looking at people if the heart of a killer beat in their breast.

Poor Jan.

I held out an arm to the contractor. "Would you mind? My knee feels like its ready to burst."

He reached down and pulled me to my feet.

"What a mess." I shook my head and leaned against the wall of the cistern. Even through the stones, I could feel the pull of the soul resting there. Thank goodness Lloyd and sons were standing in the vicinity. Otherwise, I'd be catatonic from fear. I rubbed my forehead. Where would I sleep until they got this thing out from under me?

A pounding came from upstairs. The kitchen door squeaked as someone entered.

"Hello?" A male voice dropped down the open stair-well.

Seconds later, the stairs shook with the weight of uni-formed figures coming to my rescue.

The first to descend was Officer Brad Walters.

I brushed my bangs to one side. He was definitely within fifty feet of me.

No biggie. I was an expert at eating crow. "I guess since we dialed 9-1-1, I can't threaten you with that re-straining order, huh?"

Brad's eyes settled on me. Behind his mask of profes-sionalism peeped a flicker of concern. "What seems to be the problem?"

Lloyd the Elder piped up. "She was poking around in

the cistern and must have bumped her head or some-thing. She's all . . . ," he held one hand suspended while he searched for the word, ". . . delusional."

"Delusional?" My voice arced up an octave. "Wouldn't you scream if you had a body in your cellar?"

I gulped for air. Stay calm, Tish. I didn't need another scene with Officer Walters present.

I wilted. My already bad day had taken a turn for the worse.

Brad glanced at the woman carrying a metal case. "Let's get some help here."

The paramedic flipped open the lid and dug around inside. She pulled out a blood pressure cuff. The ripping of Velcro filled the uncomfortable silence.

"I'm fine," I said. "I think you're a little too late for the person who really needs you." I jerked my head toward the cistern.

The woman continued, undeterred. She pumped the bulb, and the cuff tightened around my upper arm. Brad stood next to Lloyd. They whispered together. Lloyd did a lot of pointing. Then he got out his flashlight and the two men, tall enough to avoid a climb, peered over the ledge into the cistern.

I strained to hear their voices over the hissing of air as the cuff loosened. Brad's face was expressionless. No clues there. I had to hand it to him. He had a heart of stone when it came to murder scenes. Of course, Lloyd had been unaffected by the incident as well.

The paramedic flashed a blinding light into my pupils. I winced. Just because the men could remain calm in the face of dead bodies did not mean that my reaction had been unwarranted. Any normal person would have screamed her head off.

I remembered the image in the concrete, the mouth open in that eerie cry for help, the hands pushing away an attacker. One missing shoe.

Another shiver struck. The poor dear hadn't died graciously. But then, when was death pretty?

I tuned in on the conversation at the cistern.

"I don't see any reason to investigate. We haven't had any missing persons reports. Must have been just a trick of the light." Brad caught my eye at the last statement.

Unable to quash the squeal of outrage begging for release, I at least managed to downgrade it to a huff of indignation. "Not investigate? You're just going to let a killer run free?"

Brad placed his hands gently on my shoulders. "Miss Amble, there's no evidence of foul play. I don't know what you think you saw, but at this point, I'm going to decline investigating for lack of concrete evidence."

I searched his face. He was serious. He planned to drop the whole thing. I flicked his hands away. "The concrete *is* the evidence. Don't you see the outline of the body? It's so clear . . ."

I snatched the flashlight out of Lloyd's hand and climbed my way up the wall, not caring what appendage suffered for it. I shone the light on the lumpy white floor. Whoever had filled the cistern had done a poor job smoothing the surface, considering what lay beneath. I angled the flashlight, searching for the pattern that had so distinctly emerged when last I looked.

"It was here," I said in a half whisper. "The mouth

41

and hands, and the feet. I'm just looking at it wrong." I scooted along the wall to my previous observation point. "There. Right there."

I pointed to a series of dips and ridges that now only somewhat resembled a mouth and hands. I shifted the flashlight again. The pattern completely disappeared. Had it really been just a trick of the light?

"You know, my wife's like that," Lloyd said. "She can look at the clouds and see just about anything. She can even make sense out of all those Greek constellations. She'd probably look in there and see two or three bodies." He chuckled.

I clicked off the flashlight and set my feet back on the ancient basement floor. I slumped one shoulder against the cistern.

No body. That was good. I didn't have to find alternate lodging. I could go forward with the project without delay. I wouldn't have to contend with crime stories when I went to sell the house. One less thing to clutter my mind.

I watched Brad scribble a report in his notebook. Even the police officer wasn't concerned about a body.

I passed the flashlight back to Lloyd. "I think there's something wrong with this thing. Time for a new bulb." I turned to the paramedic. "Sorry to trouble you. I'm fine. Really."

Before leaving, the woman gave me a rundown of symptoms that would prompt a visit to the emergency room. "And it wouldn't hurt to see your doctor. You don't want to mess with head injuries."

I didn't bother to correct her. I turned to Brad.

"Officer Walters." I crossed my arms.

"Miss Amble." Brad gave a terse nod.

I loosened my guard. I might not like the man's invasion into my privacy, but that didn't mean I had to treat him like mold on my tub.

"Tish," I said. "Go ahead and call me Tish. We're neighbors, aren't we?"

"Tish." He said my name slowly, as if trying it out for the first time. He nodded his approval.

I cleared my throat. "Thanks for looking in."

"Anytime you need me." He tipped his cap and left.

"Well." I relaxed my arms and turned to Lloyd. "I guess that about covers it for the basement today. Work on getting that permit so we can get rid of that cistern once and for all."

"Come on, boys." Lloyd bolted upstairs, cohorts close on his heels.

"See you tomorrow!" I called after them.

I stood alone in the basement. I'd grown accustomed to its dank odor in the past hour, but with all distraction gone, my nose once again detected the smell. And it was colder now that I wasn't moving around. I rubbed my arms and turned in a slow circle. The plans I'd discussed with the builders flipped through my mind. Mechanical room, clean storage, open area, get rid of the cistern . . .

I stared at the crescent of rock. I hadn't given it a moment's notice on my first tour of the place several months ago. I hadn't even looked inside. It was just a detail to handle.

But now it radiated energy.

A big pile of rocks. That's all it was, hiding in the black shadows behind the steps. A big, *empty* pile of rocks.

Look, Tish, look inside me, it called.

I had already looked. And while my imagination had been in overdrive at first, there hadn't been anything to see the second time. There was no body in my cistern. No ghosts in my house.

Just me. Alone. And it wasn't likely to change anytime soon, so I might as well adjust.

I dared myself to hold my ground, resisting the urge to run, denying the fear that pulled at me with tangible fingers. The clammy silence crashed in my ears.

Behind me, the furnace kicked on.

I screamed and scrambled upstairs.

I slammed the door to the basement and fumbled with the bolt. I wasn't taking my chances. Body or not, this was one door that would stay locked.

6

I couldn't bring myself to do anything the rest of the morning except lie on my cot and stare at the ceiling. I traced the lines in the plaster with my eyes. One section had cracked in the shape of my old cat Peanut Butter, who'd shown up at my house when I was a kid. A shadow gave the image a scrawny tail. A jagged ridge made two pointy ears.

Maybe I *had* received a few too many knocks on the noggin in my life. When you start seeing bodies in the cistern and family pets frolicking overhead, you have to question if you're really all there.

Was I all there? Not likely. I was scattered far and wide. Pieces of me littered the state. I'd left a big part of myself up north, a decent-sized chunk in Walled Lake, and a generous portion in Pontiac. Everywhere I'd gone, I'd carelessly left a bit of my essence, a fragment of the human named Tish Amble.

With any luck, I'd exit Rawlings with what was left of me still intact.

I shifted my gaze to a sagging section near the windows. A spiderweb of lines radiated from a missing chunk of plaster. It wouldn't be long before the vibrations from the train spread the stress. Soon the weight would be unbearable and the whole ceiling would come crashing down. And to think, a hundred years ago the thing had been an unblemished surface.

I had been whole once too. It was before Peanut Butter had shown up on the back porch. Before my mother had driven the pickup headlong into Mead Quarry. Before Grandma had gotten sick. Long before I had done the unthinkable.

That would make me about seven years old the last time I had my life together.

Seven. I'd been in second grade. My best friend Anne had fought by my side when Mikey Palmer pelted us with snowballs on the way to school. At least Anne had decent aim.

I smiled at the memory. I turned on my side and stared out the picture window at the maple speckled with a few persistent leaves. Anne's cable TV had been a big plus too. Where else could I have enjoyed hours of *Star Trek* reruns and Movie of the Week television premiers? Even so, cable had been my first introduction to fear. Seven was too young to be watching Injun Joe pursuing Tom Sawyer in the caves. Anne had walked me home across the alley that night. I'd been terrified that Crazy Joe was lurking in the garage waiting to leap out at me with that long, curving knife.

A sunbeam bounced off a passing car and caught me in the eye. I blinked back a tear. Seven short years of bliss. Then, it was as if God had let loose a whirlwind in my life.

My stomach sent out a resounding gurgle. Grateful for an excuse to avoid the tour of days past, I jumped up and pulled on my jacket. Grocery shopping couldn't be put off another minute, or I'd never live to see another day.

I brushed my hair and a few minutes later turned out the drive onto Main Street and slowed at the tracks. Deucey took the rails like a ship on rolling seas. The car behind me tooted with impatience. I looked in the rearview mirror. Sun glinted off the windshield of a red midsize. I'd have to remember the vehicle for future reference. Its owner was completely rude.

At the next block, I stopped at the traffic signal. The clock tower on the adjacent corner read 1:15. It was surrounded with corn stalks to mark the season. I marveled at the quaint details that drew tourists to Rawlings by the droves.

Beside me, a store window caught my attention. HOME SWEET HOME, the sign above the door said. Antiques and accessories were arranged behind the plate glass with irresistible charm. A brightly colored quilt draped the chair beside a spinning wheel. A drop-leaf table was set for tea.

I hummed a sigh. Too bad I always rented furniture. This was one home I'd love to decorate with Victorian era knickknacks and uncomfortable straight-back upholstery. But it would never fly at the open house. I had to portray a feeling of casual, carefree living. Victorian was definitely too stuffy.

The bad-mannered driver beeped again, and I realized I'd daydreamed well into the green light. I pushed on the gas and cruised toward my destination. A few lights later, I turned into the parking lot of Goodman's Grocery.

I put Deucey in park and stepped onto the asphalt. To my annoyance, the red car pulled into a spot in the opposite row. Just my luck. I'd have to face my tormenter.

David, my oh-so-handsome neighbor, got out.

I was torn between the beauty of his face and the ugly of his attitude. Still, I waved when he looked my way.

"Tish!" He seemed overly pleased to see me. No doubt embarrassed to realize I'd been the slowster in the car ahead.

He walked toward Deucey. I clutched the open door like a shield between us.

"Did you see me waving?" he asked. "I tried getting your attention, but you were too wrapped up in the scenery."

I remembered the sun's glare on the windshield of his car. If he had been waving at me, I wouldn't have seen it.

"When that didn't work, I blew the horn." He skirted the door and went to the trunk. "You've got a cord hanging out the boot, and I wasn't sure it was rainproof."

I closed my door and followed him. A black strip of fabric dangled out Deucey's back end.

"It's a good thing I wasn't going to Flint today," I said. "Would you have followed me all the way?"

"Whatever it took."

I looked to see if there was a tease somewhere in those depths. But it seemed he was serious. I let down my guard. I couldn't hold a grudge against a guy who'd go to such lengths to watch out for me.

I stuck in the key and opened the trunk. Inside were

the remains of my nomadic life. I'd brought the necessities into the house the night before—personal care items, essential clothes, and sleep gear. But the rest would hole up in the car until needed.

A tapestry suitcase, containing the testimony of my existence, took up the back half of the cavernous trunk. Bills, old checkbooks, tax returns, and the clown I'd sewn for a junior high project were wedged in so tight, I'd broken the zipper trying to close it.

In front of me, tucked close to the bumper, was a backpack that just missed getting crushed the last time I'd slammed the trunk closed. Its adjustable strap hadn't been so lucky.

I looked at the sky. Good thing nylon was waterproof. The cloudless morning was about to give birth to an overcast afternoon. A bank of storms piled high on the horizon. The sun had only a few short hours before it would be swallowed by the cranky newborn.

"You're right." I locked eyes with David. "We're in for some rain."

Tearing away from his gaze seemed impossible. I'd always appreciated blue eyes on a guy with a square chin and full lips. And standing tall in his knee-length woolen coat, he looked so important, so exceptional. I wished I could figure out how to dress to impress. But in my line of work, it was too much trouble to change out of my grungies every time I left the house.

I bent over the trunk, fumbling around trying to arrange things. With the strap tucked away, I went to close it.

"Allow me," he said. He raised his arm to slam the lid. His fingers brushed mine, sending a jolt of electricity

49

tingling up my arm. I couldn't be sure if it was magnetic attraction or static cling.

"Would you like to share a buggy?" David asked. "I just have a few things to buy and I'd love the company. I won't take much space, I promise."

Share a shopping cart? I hardly knew the guy. But he was a neighbor, and I hated to be rude.

"I'd love to," I said.

We wheeled down the produce aisle.

"So, where do you get your accent?" I slung a bag of Macintosh apples into the cart.

"I come by it naturally. I grew up a bit south of London."

I smiled. "I love the way it sounds."

"Most Americans do. It's only fellow Brits that detect a hint of commoner."

"Commoner?" My gaze swept across his face. "We don't have any of those in America. We're all royalty as far as we're concerned."

"That's why I love it here."

An enormous golden grapefruit caught my eye. I put it in a plastic baggie and set it in the cart. Next to it I dropped some grapes and my favorites—plums. I crossed over to the veggie aisle and loaded up on salad supplies.

"How long have you been in the U.S.?" I asked.

"Five years or so," he said.

I reached for a bunch of celery to supplement my peanut butter craving. The red rubber band holding it together clung to the stalk beneath, and it stuck in place. I leaned forward to free it and got an eyeful of my hairdo in the mirror over the vegetable display. My brush-n-go styling had decided to hover like a halo around my face. I looked like I'd spent the morning plugged into a light socket.

Behind me, David scooped peanuts from a barrel into a paper bag. I leaned close to the mirror and tried to flatten my flyaways. Just then, the vegetable sprinkler system kicked on. I leaped back, but not before my face got sprayed. I wiped the drops off with my fingers and ran them through my hair. At least it would behave for the moment.

When I turned around, David was talking with a woman who looked like she'd spent the morning under her hair dryer. I'd never seen such a perfect flip-do. Even her lashes curled in the right direction, held in place by just the right amount of mascara. And while I couldn't detect lipstick or blush on her cheeks, that was only because it was so cleverly applied. No woman could look that good without help.

I could feel those primordial female hackles rising. To the casual observer, it would seem I had no reason to stake a claim on David. But anyone with eyeballs could see we were sharing a shopping cart. Couldn't she take a hint?

She smiled at David and gave a tacky giggle. David smiled back and said something that got an even bigger guffaw out of the petite blonde.

Come on. Couldn't he see that blatant flirtation for what it was? Maybe I'd given him too much credit.

I was just about to splat him with an avocado when the beguiling creature turned to me. Her perfectly plucked eyebrows nearly disappeared into her hairline.

51

"Oh!" Her hand froze in place over her mouth.

I guess my frizz rendered her speechless.

I was sure that somewhere behind her enlarged pupils, a brain churned. I decided to keep quiet to see if any thoughts rose to the surface. Finally, she lowered her fingers.

"I don't mean to stare. It's just that you look so much like someone who used to live around here."

I was impressed. She spoke in complete sentences.

I gave a big, overzealous smile to match her own fakey attitude. "You are the second person that's told me that today. Guess I've got that all-American look."

She scrunched up her face. "No. It's not that. You just remind me of someone who left town at least a year ago. I should have known you weren't her. She'd have to have guts to show her face around here again."

Great. I was the unsuspecting twin of some small-town pariah. I hadn't thought anyone else's face could be as featureless as mine.

"David said you're new in town." She extended a perfectly manicured hand. "I'm Tammy Johnson. I own the Beauty Boutique on Maple Street. Stop in some day. I'd love to get to know you."

Right. I squeezed politely and dropped my arm. What she really meant was that she'd love to get her hands on the overgrown haystack on my head. My stubborn streak vowed that her clippers and callus-free palms would never touch a strand.

"I'll be sure to stop in. I'm Tish Amble. Nice to meet you."

She'd done a great job keeping eye contact during

our conversation, but now she gave me a fast once-over before turning back to David.

My insides tightened. Not everyone could be as put together as her little prima donna self. She could cut those of us with a fashion handicap a little slack.

"I meant to ask you, David," she said in a silky-smooth voice, "any word from your wife?"

Air drained out of my lungs in a surprised gush. My eyes poked out and my cheeks sucked in. I felt like an astronaut who'd just lost atmosphere.

Wife? I was sharing a shopping cart with a married man? Gee, when had he planned on telling me that tidbit?

At least he had the good sense to look embarrassed.

He shifted his weight to the opposite leg as his fingers did a quick tattoo on the handle of the cart. "No. I haven't heard from Rebecca lately."

My eyebrow twitched. Another case of wayward wife. Must be an epidemic in Rawlings.

Tammy ducked her head in a show of repentance. "Sorry. Didn't mean to bring up a sore subject. Got to run."

She flashed me a parting glance as she walked up the aisle and out of view.

I leeched onto David's eyeballs with a glare of accusation. But my anger fled when I saw the look on his face. His brow was furrowed in sadness and a cloud of emotion gathered in his gaze.

I couldn't help but feel sorry for him. He obviously hadn't gotten over the woman who'd left him. I was searching my Miss Manners data bank for an appropriate comment, when he saved me from uttering the inane words.

"Tammy means well. We all miss Rebecca." His voice sounded thick. "It's hard. Every time I open the mail, I expect to see divorce papers."

He wheeled the cart into the next aisle and I followed mutely behind.

Ahead of me, David put a box of Sugar Puffs in the cart. My heart did a flip-flop. Here was a guy who needed a woman to watch out for him. No one should consume that nasty sweetened cardboard.

"Here, try this granola," I said, passing him my brand. "You'll love it. And it's good for you."

He took the box from me and set it in the cart. With a moment's hesitation, he put the Sugar Puffs back on the shelf.

I admired the way the ligaments played along the back of his hands. I could picture how well-suited those long fingers were for a computer keyboard. I knew they would be soft, gentle . . .

I cleared my throat. It didn't seem fair of Rebecca to just leave him hanging like this. If she didn't want to patch things up, she ought to at least give him the dignity of setting him free. She could step aside and give someone else a chance to erase the sorrow from his features.

My mind slid back to Tammy's perfect figure. Unless I was mistaken, I wasn't the only candidate interested in taking on the job.

Maybe I'd stop by the Beauty Boutique after all.

7

A song rolled off my tongue as I grabbed my groceries from the backseat and headed toward the house. I had more fun shopping today than I could remember. David was ever the gentleman. He didn't ask too many questions, didn't talk too much about himself. We'd been content just pushing a cart together.

He'd helped me load my supplies into the car at the grocery store, then followed me home, giving a friendly *beep* of farewell as he headed down the street to his own driveway. I could hear the slam of his car door two garages over even now.

I smiled, breathing in the bitter scent of crushed autumn leaves. It felt good to dip my big toe back into the pool of human companionship.

I paused at the steps to the back porch and wrinkled my nose at the cedar growing out of control against the house. I made a mental note to replace it with a short, tame barberry and plenty of wood chips. Then buyers could better appreciate the beauty of the turned spindles that followed the length of the rail, especially once all the trim got a fresh coat of white paint come summer.

I continued up the steps, reaching for the keys while trying to keep hold of the paper bags in my arms. The ring jangled free of my pocket. At the same moment, my toe kicked something soft.

I jerked back, expecting to see the mangled corpse of a jack-o'-lantern, a prank in keeping with the season. Instead, a cloth sack filled to the brim with ripe, juicy tomatoes awaited discovery.

I glanced across the fence to Brad's backyard. Obviously, he decided to follow through on his promised delivery despite my less-than-stellar behavior. How sweet.

As I put away my grocery items, I replayed my afternoon with David. He'd been so attentive, unloading the cart at the checkout lane. I found it hard to believe he'd been raised a "commoner," as he put it. David was nothing if not well-bred. And it had been a good long time since a man went out of his way to treat me like a lady. I knew better than to get my hopes up, but it never hurt to dream.

I went to the porch and retrieved the gift tomatoes. I unloaded at least a dozen of them into the veggie bin. I'd probably look like a tomato by the time I got done eating them all. If Brad had mentioned this peace offering before I went shopping, I could have saved a buck eighty-nine.

I closed the fridge. Outside, rain began pelting the earth. The wind blew a sheet of water against the kitchen window.

A crash of thunder ripped through the house, shaking

the floor beneath me. Lightning followed close on its heels, flashing a brilliant white against the door to the basement as I passed by. For a split second, the outline of a woman appeared on its painted surface.

I screamed and fell backward. My head bumped against the wall behind me. The lightning flashed again. The panels were bare.

I gave a laugh of relief. I'd been nearly knocked unconscious by my own shadow. I rubbed the back of my head.

"Pull it together, Tish," I said to the empty room. I stood up and patted the dirt off my backside, hoping to brush off a little imagination with it.

It had been only my shadow on the door, not some specter beckoning to free her wronged spirit. With Officer Brad and Lloyd & Sons as my witnesses, there was no body in my basement.

From where I stood, I could see that the bolt still secured the door. Even the swamp monster couldn't get up here. Still, I wasn't feeling very brave. I inched my way past, never taking my eye off the doorknob, expecting to see it turn any second . . .

I made it to the bathroom and flipped the lock.

How had I gone all afternoon without thinking of the body that was not in my basement? Obviously, being in David's company helped. I could only hope that I'd get to spend more time with him—I had to do something to keep my sanity. It would be pathetic if the neighbors found me one day, locked in my bathroom, rocking back and forth on the toilet seat and ranting about a body in my cistern, when of course there was no body in my cistern.

The flush of the toilet blended with the peal of a train whistle as an engine flew past. Funny, a sound I'd dreaded only last night was a comfort to me now. The blaring notes were rooted in reality. They strengthened me enough that I could open the door and walk back into the kitchen. There was no need to be nervous.

There was no body.

That night, after an evening topped off by a tomato salad and a romance novel minus the ghosts, I fell asleep to the sound of rain. I woke the next day to the *coo* of a mourning dove. Somewhere in between must have been more ear-splitting whistles, but my only conscious memory was of a dream that had me trapped in Deucey's front seat, with Grandma driving.

"Your mother was always a good girl," she said, smiling at me. Her white hair was arranged in perfect curls around her face. Red lipstick and drawn-on eyebrows made her seem younger than her years.

When I looked at her hands, wrinkled and old, gripping the steering wheel, that "something's amiss" feeling came over me—the one you get when you meet someone in a dream, and all of a sudden you remember that in real life the person is dead. Suddenly I was scared. My legs and arms felt bolted to the bench seat. I watched, helpless, as Grandma's face became an oozing mass of color, as if an artist had swirled his brush on the canvas to blot out a mistake.

The contorted mouth talked to me. "Why couldn't you have been more like your mother?"

Then we were airborne, with the bottom of Mead Quarry racing up to meet us.

I was awake now, more so than after my usual two cups of coffee. And a good thing too. It was time to roll up my sleeves and get to work.

Milk sloshed over the edges of the bowl as I ate a hurried breakfast. I decided to strip the wallpaper from the front entry while waiting for Lloyd & Sons to arrive. I could accomplish the modest-sized project before lunch and feel like I was at least headed in the right direction.

I painted water over the '70s pattern, gave it a few minutes to soak in, then scraped the layers off with a wide, flat-edged putty knife. It wasn't the most effective way to rid the walls of their covering, but the obsessive-compulsive in me loved the way the paper came off in long spirals that piled up on the floor.

One wall was stripped bare when I realized Lloyd hadn't arrived yet. I flipped open my phone and dialed up his cell.

"Lloyd here," he answered in tandem with crackling airwaves.

"Tish Amble. I thought we were on for today."

There was a pause while he tried to come up with a good excuse for stiffing me.

"Got tied up . . . *crackle* . . . deck repair . . . *crackle* . . . *crackle* . . . get the permit?"

"Permit for what? I thought you were taking care of all the permits."

I could barely hear his reply as the signal cut in and out.

". . . get the permit . . . for the cistern . . . by tomor-row."

"By tomorrow? Fine. In fact, I'll take care of it right now."

The line was nothing but static as I jammed the disconnect button with my finger. What kind of contractor didn't pull his own permits? It's not like it took a college degree to get permission to knock down a stone wall.

I picked up the soggy paper shavings and dropped them in a plastic bag. Now I'd have to get cleaned up and face the village guardians myself.

But it would be worth it if it meant getting rid of that creepy pile of rocks once and for all.

8

The brisk October wind blew cold fingers of air down the neck of my jacket, slowly cooling my boiling blood as I stomped two blocks down to the village offices. Lloyd's reliability quotient had dropped to a solid zero. What was I paying him for? I should fire him and use the money on a one-way ticket to Fiji. I could renovate a grass hut as my next project.

Leaves danced circles around me, then piled up in exhausted heaps against the brick storefronts. I pushed open the heavy glass door to the Village of Rawlings headquarters and stepped into a workplace as hushed as a morgue. The smell of new paper and copy toner greeted me. Behind the reception counter, a woman was absorbed with a collating project that involved six or seven multicolored sheets and an electric stapler.

I crossed my arms and waited. She showed no sign of slowing. After a few moments, I cleared my throat.

Without looking up, the clerk droned, "I'll be right with you."

My fingers tapped the denim of my sleeves. The pile

that consumed the woman's attention hadn't shrunk a millimeter since I'd been standing there. I wondered at what point she would decide to do her job and assist me.

"Uh-hmmm," I said with more insistence.

The nameplate on the counter identified the woman as Laura Boyd. I was about to say her name in not-very-nice tones, when she huffed and laid down the papers overflowing her fingers. She gave me a sharp glance.

"Can I help . . ." Her voice petered off into stunned silence. From her goggle-eyed stare, I concluded my notorious twin had preceded me once again.

No time for flabbergasted clerks. I had a deadline.

"I need to apply for a permit." I flopped my elbows on the counter and leaned toward her. "My name is Tish Amble and I'm at 302 South Main Street."

"T . . . Tish Amble?"

"That's my name."

Ms. Boyd backed up into a desk, knocking over the pencil holder. She swung around, made a half-try to pick up the mess, then practically ran to a back office and shut the door.

I hoped that meant she was getting my application.

Her absence dragged on. An old-fashioned bell, the kind you ring for service, was sitting on top of a stack of last week's local newspaper. My patience came to an end, and I gave the ringer a good workout. The *ding, ding, ding, ding* lowered my frustration level considerably, though whether it had the power to procure my application was yet to be seen.

From the direction of the back office, bobbing between bookshelves and file cabinets, came a head shaved smooth as a plum. I had only a moment to wonder if the owner used a double-blade or some kind of cream, before the man's face, purple-veined with anger, wiped all curiosity from my mind.

"Laura tells me you need a permit." His voice resonated off the plate-glass windows behind me and rattled my rib cage.

My body stiffened in defense. "That's right."

"At 302 South Main?" he asked.

"That's correct."

"For what?" The guy sounded like a grunting monkey.

"Removal of the cistern."

"Nope. Can't do it." He thumped his fist on the counter.

"Pardon me?" My heels dug into the carpet.

"You heard me—302 falls in the Historic Preservation District along with the rest of Rawlings Township. Can't touch the foundation."

"Thankfully, the cistern isn't part of the foundation." I made my best attempt at a smile, but I'm sure it looked more like a grimace.

"It's part of the original stonework. The committee won't let you touch it. Believe me." His head angled down and his brows angled up.

"Perhaps you could give me the chairperson's name and I'll check into it myself." No village tyrant was going to deter me from reaching my goal.

"Sure. Martin Dietz."

"Where would I find Mr. Dietz?"

"You're looking at him."

I drew a deep breath. First a cop for a neighbor, then a body in the cistern, now some demon-possessed zoning

63

official. I needed to go home and ask God what I did to deserve all the potholes on my straight and narrow road.

"Mr. Dietz, what I need from you is the permit application. I'll let the committee review it for themselves and make the final decision."

Dietz flashed an evil smile. "It'll be a waste of two hundred and fifty bucks, but suit yourself."

He set the application between us on the counter. His look dared me to take it.

My fingers hesitated a bare instant before snatching up the triplicate form. He shouldn't be so cocky. I'd faced officials with more hair and come out a winner. There was no way he could stop my project from going forward. I knew all the ins, outs, and secret passages of zoning laws. Completing the application and getting denied was a mere formality.

I gave him a final taut-lipped look and turned to go out. The coming victory would be one more notch in the holster of my staple gun. I couldn't help but smile at the challenge ahead.

Lloyd the contractor arrived first thing the next day.

I greeted him with crossed arms and a tapping foot. I wasn't about to let him off easy. "I couldn't get the permit."

"Permit? What permit?"

I rose up on my tiptoes to gain some height. "Hello? The permit for the removal of the cistern."

"Huh?"

This guy was losing it. "You know. The one you told me to get when I called you yesterday."

I couldn't believe he'd forgotten our conversation already.

"I told you *I* would get the permit," he said.

I wanted to knock on his cranium to jog his memory. "No. You told me to get the permit for today."

His eyelids peeled back in a look of panic. "I said I would come by today. You went down to the village office?"

"Yeah. Why the big deal?"

"You saw Martin Dietz?"

"Yeah."

Lloyd slapped himself in the temple. "You'll never get the permit now."

"What do you mean?" I was pretty sick of him raining on my renovation parade.

"I guarantee he took one look at you and decided you weren't going to get a permit to flush the toilet, let alone remove a cistern."

"Mr. Dietz is a public servant. He can't deny me based on frivolous logic."

"Mr. Dietz is a public tyrant. He'll make your life so miserable, you'll wish *you* were the one buried in the cistern."

I stopped breathing. Did Lloyd think there was someone under the concrete in my basement?

He shifted his feet. "I don't mean to say there's a body in your cistern. I was just giving you fair warning. Don't go after the permit. Box in the cistern and forget about it. Let it lie."

My skin crept with déjà vu.

Let it lie. I'd heard those words before; three simple words that always rousted the rebel in me.

The cistern didn't have a chance.

9

Good old Lloyd stomped off without pounding one nail.

Get the permit and remove the cistern or wall the thing in were the only two options the man would entertain. My idea to sneak the big rocks out disguised as trash only served to hasten my star contractor's departure. Apparently, Martin Dietz gave no quarter to code violators, and Lloyd wasn't about to suffer the tyrant's wrath.

Moratorium declared, I slunk off to start work on the back staircase. I peeled, primed, and papered until the narrow passage looked like it belonged in the twenty-first century. Then I pried and pounded until the steps were squeak-free.

By the time the big fall holiday arrived a few days later, I had worked off my frustration over the uncooperative Lloyd and was ready to enjoy the occasion.

I was just tucking the final section of my costume masterpiece into place when the doorbell rang and the first little voices of the night wafted into the kitchen.

"Trick or treat!"

66

I dumped pencils and stickers into a bowl and headed to the front door to let the rascals help themselves. I smiled on the way through the dining room. I'd survived my first weeks in the new neighborhood.

But though my gray matter was intact, my house still looked as if it were a creepy old asylum. Even if things weren't moving as quickly as I hoped, I nevertheless felt satisfied when I reviewed my progress.

I glanced around the vestibule before opening the door. Utterly perfect. I'd painted the walls a creamy off-white and rubbed the natural oak woodwork until it shone. An ornate Victorian three-bulb fixture gave off a welcoming light.

I pulled open the door and stifled a giggle. A waist-high pirate pointed a plastic sword in my direction. Next to him, a dainty princess held up her sack in expectation.

"What are you supposed to be? A mummy?" the pirate asked.

"I'm Lazarus," I answered. I secured a stray white strip wrapped around my head.

"Who's Lazarus?"

"He's a guy from the Bible. Jesus raised him from the dead. Lazarus, come forth!" I said, lurching sideways in my best imitation of the newly risen friend of Christ.

Three summers of Vacation Bible School when I was a kid were the entirety of my religious training. I'd gleaned enough to know there was a God. And I couldn't have survived to adulthood if I hadn't held on to the hope that Jesus really existed. Sadly, a few years in the church I attended as a teen with my grandmother were enough to sour my attitude toward organized religion and keep me from wanting to know more. Now

67

at least I browsed the Bible, even if I didn't always understand it.

Across from me, the chaperone forced a smile. "Kids, pick out a treat. We have a lot more houses to go."

I smiled back through the wadding that covered my face. The pirate rested on his sword. "There's no candy in here and stickers are for babies."

"Jason!" The mother swatted at him. "Mind your manners."

"How about a pencil?" I asked, almost wishing I'd conformed to the tooth-rotting Halloween tradition. "Here's one with 3-D lettering."

I handed the little thug his prize, and he toyed with the image for a moment.

"Cool." The pencil went into his pillowcase. Then he pushed back his patch and looked up at me. "Brandon says your house is haunted."

"Jason!" His mother grabbed at his shoulder and half dragged him off the porch. "Thank you!"

The princess ran after them into the night.

I sagged against the doorway.

Haunted? Perhaps.

There was always the possibility that my house was inhabited by the restless spirit of some murder victim. But what were the chances, really? Other than a vague glance over my shoulder now and then, I hadn't given the ghost another thought. Nor had the apparition shown itself again. True, I hadn't been in the basement since the day of my "vision," and neither had anyone else. Lloyd had fed me one excuse after another for not getting to the job downstairs.

Most likely, what I'd seen was a result of my own guilty conscience projecting an image from my past onto the concrete, hoping I'd face up to my deeds.

Nah. Too Freud.

I watched through the storm door as another group of trick-or-treaters came up the sidewalk, wearing costumes that stood the test of time.

The five oversized kids gave their call in unison, then edged in toward the bowl. Hands hovered, then halted.

I definitely should have capitulated and gone with the standard sweets.

"Pencils?" the vampire asked through his fangs.

A vein in my neck throbbed. "Here. Try this one. It's 3-D."

He twisted it in his fingers. "Is it legal to pass this stuff out on Halloween?"

I lost my cool. "Aren't you a little too old to be trick-or-treating? You're lucky I let you stick your fingers in the bowl."

"Sorry," he moped, dropping a pencil into his bag. He backed off to make room for his friends.

A white-sheeted teen peered over my shoulder into the house.

"Have you seen it yet?" he asked, his voice low and gravelly.

"Seen what?" I turned to look behind me.

"The ghost."

A prickle crept up my scalp and raised the hair beneath the strips of cloth wound around my head.

Tish, Tish. I could almost hear a voice calling me, rising from the concrete, curving up the basement steps, seeping under the door and floating to my place in the vestibule.

Behind me, the kid let out a snort. "I'm just playing with you, lady. *I'm* the ghost. Get it? Man, you look like you thought your house was haunted or something."

There was laughter. The bowl jostled in my hands. Then the porch was empty.

I clutched the Tupperware to my chest. Tears welled up and one of those big lumps stuck in my throat.

Life didn't seem right anymore. I'd managed well enough in my other neighborhoods. Lonely, but content. I had felt, or maybe just hoped, that a change was coming with this move to Rawlings. But things were worse here. Now, even the kids taunted me.

I dabbed at a nasal drip with a dangling bandage.

In my side vision, a dark figure moved across the lawn toward the porch. Probably another rude kid looking for a handout.

It was David.

My face burned beneath my wraps as I tried to find a place to hide. I absolutely could not let him see me looking like the victim of some toilet paper prank.

"Hello," he called from grass glistening in the light from the porch. "Is that you under all that tissue?"

There was no hiding now.

"Hi." I tried to put a smile in my voice. "I'm just getting into the holiday."

He sprang up the steps. "Are you The Mummy?"

I cleared my throat, trying to get the lump down to a manageable size before I croaked like a frog.

"Yeah. The Mummy."

As soon as I said it, I felt like crawling into a tomb somewhere. Apparently my courage had escaped out the front door at the arrival of my adorable neighbor.

I gripped the Tupperware like a life preserver.

"What's in the bowl?"

He was probably hoping for a candy bar too.

"Pencils." The bowl started to shake in my grasp.

"Superb idea. Why rot the little angels' teeth?"

My knuckles relaxed. At least someone agreed with my logic.

"You're not passing out treats at your house?" I asked.

He tucked his hands in his pockets. "Trick-or-treat is strictly an American tradition. And with Rebecca gone . . . Well, I thought if I turned out the porch light, the kiddies would take the hint. But there's no dissuading them. They wouldn't quit ringing the bell. And when I opened the door to tell them the bad news, they gave me such devilish faces, I thought I'd better come over here to be safe. Perhaps I can hide behind the pencil bowl."

I grimaced. "I'm not having any better luck than you bribing a smile out of those ungrateful little monsters. I'm getting the idea that pencils and stickers don't qualify as treats in their mind. Tricks, maybe."

He looked over his shoulder as the next batch of hooligans walked up the sidewalk.

"Let me give it a go." He came up the steps and took the bowl out of my grip. "I'll get rid of every last one of them."

My brow furrowed. Get rid of the trick-or-treaters? This was my once-a-year missionary opportunity.

"The pencils, I mean," he said, and shook the bowl.

The new arrivals gave the call and came close to collect their prize. Their hands pulled back in hesitation.

"I can't believe what I'm seeing," David scolded them. "These pencils will be valuable antiquities one day. Put one in your trinket box, and I guarantee when you graduate from high school, you'll be able to sell it on eBay and pay your way through college."

At his words, tiny fingers grabbed indiscriminately at the bowl, rushing to take more than one goody.

I giggled into my hand, pleased with his clever sales job.

"It's definitely a different world than the one I grew up in," I said as the kids left and made their way to less future-oriented porches.

David crossed his arms and leaned against the vestibule wall, shaking his head. "Today's kindergartners are more versed in computers than most adults."

I looked to the ground, embarrassed by my own ignorance. "I guess not everybody's had the opportunity to be around one."

His hand touched my chin. I met his eyes, fascinated by the pale, yet piercing, blue.

"I didn't mean to offend you," he said softly. "A career in computers was my dream as a kid. I feel very fortunate that I was able to make that dream happen."

More goblins and hobos came to the door and David made his pitch. Only five pencils remained when the last trick-or-treater disappeared into the night. I tore the Lazarus wrap from my head, glad to be liberated. "Thanks for helping out," I said, walking after David onto the porch.

"My pleasure." He paused on the top step.

I smoothed my hair. "I never could have gotten rid of all those pencils without you."

He turned and started down the stairs, but paused and looked back.

"Tish, would you have dinner with me next Friday?"

My heart slammed to a halt.

His words transported me to Single Woman's Euphoria. His was my second invitation to dinner since I moved in. Poor Brad hadn't had a chance, of course. Lousy timing, along with a poor choice of occupation, had doomed him from the start.

David came up the steps and leaned close, his mouth magnifying before my eyes. My breath drained out as I imagined those lips against mine.

"Dinner? Next Friday?" I couldn't think of a single conflict, besides the fact that he was a married man.

I grabbed hold of my enthusiasm and stuffed it in under a rock. "You know, David, normally I'd love to go to dinner with you. But, um, you're really not free to ask."

Sadness welled up in his eyes. "The divorce papers came today. It's officially over between Rebecca and me."

My breath caught.

"I'm so sorry." I couldn't begin to imagine his pain. "Are you sure you're ready to go on a date?"

He swallowed and nodded. "It's been a really lonely year. We could get together and just talk."

"Okay. Sure. Dinner sounds nice."

"Thanks, Tish. How's seven o'clock at the Rawlings Hotel?"

Sheesh. Brad had wanted to take me to the Rawlings. I

bit my cheek, allowing the sharp pain to chase away the guilt that threatened to ruin my triumphant moment.

"I would love to join you at the Rawlings Hotel."

A smile lit his face. "You won't be sorry. The beef Wellington is superb." He trotted down the steps and across the lawn toward his own yard.

I watched until he disappeared into the shadows.

Alone again, I rubbed my arms to ward off the dampness of the black night.

"Can I lend you my coat?" The unexpected voice came from the darkness beyond the porch.

A scream tore from my throat and my hands flew to my neck in panic.

Officer Brad stepped into view, laughter on his face.

"Do you know what night this is?" I said through injured vocal cords. "Never sneak up on somebody on Halloween. They're liable to drop dead from heart failure."

His smile faded to a barely restrained grin. "I'm sorry. I raced over as soon as the insanity ended. I wanted to make sure you locked things up good tonight. Even Rawlings has its undesirable element—especially on Halloween."

"How long have you been standing by the porch?" I asked.

"Long enough to know that you'd choose dinner with a pretty face over dinner with a man of impeccable character."

I slumped into my waist.

"I was afraid you'd heard that. Are you mad?" Brad was nice enough to come over and make sure I double-bolted my doors. I hated the thought that my flat-out refusal of his dinner invitation earlier in the week had just gotten rubbed in his face.

"I'm a patient man, Tish. I figure once you get over the fascination of his good looks and English accent, you'll be ready for a guy who actually has a personality, not to mention a green thumb."

"Oh, yeah. Thanks for the tomatoes."

He plopped down on the top step and looked out at the street. "And there's the added benefit that I'm actually available."

I sat next to him on the stairs and bit my tongue. It was none of his business that Rebecca finally got around to sending David divorce papers.

He tapped his fingertips together. "You look great, by the way. Who are you supposed to be—Lazarus?"

I squealed and gave a giddy clap. "You're the first to guess right."

He turned toward me. "You know, when you smile like that, you kind of look like you've been raised from the dead."

"I'll take that as a compliment," I said, squeezing myself in excitement. Even Brad could tell I was feeling resurrected tonight. It would take a hammer and chisel to knock the smile off my face before next Friday.

A sigh of contentment snuck out. My first real relationship in my adult life was just over the horizon. Rebecca's loss would be my gain. I twirled a coarse strand of hair around my finger and made a mental note to set up an appointment with a beautician. Funny how Tammy Johnson's smirking face leapt into my mind. I couldn't help but smile at the crushed look that was sure to come when I told her of my special occasion. Talk about heaping burning coals on her snobbish head.

Brad cut into my victory dance. "I know it's none of my business, but are you sure you want to get involved with a guy you barely know?"

"Gee, Brad, I barely know anybody. I think that's the point of going to dinner. To get to know each other. It's not like he asked me to marry him."

Brad harrumphed. "Don't be surprised if he does."

I shot a look at him. "What's that supposed to mean?"

He clamped his lips together.

My breath quickened. Brad had a real talent for bringing out the beast in me.

"You know"—my voice rose to across-the-street levels—"it would be an honor if the guy did ask me to marry him."

"I'm sure Rebecca felt the same way, once."

I felt like slapping him. "So? She changed her mind. From what I can tell, the whole divorce thing was her idea. David seems like the kind of guy who could love a woman 'til death do them part."

Brad snapped his head in my direction. "What's this about a divorce?"

"He got the papers today. Rebecca's finally decided to give him another chance at love. Sure took her long enough."

Brad bounced his thumbs off his lips in silence, staring at some crack in the sidewalk below.

His voice came softly. "It hasn't even been a year, Tish."

I met his eyes. Plain brown circles stared back at me.

I stood up. "Well, thanks for stopping by. I promise I'll check my locks twice."

He jumped to his feet. "If you don't mind, I'd like to have a look around for myself."

I crossed my arms, debating. The guy was a police officer, not to mention my neighbor. And it wasn't as if I had anything to hide that he didn't already know.

I gave him a smart-aleck look. "You're not afraid to be alone in a house with me?"

"Should I be?" he asked, not rising to the bait.

My heart softened. At least he wasn't the type to throw my past in my face.

I opened the door and he followed me in.

10

Once through the door, Brad took the lead, walking with purpose to each window, jiggling sills and checking latches. I raced to keep up with him as he took the steps two at a time to the second floor and repeated the motions, then thumped down the back stairs to the kitchen.

He walked toward the cellar door.

"Wait," I hollered when I realized his intentions. "That door stays locked. There's no reason to go down there."

He paused with his hand on the knob. "Let me do my job, Tish. I want to get some sleep tonight."

I crossed my arms. "Fine. I'll wait up here."

"No problem." He turned the latch and stepped into the gloom beyond.

The sound of his footsteps diminished as he reached the dusty floor of the basement. I crept away from my safe haven by the kitchen sink and over to the door. I leaned against the trim, peering down at the dim circle of light on the gray floor below.

I listened for movement. Only an occasional *shuffle*

78

and *thud* reached me. A soft breeze drifted up from the cellar and brushed against my cheeks.

Panic rose in my throat.

A ringing filled my ears—the same high-pitched inner whistle I'd experienced the last time I'd braved the basement. And just as before, I felt more than heard a soft, haunting plea.

Help me, Tish.

I shuddered. A voice from the past, nothing more. Why couldn't she leave me alone? I'd done what she'd asked of me. I'd made the ultimate sacrifice so she could rest in peace. So why couldn't Grandma just leave me alone?

I put my foot on the first narrow step.

What was taking Brad so long? I threw a glance over my shoulder at the empty kitchen. Hanging out in the basement suddenly seemed more appealing.

I went down another step.

My breath came in panicked gulps.

Memories of the image at the bottom of the cistern forced themselves into my head. The open mouth, the clawing hands, the flailing feet . . .

I wrapped one arm around the railing and shrank against the wall.

"Brad!"

He appeared at the bottom of the steps and started toward me.

"Everything okay?" He gently untangled my elbow from its mortal grip on the handrail and helped me up. "You look scared to death."

I cleared my throat. "I must be shook up from earlier this week. I guess the cellar still spooks me a little."

"Everything checks out. We should both be able to sleep better."

He helped me to the kitchen, and for the first time since my arrival in Rawlings, I wished I had a chair to sit in.

I leaned against the counter instead. "Thanks. I appreciate you looking the place over."

He walked to the back door. "Lock up after me."

I followed him and watched as he stepped onto the porch.

His eyes met mine. "Good night, Tish."

I shook off the rush of longing his whispered words sent through me.

Those teenage prickles that dotted my skin were reserved for David alone.

I faced the mirror the next morning and noticed a crop of flyaway grays that hadn't been there the day before.

I dialed the Beauty Boutique and was greeted by the chipper voice of Tammy Johnson.

I tried not to gloat as I arranged a Tuesday appointment. "I've just got to have my hair done before Friday. David Ramsey is taking me to dinner."

Tammy's silence told me I'd hit the mark.

I spent the rest of Saturday staying clear of the cellar door. Since the front bedroom in the second story needed only a fresh coat of paint, I made that my weekend project. By Monday night, the walls, ceiling, and trim were painted, and the room was ready for new flooring.

I woke with a tremor of excitement on Tuesday morning, maybe from the promise of a new me, maybe from smugness. Either way, I arrived at the salon at 10:00 sharp and plopped into the twirly chair at Tammy's station. The sharp smell of perm solution lingered from a previous client.

I took a moment to admire the distinctive touches that were in keeping with the town of Rawlings' historic theme. Dark trim traced the lines around the ceiling and floor. On the wall behind me hung a tapestry depicting seventeenth-century women wearing tall hairdos and poofy gowns. A floral swag in burgundy and cream draped the mirror at each work station.

I focused on my reflection as Tammy fingered my frizz. One side of her mouth curled, giving away her apparent distaste.

My stomach twisted. It hadn't occurred to me until that moment that Tammy was probably the last person I should let touch my head.

I smiled, hoping to disarm her. "So, what do you recommend?"

She stared at me in the mirror and continued to play with my hair. My fingers started to twitch. I contemplated the best escape route if she should come after me with the clippers.

Finally, she dropped my locks. "I'd say you should go with a classic shoulder-length cut. But, I'm afraid you'd resemble Sandra even more."

"Sandra?" I echoed, even as I realized she must be referring to my elusive twin.

Tammy sighed. "Not everyone will appreciate your resemblance to her. We don't want to make the situation worse. Could you stand a chin-length style?"

81

She showed me a picture of one she had in mind.

I glanced at the glossy magazine. The model looked pure chic. I figured I'd give it a try. I'd look classy next to David's distinguished form come Friday night.

Tammy led me to the washtub. The soothing massage action of her extra-long fingernails against my scalp lulled me into a state of serenity.

"So what restaurant are you going to Friday?" Tammy's voice filtered through the sound of spraying water as she rinsed my hair.

"The Rawlings Hotel." I wondered if she was jealous, and thought a change in subject might be wise, at least until she was done with the cut. "So, tell me about my twin. Why does her face cause such an uproar around town?"

She toweled my hair and draped a black plastic apron around me, then sat me back down at her station.

"Sandra." Tammy shook her head. "She's one of those women who can cause a commotion wherever she goes. Beautiful, spunky, driven . . . you know the type."

Yeah. Sandra sounded like the person I'd dreamed of becoming, if only things had gone differently.

Tammy picked up a brush and ran it through my hair. "Sandra and I went to high school together. We were both on the cheerleading squad, in student government, and tied for Most Likely to Succeed."

The brush slowed and Tammy's gaze became distant, as if she were lost in memory. "After college, a bunch of us came back home and started up our own businesses. I was content to operate the salon and have time to do other things. Sandra, on the other hand, was totally devoted to building her marketing company. She was based here in Rawlings, but her clients were spread all over the Detroit metro area."

Bristles snagged in my hair. I blinked back tears.

"Sorry," Tammy said, untangling the mess. "Anyway, Sandra definitely wins the Most Successful award. She ended up on the campaign team for some guy running for mayor in one of the big suburbs. He gave her credit for his win, and she pretty much wrote her own ticket after that. You can't beat a six-figure income at the age of thirty-three."

Tammy put the brush in a drawer and slid it shut with a bang. "I'm lucky if people remember to leave me a tip."

I frowned in sympathy. I couldn't blame Tammy for feeling disappointed at the follies of life. My own forgotten dreams were enough to make me resent everyone I'd gone to school with. I hadn't kept in touch with any of them, but somehow I was sure their lives were going along without a hitch, while mine had bottomed out long ago.

A comb scraped against my scalp and scissors crunched through my hair. I tried not to cry as four inches of split ends dropped to the floor.

Tammy yanked up another section. "Then a few years ago, Sandra hooked up with a guy even more driven than she was. They fell in love, if you can call it that. Anyway, their careers ended up on a collision course, and before you know it, she broke off the engagement. Not long afterward, Sandra left town, never to return."

I wondered if it was completely rude to ask more specifics. I decided I had a right to know. Sandra's messy life had spilled over into my own.

"Who was this guy and what happened?" I asked.

"I probably shouldn't be telling you this. It comes dangerously close to being gossip." She lifted another section of hair. The scissors hovered, then I heard the *snip*. "But I better mention it so you don't find yourself on the wrong side of Sandra's ex-fiancé."

"Would I know this person?" I asked.

"You would if you've tried to get anything through at the village." She cut off a chunk of fluff. "Martin Dietz."

My fist hit my forehead. At the sudden move, Tammy jerked her scissors clear.

"Martin Dietz, huh?" That explained why the man was so barbaric at our first run-in. If this Sandra had jilted him, my face could only bring back the most painful of memories.

But was that reason enough to deny me a permit to knock down the cistern? It seemed he was letting personal grumps get in the way of his job.

"I take it you already ran into him," Tammy said.

"This past week. No wonder my contractor yelled at me for going over to the village offices."

"I hope you don't get the wrong impression. Like I said, it's just because you look so much like Sandra. Martin's really not that bad. He's just getting over a broken heart. I think he's taking positive steps toward improving his attitude. For one thing, he's been a big financial backer of our church's youth group over the past year."

I almost guffawed at the thought of Mr. Dietz being

charitable. More likely, he was trying to buy his way to heaven.

Tammy turned my chin back toward the mirror. "Almost done."

I hardly recognized the woman staring back at me. I had a neck. And eyebrows.

I tucked one sleek strand behind an ear. I had a face again, and it was pleasant. Pretty, actually. I could even see the green of my eyes now that all the perm and highlights from last year's visit to the salon were cut out and my hair was back to its original chestnut color. The glaring grays I'd obsessed over this morning had disappeared with the fresh look.

"Wow. It's great." I smiled at Tammy in the mirror.

I wondered if she could perform the same miracle with my insides. Snip off a little guilt here, a tortured conscience there, and voilà, I'd be as good as new.

Yet somehow I knew it would take more than a trim to cure my problem.

11

Tammy dried my hair, then suggested a manicure as a finishing touch. I looked down at my jagged nails. The last remaining runt had peeled off this morning when it snagged my paint-splattered sweatshirt.

I pictured myself across the table from David at the Rawlings Hotel, lifting my glass in toast to a possible future together.

I slumped at the vision.

The only lipstick I owned had to be at least three years old; I'd never had my nails done professionally; and I couldn't remember the last time I'd bought a new outfit. Goodwill clothing had always served my renovator lifestyle just fine.

Before my thoughts degenerated into an all-out pity party, I reminded myself that David had asked me out before I cut my hair or bought new clothes. He appreciated me for qualities beyond my outer appearance. What those qualities were, I couldn't yet fathom, but I hoped to discover that on Friday.

Still, stick-on nails with a glossy coat of polish could only enhance my inner attributes.

"A manicure sounds good," I said.

Tammy led me to an oblong mahogany table near the window. A display rack filled with nail colors took up one end. I sat in a floral-patterned chair and lay a hand on the vinyl pad opposite me. Tammy picked up a file and went to work. White dust gathered on the black surface beneath my fingers.

I peeked at Tammy's own perfectly manicured hands and wondered how she'd managed to dodge a wedding ring through the years.

"It sounds like you were pretty involved in high school. Do you still stay busy?" I asked, interrupting the steady *ssht ssht* of the file.

"Absolutely. I spend most of my time with the teens from church. You wouldn't believe how many hurting families there are in this town. And most of them live in the pretty houses."

I nodded. I hadn't lived in one of the pretty houses, as Tammy put it, but I'd endured the lingering pain of my mother's suicide. I'd probably never forgive Mom for leaving me to be raised by my grandmother.

"Your mother would be spinning in her grave if she knew you were hanging out with that girl," Grandma would scold. "And look how you're dressed. Nice girls don't wear clothes like that."

It seemed Grandma never approved of anything I liked—my friends, my music, or even the books I read. I finally figured out that life was simpler if I did things Gram's way.

College had been my first taste of freedom. Unfortunately, it hadn't lasted long. I remember the sound of

Christmas music playing on my roommate's stereo and the smell of homemade gingerbread cookies from a care package as I answered the phone in my dorm that day more than ten years ago. Nat King Cole's rendition of "The Christmas Song" became a surreal requiem in light of that brief conversation.

"I've got some bad news, sweetie." Grandma's voice was filled with false bravado as she told me she was given only a few months to live. "Come on home and we'll talk about it."

"Which color do you prefer?"

My head snapped up at Tammy's question, and I realized I'd been staring vacantly as she'd applied my nail tips. I looked at the myriad of opaque, gloss, and pearlescent polishes on the rack beside me.

Choices.

I excelled in a one-color scheme in all my renovation projects: off-white. When dealing with discerning homebuyers, walls the color of cream cheese frosting were the safest, least offensive choice.

But that seemed far too tame a shade for a Friday night at the Rawlings Hotel.

Tammy leaned her elbows on the vinyl pad. "What will you be wearing? That's the easiest way to decide."

What will I be wearing? I chewed my lip. Jeans and a tee would never do.

"What should I wear?" I asked. After all, she was the professional.

She cocked her head and poked her lips to one side. "Hmmm. How about something blue? That will show off your hair and eyes."

The suggestion brought to mind an exterior paint chip card I'd been contemplating for accent colors at the Victorian. The shade was a rich, medium blue, like the sky over Lake Michigan on a summer morning.

I wrestled my mind back to the moment. I could probably track down some bluesy outfit at one of the local clothing stores.

"Blue it is," I replied. "Which polish choices does that give me?"

"I hate to do this to you." Tammy reached for a bottle filled with a pale fleshy-mauve tone. "This is Rebecca Ramsey's favorite shade. The woman might be a witch, but she has impeccable taste."

I tested my new nails on the mahogany tabletop, enjoying the *clickety-clickety* sound of the long tips. Somehow from David's puppy-dog eyes back at the supermarket, I hadn't figured Rebecca for a witch. And he'd seemed sincerely remorseful about the divorce papers arriving the other day. But then again, what kind of woman disappears for a year and then writes home with a divorce decree?

"Impeccable taste or not, I can't imagine wearing her shade to dinner with David." I searched the rows for a color I could call my own.

The sheer pressure of having to choose a single shade had me swallowing to chase down the acid climbing my esophagus. I panicked, settling on a Flamingo Pink in the second row.

Tammy opened the bottle and painted a stripe down the center of one nail. She paused, waiting for my approval. The bright fuchsia had me squinting. The color went completely against my personality, but I was open to fresh ideas.

"Perfect." I nodded for Tammy to continue. Ten minutes later, she showed me to an overstuffed chair by the window where I could sit and let my nails harden. I folded my legs under me and relaxed.

Just as my chic new hairdo hit the fabric behind me, the hat-clad head of Martin Dietz bounced past the plate glass and up the steps of the Beauty Boutique. I sat up and gripped the armrests, forgetting the still-wet polish on my fingers.

A pinky nail popped off and landed on the floor with a tiny *clink*. I stared at my mutated hand. That man was nothing but bad news. If I scrunched up small enough in the chair, I could probably go unnoticed.

I sensed him as he walked in the door. The loud jangle of bells punctuated his entrance, giving clear warning of a black mood.

I hunched lower and listened for his bellowing voice.

Instead, I heard a low rumbling sound that seemed soft and sensual. "Good morning, Tammy."

"Hi, Martin," Tammy returned with trademark cheeriness.

I peeked around the tall back of my chair to double-check that I hadn't been transported to an alternate universe.

Dietz was leaning across the front counter, practically gazing into Tammy's eyes.

Where was the evil zoning official who had given me such a rude welcome to Rawlings the other morning? I watched, amazed, as he hung his coat and hat on the rack by the door, seemingly laid-back and friendly.

He rubbed his scalp and smiled. "Time for a trim."

Tammy giggled.

I tried not to puke.

I turned back toward the window, holding my stomach. I couldn't believe what I was witnessing. It seemed the local ogre had some budding attraction for the local hairdresser. That explained Dietz's out-of-character generosity toward the church youth. I didn't peg Tammy as the Beauty-and-the-Beast type, but I figured she could flirt with whomever she wanted as long as she wasn't hounding after David.

I plucked at a nail tip. It seemed secure enough. Time to get back to the house and start on another upstairs bedroom. Once I got the second floor done, I'd have some furniture brought in and could at least enjoy a mattress and a fluffy pillow at bedtime. With a decent night's sleep once in a while, I should be able to get the rest of the house done by selling season.

I fished under the chair for my pinky nail, tucked it into my jeans pocket, then walked over to the counter to pay the bill. As I approached, Dietz dropped his relaxed pose and stiffened to full height.

I squinted into his eyes, daring him to make some comment.

He glared at me, his bald head bulging with veins. I half expected him to snort and paw like a raging bull.

Tammy dove between us. "Doesn't Tish look great, Martin?"

She touched a strand of hair that followed the line of my jaw. "With a little restyling, we've uncovered the real Tish Amble. And she's beautiful."

Tammy turned toward Dietz. "Isn't she, Martin?"

The red drained out of his face and he cleared his throat.

"You certainly look like a different person," he said to me.

I stood flabbergasted. It seemed Tammy had already tamed the beast. I gave a half smile, slapped enough money on the counter to cover the bill plus tip, and headed for the door.

I practically sprinted the half block to the Whistle Stop Coffee Shop, hoping to put some fast distance between Dietz and me.

The scent of fresh, hot coffee calmed my jostled nerves.

"Brrr," I said to the bejeweled attendant inside. "Feels like January out there."

"It's supposed to get colder this weekend." The girl's diamond lip stud flashed with each word.

"Great." I rolled my eyes. "I guess I better warm up with a café mocha. A drop of raspberry in that too, please."

"Whipped cream today?"

"Absolutely."

Coffee Girl blended and poured and stirred until my order was steaming in front of me on the counter.

"By the way," she said, "I watched it."

I looked at her, perplexed. "Watched what?"

"*Casablanca*. I didn't like the ending."

I cocked an eyebrow. "Why not? Rick did the right thing."

"I know, but he loved Ilsa. They should have been together."

"Ilsa didn't love Rick. She loved Victor."

Coffee Girl leaned over the counter toward me. "Victor Lund was an idea, not a man. Rick was real. I wanted her to love Rick."

I'd never seen such passion in the usually complacent young woman.

I shrugged. "Ilsa made a tough choice. We can only guess at the outcome." I picked up the Styrofoam cup. "Thanks for the coffee," I said over my shoulder as I walked out the door.

The sharp November air sliced through me like hedge cutters. Though it was only noon, dark clouds had moved overhead, creating a perpetual twilight. The first snow of the year would surely grace us by the end of the week.

I came around the rear corner of the house and headed to the garage for the snow shovel. The back porch would be the best place to lean it for the next five months or so.

One foot caught on a ridge in the blacktop driveway and I stumbled. The cup of café mocha flew out of my grasp and settled lidless on the pavement. I caught myself with outstretched palms, saving my secondhand jeans from a bigger hole in the knee. I dusted my hands off and watched the last drops of coffee drain onto the ground. In my side vision, I caught that "something's not right" feeling. I turned toward the rear of my towering Victorian.

My eyes rested on the basement window, the one just above the spooky old cistern. A stick protruded out the bottom sash, propping open the flip-out window half an inch.

I froze to the pavement. Icy wind forced its way into

my lungs. At least I wouldn't die from lack of oxygen while I waited for my senses to come back on line.

I stood there breathless, trying to figure out how that window ended up open. Just a few nights ago, Brad had assured me everything was locked up. So when had a stick magically appeared in the sill?

12

I stared at the propped-open window and remembered the body I'd imagined beneath the concrete. I wondered what I'd see if I peered through the glass into the cistern. Human features twisted in suffering? I fought a swell of vomit at the idea . . . Behind me in the yard, the ancient catalpa tree groaned.

Breathe, breathe, breathe, breathe, I told myself.

A car clattered across the tracks. From a nearby garage came the hum of an automatic door opener. The sounds of everyday life prevailed over the dizzy whirl of my brain. There had to be a rational explanation for the stick in my window, if not for the face in my cistern.

I peeled my feet from the pavement and spun toward Brad Walters' house. He was the last person in that cellar. He'd better have good justification for the piece of wood that made my house accessible to any crazed axe-murderer in Rawlings.

I banged on Brad's front door three times with my fist. The sound of my impatience made me take a step back. I didn't want Officer Walters to think I was some hot-tempered psycho-chick, at least not until I had definite proof that he was behind the open-window incident. Then he'd get a piece of my mind.

I concentrated on my air intake while I admired the tidy exterior of Brad's home. Bright white trim and dark gray shutters accented cheerful yellow siding. The grass was cut back from the smooth sidewalk, and a row of cone-shaped evergreens lined the front of the house. I looked down at the cement porch beneath me and made a mental note to tell Brad he'd better fix the cracks or potential buyers might count it against him. I couldn't fathom why he hadn't replaced the porch the same time he'd had the sidewalk done, which was no doubt within the last couple years.

A faint thudding came from inside the house. I looked toward the door just as Brad opened it. If it hadn't been almost lunchtime, I would have sworn he was still in his pajamas. He wore a sleeveless white tee and clingy black sweatpants. His hair stuck up on one side like it had recently been mashed against a pillowcase. One of those sleep-induced lines ran down his cheek, and that moist area on the side of his mouth could very well be drool.

One bicep, thick as the pillars holding up my front porch, blocked the doorway. My eyes traveled over the hump of solid muscle. Funny, Brad hadn't seemed so huge with clothes on.

I tried choking out a hello. Instead, my mouth dropped in dumb awe.

What was wrong with me? I'd seen plenty of well-endowed Uniforms before. I'd seen big, bare-muscled hunks on TV. There was no reason to stare at a man's body just because it had obviously been put to good use. And let's face it, I was hitting middle age. I shouldn't even blink twice at the sight in front of me. I took a step back.

"Everything okay?" Brad asked.

"Ummm . . ." I knew I was here for a reason, I just couldn't think of it at the moment. I looked at my feet. A crack led up to the door, then branched back in two directions, like a big arrow pointing at Brad, saying, "He's the one. He's the one."

He was the one, all right. Now I remembered what I was here for. I put my hands on my hips. "Everything is not okay. When you walked through my house the other night, you somehow missed the log propping open the basement window. Anybody could have gotten in there. I'm lucky I didn't get my throat slit in my sleep."

"Whoa." Brad crossed his arms. "What are you talking about? What log?"

"Not a log, exactly. More like a stick. But either way, that window isn't secure. And I want to know why."

Brad ruffled a hand through his hair. "Hang on. Let me get dressed."

He shut the door, leaving me alone on the porch. I stared at the six panels of glossy white. If it had been my house, I would have asked him inside. I felt a little put out having to wait here, especially since I hadn't yet grabbed my winter coat out of the trunk of my car.

I sat down on the first step and scrunched up to keep warm. Directly across the street, the railroad tracks stretched east and west. Behind them lay an unkempt

97

field of grass, then began the first buildings of down-town.

I shook my head. The inferior view coupled with the ear-blasting trains that ran rampant through town would definitely count against poor Brad upon resale. He'd have been smart not to get shackled with the home in the first place. But hey, not everyone was as house-savvy as me. At least my house had a row of shade trees hiding the rail-road tracks. And if I were lucky, the next owner wouldn't even notice the tracks until the papers were signed.

I wondered how Brad had ended up in Rawlings. Where had he grown up? Why had he become a cop? Why wasn't he married?

I sighed. Maybe I should have said yes to his dinner invitation. He seemed like a nice enough guy, even if he was a Uniform. He'd probably just wanted to welcome me to the neighborhood like he'd said, not quiz me on my pathetic past. In fact, Brad didn't even seem to care that I'd done time. That alone said heaps about his in-tentions. If he were looking for a long-term relationship, he sure wouldn't pick me.

I leaned on my hands and sighed again.

Yep. I was safe with Brad.

The door opened and I turned to see him dressed in work boots, blue jeans, and a gray sweatshirt. Though he still looked built, his jaw-dropping features were now safely covered with fabric.

"Why don't you show me the problem," Brad said, coming down the steps.

When he got to the bottom, he turned and looked at me. Tall as I was, my head only reached his shoulder.

"By the way, your hair looks great," he said.

I touched my new do, suddenly appalled by its lack of length. It seemed anybody could see right to my core without those fluffy flyaways to hide behind. And though Brad's eyes had appeared dull brown on Halloween night, they were definitely sparkling with x-ray vision today.

I pursed my lips, determined not to be sidetracked by eye color observations. Especially since there was a pair of beautiful blue ones waiting to take me out Friday night.

"Follow me." I led him up Railroad Street to the edge of his property, then angled through the crackled-white picket gate onto my own land. I kept close to the fence line, which was thick with out-of-control weeds and infant trees mixed with a border of daylily greens. Jan Hershel apparently hadn't cared much for gardening. The unsightly mess could only come from years of consistent neglect. I was tempted to take a rototiller to the whole yard and start fresh.

But the grounds would have to wait until after I brought the gasping-for-life Victorian back to health. I halted on the pavement and pointed to the basement window. Brad moved past me and knelt down, squinting at the weeds and dirt surrounding the foundation. He stared at the stick in the sill for a minute, patting his fingers to his lips.

"It's nothing more than a twig, really. I'm surprised you even noticed it. Let's have a look inside." He stood and walked toward the back porch.

"You don't need me down there, do you?" I called.

He gave me a wry glance. "You'd probably know better than I would if anything is out of place."

He was right. I hustled after him, though I dreaded another glimpse of the cistern and its gruesome contents. At the mere idea, my breath flew into hyperdrive.

We crossed the kitchen and neared the cellar door, my only goal to make it downstairs and back without losing my cool.

Nearly gasping, I slid back the bolt.

What was I so afraid of? It wasn't as if there was really a body in the cistern. The most we might find besides lumpy concrete would be a little dirt if someone had tried crawling through the window.

I stood aside and let Brad go first.

We approached the bottom. Each riser yelped, as if screaming a warning.

I shot a glance at my feet, convinced that someone was hiding behind the staircase. I could almost see a gnarled skeleton hand grabbing for my ankle through the open space at the back of the step.

My ears started to ring.

I gripped the rail.

All I could think about was jumping piggy-back onto Brad.

Before I could act on the impulse, Brad reached the concrete and pivoted toward me.

"Tish." The urgency in his voice had me convinced some ghoul was ready to attack.

I whipped around on the narrow step, ready to defend myself from whatever supernatural force came at me through the staircase.

The momentum from my spin carried me to the opposite rail and my hip bounced off the ancient wood. Flailing, I tried to catch hold of a rail or beam but grabbed only air.

Time shifted into slow motion as I tipped backward. Through the steps I got a clear view of the stony cistern. The window above it flashed strobe-like as each riser crossed my line of vision. Brad grabbed at my arm, but I fell through his grip.

I heard a thud and realized I'd landed spread-eagled on the basement floor.

13

Pain shot up my leg.

Brad lifted me to a sitting position. "I would've caught you, but that funky little spin threw me off."

"Why'd you say my name like that? I thought the boogeyman was behind me." I tried for a smile, but flinched instead.

"I was worried you were going to pass out. Your face was all white."

I held my ankle, rocking and rubbing the twisted joint. It finally registered that the little squeaky sounds I'd been hearing came from my own efforts not to cry.

"Here. Let me take a look," Brad said.

He manipulated my ankle, sending me into star-punctuated spasms.

"Okay. That's enough," I squealed.

This couldn't be happening. I needed all my limbs intact. There was no time for debilitating injuries or whacky hallucinations. I had to get the job done and move to the next project, before I fell in love with Rawlings . . . or whomever.

"Help me up." I held out my hand and Brad pulled

me to my good foot. Spirals of color flared in my side vision. There had to be a broken bone in there somewhere. Sprains didn't hurt like this.

I gritted my teeth. "I think I can walk."

Brad guarded my back as I hobbled up the stairs using one foot and the handrails. I crawled across the kitchen floor, content to lean against the cupboards for lack of a chair. It was one of the few times I regretted traveling light through life. A big, soft, sink-down-in-fluff-up-to-my-chin love seat would really fit the bill about now.

Brad stood above me in the empty room.

"Well," I croaked, "you'll have to investigate on your own. It might be awhile before I can make that trip again."

"I'd feel better if we got that looked at," Brad said. "There's a walk-in clinic just north of town. Tell me where your keys are and we'll take a drive."

My foot hurt too bad to argue with him.

A somber display of bare forest and gray fields rolled past as we drove. Brad's easy chatter about area history and childhood escapades kept my mind above the ankle.

He pulled into the circle drive of a brick-and-vinyl-sided building, popped Deucey into park, and set out for a wheelchair.

With Brad as my entertainment committee, the wait in the lobby flew by. A nurse wearing a smock smattered with coconuts and palm trees ushered us into an exam room. A few minutes later a man in his late fifties entered.

"I'm Dr. Phillips." He smoothed down the back of his

long white cover-up and sat on a stool. He wheeled over to my place on the table and took my dangling bare foot in both hands. "A little swelling. Some discoloration. Most likely gave your sciatic nerve a good twang. That'll cause a buzz in your leg that could take a few weeks to settle down. I'll write you a prescription that should help calm things."

"How soon before I can walk on it?" I asked.

"I'd give it a few days." He squinted at my foot and craned for a closer look. "Let's have you remove your other shoe."

Brad helped do the honors.

The doctor compared the soles of my feet. "There's some discoloration on your good foot as well. Where do you live, Patricia?"

"Almost right downtown Rawlings. And please call me Tish."

"You may have been more bruised from your fall than you realize. Or . . ." His brow wrinkled. "No, it couldn't be."

I gave him a questioning look.

"I served as a missionary doctor near Bangladesh a good number of years ago. Saw a fair number of people suffering from arsenic poisoning, from water right out of the village wells."

My eyes widened.

"I'm not saying that's what this is. You may want to consider a water filter system, just to be safe. If the bruising doesn't clear up in the next week or two, come back in for testing."

I gave a laugh of relief. "I'm sure it's not arsenic poisoning. I only drink bottled water. I read all about the township wells before I moved to the area."

"Like I said, just keep an eye on things." Dr. Phillips wrote the prescription.

Brad and I rode back to my house in near silence, stopping at Goodman's Grocery to fill the prescription.

Brad helped me into the house. I downed a pill with a glass of purified water the moment we walked in the door.

"Let me get you situated," Brad said. "Then I'll go downstairs and check out that window."

He saw that I made it to my humble portable bed.

When he left, I lay on my cot taking short little gasping breaths, waiting for the drug to do its job. I wondered all the while what Brad would find in the cistern.

Why would someone prop open my basement window, anyway? There wasn't a stick of furniture in the house, no valuable electronics, not a dime in cash lying around. The most anyone could hope for was the thrill of sneaking in and out of a "haunted house." But after the strange crew of trick-or-treaters I'd gotten the other night, it wouldn't surprise me if a couple of them had become daring.

I leaned up on one elbow and stared out the big front window. Across the street, the neighbor lady was at it again, raking, clipping, and sprucing up her lawn. I had a big job ahead if I was going to compete with her neat-freak yard.

I gave a little chuckle despite my pain.

Just wait 'til spring. The woman wouldn't know what hit her. She might be the reigning queen of the block when it came to fine flora, but I'd unseat her in a heartbeat with my guaranteed curb-appeal strategy.

That is, if my injury didn't put me back too far. To stay on track, I had to get the upstairs finished by Christmas. Then I could get to work on the first floor. And if Lloyd & Sons ever got back on board, their portion of the basement renovation should be completed by Valentine's Day. That would leave me three months to finish up the cellar plus do the exterior. By the time June rolled around, I could get the furniture in and be ready for the first buyers of the season.

I groaned and lay back down on the cot. Unfortunately, the way I felt, there was no chance that would happen.

The pain seemed to come in waves, starting at my ankle and washing up to my hip. I transported my mind elsewhere and joined Jan Hershel on the beach in Cancun, or wherever she was healing from her marriage-gone-sour. I reclined on the wooden lounger next to hers and listened to the crashing surf. The sun beat down on my gimpy leg, heating it through, soothing the pain.

Total relaxation.

The ocean breeze kicked up. A puff of white dust landed on my baby-oiled skin. I looked over to see where it had come from. Jan was covered in the white stuff. She scraped at it and beat at it, but it stuck to her like . . . concrete.

I jerked upright on my cot, grateful for the sharp pain that snapped me back to the gloomy Michigan afternoon.

Hold it together, Tish, I chided. Jan Hershel is not buried in your cistern.

In fact, nobody was buried in my cistern. And why my line of thinking kept heading in the body-in-the-basement direction was beginning to be a source of concern. If I weren't in such a rush to get out of Rawlings, I'd consider taking a full-time job to keep my mind off the past, present, and future.

But I'd come to the realization awhile back that I was completely unemployable. Three years of forced menial labor had cured me of the job market forever. And when I'd finally collected my two-bedroom inheritance and enough money to pay my attorney bills, I'd leveraged my way from that first broken-down house in Walled Lake to this veritable mansion in Rawlings.

The windows rattled and I knew Brad was making his way up the basement steps.

He stopped in the doorway of my future master suite.

I gave him an arched-eyebrow look that demanded he tell me everything.

"Probably just kids looking for thrills," he said. "There was no damage, so I locked up. You're good to go."

I found it interesting that whenever somebody said something I didn't want to hear, I got this chokey little ball in my throat. Right now, Brad was lucky I couldn't go after him on two feet.

I swung my legs over and gripped the edge of my cot. "What do you mean, I'm 'good to go'?"

In my book, a stick in the window was as close to a break-in as they come. Brad had better track down the offenders, or I'd contact his superiors and let them know that Officer Walters was a dud.

"Look." Brad crouched down to my level. "There was

a stick. That's all. There was no sign of an actual entry. I'll make sure the department steps up its drive-bys on this corner."

"That's it?" I asked.

Incredible. And not acceptable.

I leaned close enough to detect toothpaste on his breath. "Run some prints. Do whatever detective stuff you guys do. I want to know who was monkeying with that window."

"Tish," he said, tapping his thumbs together, "Rawlings is a small town. All that detective stuff costs money. If there had been a murder or grand theft or something, I'd consider it. But there hasn't even been a crime committed other than possible trespassing. The latch on the window isn't even damaged. If I didn't know better, I'd have thought the stick was put there from the inside."

His voice was gentle and soft. Mesmerizing. Convincing. It made me want to forget that Brad was the last one in the basement . . . the only one who could have put the stick in the window from the inside.

14

I didn't want it to be true. A big part of me wanted to believe that Brad was the one good cop I knew, the one Uniform that was also a decent human being. We'd spent such an enjoyable afternoon together, despite my injury. But as I met his steady gaze and followed the faint creases that lined his eyes, I realized I really knew nothing about the man, other than the fact that he went to church on Sundays and could tell a good story.

Any motive he might have for entering my basement through that window was beyond me. A dark, paranoid imagination might suppose that he wanted access to the body in the cistern, maybe to do a better job of hiding it. But a realistic, facts-only look at the situation concurred with Brad's take on things: the perpetrators were just naughty, nasty, rotten, stinky kids looking for a thrill.

Besides, if Brad were the murderer, who was the victim?

Brad must have caught me squinting at him. He pulled back and stood up, staring at me for a few seconds with an expressionless face. Then with a slow blink, he said goodbye.

I listened as he left the house through the back door. A squeak of the screen, the crunch of metal as the door slammed shut, then all was silent.

Except my brain.

As long as shock waves continued rippling up my leg, I had nothing better to do than lie on my cot and replay the Brad-as-murderer theme while I waited for the prescription to kick in. But please, Brad just wasn't that kind of guy. Look at his tidy yard and neat gray shutters. That was the sign of a sane, well-organized mind. Of course, there was the cracked concrete on his front porch . . .

I sat up. I couldn't take it anymore. I'd been lying here idle for ten minutes, and my mind had taken a bizarre digression. Clearly, having a leg injury was bad for my mental health. I had to get up or I'd drive myself crazy thinking about a murder that never happened.

Sighing, I recalled Brad's gentle features. A pleasant-looking guy like that with those straight, serious lips could only be taken at face value—at least for now.

In any case, the burden of proof was on me. And I had no intention of proving anything about anybody. All I wanted to do was finish the job at hand and move on to whatever vacant, decrepit building was in store for me next.

Still, as long as I was disabled, it wouldn't hurt to hobble across the street and meet the neighborhood watchdog. It would be my first, long-overdue step in moving from a *Silas Marner* way of thinking to an *Emma* frame of mind. And if the old gossip gave me any local scoop, so much the better.

I held on to the wall as I put weight on both feet, standing inch by inch. Each jolt of pain reminded me that I was indeed alive. And that was better than some people.

I slid carefully into my jean jacket, clenching my teeth to stay focused. By the time I reached the front porch, I was out of breath. And despite fall's sharp bite, beads of shock-induced sweat broke out on my forehead.

Maybe now wasn't the right time to pick my neighbor's brain.

I collapsed to the top porch step. I rested my head on one knee, listening to a swirl of noises. The far-off beep of a car horn. The distant slam of a screen door. The rumble of a truck over on Maple Street. A faint whistle, foretelling the train to come.

I groaned. The doctor's assurance that my leg would only hurt for a few weeks seemed shortsighted. The way I felt, a year was probably more accurate. Which meant that Friday night's date with David wasn't going to be the perfect romantic evening I'd had my heart set on, not with me gritting my teeth between every bite.

On the bright side, if I couldn't work, I couldn't lose any more fake fingernails. But on the downside, I think I'd been counting on them all falling off before Friday. Could I truly go out in public with Flamingo Pink anywhere on my body?

I pity-partied the whole time the train blew past, wallowing in the bone-jarring vibrations, holding fast to the revolting but undeniably authentic sound of my reality.

At the last ding of the warning bells, I lifted my head. And there she was, staring at me, right at the foot of my front porch. The neighbor lady, Ms. Watchdog.

At close range her gray hair was more like wisps of pure black mixed with chunks of pure white. In between were pale patches of bare scalp. Her face seemed almost blue from the labyrinth of veins showing, with skin pulled tightly over a bone-thin nose. Her lips withdrew into her mouth, and I wondered if she'd remembered to pop in her dentures that morning.

"Looks like you're in some pain," she said in a soft, surprisingly youthful voice. I had expected the cackle of an old hag.

"I twisted my ankle going to the basement." I paused to catch my breath.

"Not surprised. Those steps are too narrow to be safe."

"Oh? You've been down there?"

"Plenty of times. My son, Jack, helped with the foundation repair after the flooding. When was that . . . about a year or so ago?"

I wanted to jump for joy. Brad wasn't the killer—Jack was. Jack had access to the basement and even worked with the concrete.

"Mind if I sit a minute?" The woman climbed to the top step and settled in, leaning against the crackled-paint siding.

"Be my guest. I'm Tish Amble, by the way." I offered my hand, but pulled back at the electric twang ripping through my nerves.

"Dorothy Fitch. You stay put." Dorothy adjusted her bulky quilted jacket. "Takes a little more to stay warm these days."

I waited for her to say more, but she simply looked at me in silence. Flustered, I glanced across the street at the Fitch residence.

"So, have you lived in the neighborhood long?" I asked.

"All my life," she replied. "Grew up in that little house next to the church a couple blocks down. My husband grew up in that house right there." She pointed to her story-and-a-half, early-1900s home. "We moved in with his mother and raised four kids in three bedrooms. Hate to say it, but the best day of my life was the day his mother died. She was a miserable, sickly woman. Only lived to torture me."

"Oh." I swallowed hard at the callous comment. "Must've been some flood last year, huh?" I said, hoping she'd move back to a less irreverent topic.

"Never saw such a downpour. Water was seeping through every crack. Rick and Jan had it worst of all." Dorothy patted the tongue-in-groove of the porch floor. "Looked like sprinklers going off from every wall of the basement."

"You were down there when it happened?"

"Jan called right away. It was the last straw for her. She hadn't wanted to buy the place to begin with." Dorothy shrugged. "Rick wasn't about to give up his baby."

I thought about Rick Hershel, almost in tears at the closing table. His scruffy beard and mustache barely hid his emotion as he penned his signature on the dotted

113

lines. At the time, I thought he was distraught about the divorce. Now I wondered if he wasn't more heartbroken over having to sell his true love.

For a second, I hoped Jan really was lying in my basement. Some people had no understanding of the connection between flesh and bone, and plaster and wood. Renovating an old home was more than just a project. It was a labor of love, almost certainly more gratifying than giving birth. Unlike a child, a house didn't have a mind of its own that came with destructive self-will. Every effort applied toward its four walls remained constant, and only powers greater than the house could change it. Time, elements, a new owner.

A gust of air rattled the windows. The cold blast brought to mind the image of perpetual suffering frozen in the cistern, and along with it came a wave of empathy. In her misunderstanding of Rick's passion for the house, Jan might have become a permanent part of it.

Or not.

I reminded myself that there was no body in the basement.

"So Jan must be happily living in a brand-new home somewhere, huh?" I said.

"Haven't heard. Thought she'd drop a note now and then, but some people are bad that way. Probably hurts too much to think about the old neighborhood."

I clasped my hands against a rearing stomach. "What about Rick? Has he stayed in touch?"

Dorothy nodded. "In a manner of speaking. I see his car drive by every so often. Probably just curious to see what you're doing to the place. Never stops in, though."

Not exactly comforting to learn that a possible murderer was casing my house. I thought about the stick in the basement window, and wondered if Rick had conveniently kept a key so he could let himself in later, prop open the basement window, then take his time patching up his lousy burial job.

Forgetting my audience, I shook my head and rolled my eyes, determined not to give valuable brain space to a ridiculous notion.

"Where'd you wander off to?" Dorothy asked.

I gave her a questioning look. "Pardon me?"

"Looked like your mind was a million miles away."

I hesitated. Spilling my guts about imaginary bodies somehow didn't seem like good Welcome Wagon conversation.

Still, for the sake of sound sleep, I took a chance.

"Just thinking about the trick-or-treaters that came through last week. A couple of them said my house was haunted." I gave an embarrassed smile and rubbed the back of my neck.

I'd hoped she'd laugh and reassure me that it wasn't true. Instead, a look of alarm flashed across her face. Her hands fidgeted in her lap.

"Oh, kids these days." She waved off their comments. "No such thing as ghosts."

I wrapped my jacket tighter to keep the frigid wind at bay and stared vacantly at Dorothy's house across the street. The curtain in the downstairs window moved to one side. I jerked upright in my perch on the top step. A zing of pain knifed down my leg.

I tried not to waggle my primped-up finger too exuberantly as I pointed.

"Who's that in the window?" I asked. I'd been going on the assumption that Dorothy was the busybody of the 'hood, but it seemed I was wrong.

Dorothy looked toward home. The curtain fell back into place.

Her lips pursed up, giving the illusion she had teeth.

"Just my Jack," she said. Her thumbs twirled together in slow circles. "Bet he'll like you just fine. Sure liked Jan when she used to live here."

A buzz of apprehension crept over my shoulders and up the back of my neck. Somehow I didn't want anything in common with cold, dead Jan.

Especially not interest from Dorothy's eccentric son.

15

I coughed at the sudden dryness in my mouth.

"Let's get you inside before you catch your death," Dorothy suggested, touching my arm.

Too weak to resist, I allowed her to help me. She led me to my makeshift bedroom and tucked me into the cot, complaining that I should have a real bed. She left the room and appeared a few minutes later with a sandwich piled high with slabs of Brad's homegrown tomatoes, cucumber slices, and cheese.

"You're not eating enough," Dorothy chastised, handing me the fare. "Hardly any food in your cupboards, and what's there is only fit for birds and rabbits."

My stomach grumbled as if in agreement. I took a bite, closed my eyes, and savored the juicy combination. A stream of pink squirted from the side of my bread, and I licked it from the back of my hand. "This is delicious. Thank you."

"You need to take better care of yourself," Dorothy lectured as she handed me a glass of milk.

I sniffed the contents before I took a drink. It never hurt to verify the expiration date.

I thought back to the shopping trip with my dreamy neighbor David almost a week ago. I'd been at the milk cooler, grabbing for the half-gallon of skim. He was at the cream cheese, picking up an eight-ounce package. Thankfully, I'd shown him the reduced-fat variety in time. He'd had that special sparkle in his eyes as he thanked me for helping him avoid a major mistake.

I sipped the cold, refreshing milk and looked forward to a future of mind-melding looks from David.

"Far too skinny for my liking," Dorothy carried on. "A few more pounds would do you good."

I handed Dorothy my glass. She was either passing out backhanded compliments or bold-faced criticisms. I tried not to let them under my skin.

"You work yourself to death." Dorothy clucked her tongue. "Rest up. I'll check back on you later."

She took the dishes into the kitchen and thumped around in there awhile. I wondered what she was doing. Then I heard the faint sound of the faucet running and realized she must be washing up for me. A few minutes later, Dorothy left the house, closing the front door softly behind her.

An approaching train provided the backdrop to my dreams as I dozed off.

I woke a few hours later, refreshed after my first nap in years. Somewhere under the pile of laundry in the corner, my cell phone rang.

I retrieved it from the pocket of last week's jeans, knowing before I answered that it must be the vagrant Lloyd & Sons on the other end. Nobody else in Rawlings, not even David, had my phone number.

"This is Tish," I answered.

"Lloyd here. How's the permit . . . *crackle* . . . coming?" The connection was no better than the last time we'd talked.

"I mailed out the application. The next committee meeting is a week from Thursday. I'm not holding out any hope. But don't worry, I've got a Plan B in mind." I leaned against a windowpane and looked at the overcast sky, completely clueless as to any Plan B.

Lloyd piped up. "While you're waiting around for approval, I've got other projects. I'll . . . *crackle* . . . and check back with you in the spring." The line screeched static and I realized I lost him.

Disgusted, I hit the off button and dropped the phone back on the pile. I steamed into the parlor as fast as my limp would let me, and paced the blue shag carpet. I relished the shot of pain zapping my nerves at every step.

Get back with me in the spring? Was Lloyd crazy? My basement was top priority. And when I lined him up last summer, he'd guaranteed my project would come first.

Looking at the situation from Lloyd's point of view, I could see where my own stubbornness to have the cistern removed, instead of walled in, was messing with our agreed-to schedule. It was my change, not his, that slowed the renovation.

Of course, when I walked through the house last July, it hadn't registered that there even was a cistern in the basement. So technically, Lloyd should include its removal as part of the project.

I fingered the banister leading to the second floor, pulling back at the stickiness of the original finish. With everything else to do, there was no time to dwell on the cistern. The matter was now up to the Historical Committee. Once I got an official rejection, and not just some off-the-cuff denial from the village overlord, I could decide my next step.

I toyed with a loose dowel along the stairwell. It would be simple to wall in the cistern as Lloyd suggested. Preferable, even. No more concrete image dangling in my mind at bedtime. No more wondering how a body ended up buried in my basement, and worse, who put it there. But somehow I knew I wasn't being honest. I already had the overwhelming urge to pick up a hammer and chisel and see for myself what lay under the concrete. A mere layer of drywall couldn't dampen innate curiosity. If I thought I could maneuver the basement steps, I would be down there even now disproving my morbid theory.

I looked up from the broken dowel to the wallpaper that lined the room. Small pink and yellow roses were arranged in tidy columns. In between each was a strip of larger bouquets tied with blue ribbons. From my place at the stairs, the pattern looked like mama flowers holding hands with baby flowers.

I leaned close to the edge of a leaded-glass window and picked at a gap in the paper with one pointy fake nail, peeling off the time-worn surface in a long strip. The next owners would have inoffensive, off-white paint interspersed with a coat of polyurethane to create a subtle striped effect.

Just for fun, I pulled off every loose section and picked at every long-suffering bubble throughout the parlor.

When I'd finally exhausted my urge, the floor was covered in curls of pastel and white paper, like the remains of a hit-and-run baby shower.

I plopped to the carpet and massaged my ankle. Pain or not, I had just made the parlor my next project. The thought of someone walking in and seeing peeled, unfinished walls reviled my sense of pride. I plotted a trip to the paint store, hoping I could still operate a car with my foot in such bad shape.

I was getting up the gumption to stand when the doorbell rang. I looked at my mess in panic, wondering if I should pretend I wasn't home. Footsteps crossed the porch and the room darkened as the uninvited guest peered in the front window.

It was Dorothy, keeping her promise to return and check up. One hand shielding the glare, she spotted me amidst the evidence of my parlor paroxysm.

Dorothy shuffled around to the door and let herself in, probably feeling sorry for the turtle thrashing around on the floor.

She waded through the shredded wallpaper.

"Give me your hand," she said with a tinge of frustration. "Thought I told you to rest."

She pulled me to my feet.

"Sorry." I brushed off little wads of sticky flowers stuck to my clothing. With all Dorothy's nagging, I could almost believe I was still living with my grandmother.

"Come get something to drink," she said.

I followed her into the kitchen, feeling like a visitor in my own home.

Dorothy turned the knob on the water dispenser, filling a glass with the refrigerated liquid. She passed it to me.

I took a long swallow. I hadn't realized a nap could be so draining. Refreshed, I set the glass on the counter.

"Better?" Dorothy asked, her pale face almost phosphorescent in the waning afternoon light.

"Much," I replied, smiling.

An awkward moment passed. I scrambled to figure out ways to be hospitable without furniture to offer.

"Thank you for all you've done today," I groped.

She nodded. "Glad you're not too laid up."

Guilt oozed in her tone.

I fidgeted with the short ends of my new cut. "You know how it is. I have to stay busy or I'd go nuts."

Dorothy grabbed a paper bag from under the kitchen sink and started toward the parlor. I hobbled after her.

She scooped up handfuls of debris and loaded them into the sack. I gave my best shot at pitching in, but fell short of her capable efforts. Her navy stretch polyester slacks rose to flood level as she bent over to pluck the last tiny speck from the shag.

"Got an old love seat for you," Dorothy said, straightening. "Need something to sit on while your foot's healing up."

I pictured a tattered, dust-mite-scented sofa. "No, thank you. Really. I've still got to pull the carpet from this room. It won't be ready for furniture until Christmas, at least."

"Never heard of anything so foolish. 'Bout as comfortable as a prison cell." Dorothy's look said volumes.

My throat tightened as my wall of defense went up. Apparently Brad had spread the news of my past. From the look of judgment on Dorothy's face, the unethical Officer Walters had filled her in with all the details.

I could only hope the news hadn't traveled to David. All I wanted Friday was a night of pleasant conversation. Fluffy, even.

I checked my stick-on nails. Nine were still intact. I might as well make the rest last until the special night. Then they could pop off in unison for all I cared. David had a one-night shot at seeing me at my girly best. After that, like it or not, I would be back to my normal, frumpy renovator self.

Dorothy headed for the front door.

"Bring you some soup tomorrow," she said.

I noticed she walked with a slight limp of her own and wondered if it was arthritis or the legacy of some injury from her mid-thirties. At the thought, a lightning bolt of pain shot up my leg, along with a heavy dose of self-pity.

It was bad enough that I was living my life alone. I could hardly handle the thought of becoming old and run-down. Still, at least Dorothy had a grown child to keep her company. I might never have one to call my own.

I watched Dorothy cross the street.

Not that I wanted a child, of course. From what I could tell, kids meant heartbreak. You could never get them to do what you wanted. And if they ever did do as you asked, sometimes the outcome was worse than if they had disobeyed.

No, it was better to be alone. My children were the homes I resurrected.

I pressed my forehead against the cool glass of the parlor window and sighed. If only someone could revive me in the same manner I revived houses.

I tapped a snappy rhythm on the window, quite certain that David was that someone.

I'd find out for sure this Friday night.

16

Friday morning showed up ahead of schedule. I hadn't even picked out what to wear and it was already the day of my big date.

Shower. Blow dry. Get dressed. I worked through my morning routine, furious with myself for putting off what I should have done a week ago. Sure, my parlor looked pristine. But tonight, sitting across from David wearing heaven-knew-what, would I care that I'd gotten the entire room done in two short days on one working leg?

I slipped into my best jeans, the ones without paint splotches or holes. With a painful tug, a nail tip dropped to the floor.

Great. Only seven remained after the one I'd shed yesterday into a can of paint.

Now, not only did I have to track down the perfect outfit before seven o'clock, but I also had to stop in to see Tammy at the Beauty Boutique for a repair job.

First, however, I'd pick up a roll and coffee at the Whistle Stop. Two days of seclusion made me thirsty for human interaction. And while the girl behind the counter was no conversationalist, at least I could look forward to the possibility that she'd added a new nose ring to her collection or an old movie to her repertoire.

I threw on my pink crochet hat and insulated coat to ward against the blustery November wind, then limped my way toward the shop. Leaves crunched in an uneven pattern beneath my feet. Limp, step. Limp, step. The pungent smell of late autumn filled the air.

I crossed the tracks, hardly glancing up, lost in analyzing the coffee girl's facial jewelry fixation. If she was willing to offer such a countenance to the community, her thinking dipped even below my own cloudy level. At least I kept my societal blemishes hidden. But I supposed there was a place for the coffee girls of the world. Somebody had to make the rest of us feel better. Compared to her, I had my life together.

The door jangled as it opened. Warm, java-scented air rushed past into the street, and I scurried to put the plate-glass door between me and the frosty morning.

The nose-ring attendant was nowhere in sight. I grabbed a Styrofoam cup off the stack and filled it with raspberry coffee. I added some chocolate creamer and stirred.

Mmmm.

The sweet steam loosened up my sinuses. A drip of condensation formed on the tip of my nose. I dabbed at it with a napkin from the counter as I waited to pay.

After a minute, I decided the coffee girl must not have heard me come in.

"Hello?" I called.

The sound of shuffling came from the back room.

126

I waited. Good service in a small town was optional.

A minute later, a young blonde with a blotchy red-and-white face made an appearance.

"Sorry about that. Can I help you?" she asked, wiping her cheeks with the back of one wrist.

"Uh, sure." I set my cup on the counter and poked around in my coat for a few dollars. "Coffee and that sticky bun back there, please." I pointed at a supersized caramel roll sprinkled with nuts.

She plucked a piece of waxed paper from a box and reached for the breakfast treat. I studied her profile, a tad envious of the gold and diamonds that dangled from her ears and neck. First impressions said she was around eighteen, smart in school, and from a highfalutin middle-class family. No facial jewelry allowed in that household.

Curiosity got the best of me. "I guess I was expecting someone else this morning. Are you new here?"

She swallowed, obviously holding back tears. "I'm filling in for the owner's daughter."

In my mind, Coffee Girl made the jump from High School Flunky to Indulged Only Child. I felt like snorting. If this were my shop, would I let my daughter wait on people with her face full of sterling silver?

I tried not to snoop, but I couldn't stop myself. "Is she on vacation?"

The attendant's lip quivered and a tear chugged down one cheek. "Casey died yesterday. I'm helping out 'til her mom gets things together."

A chill swept through my body. My legs tried buckling beneath me. I grabbed the smooth wood countertop and steadied myself.

The coffee girl had a name. Casey. I'd never even introduced myself.

Every unkind thought I'd had toward the girl swirled through my mind, and I knew that she would have been ten times harder on herself.

Please don't let it be suicide.

I blinked hard and took a deep breath. "I am so sorry. Was there an accident?"

A million ways to die flashed through my mind. Quick and painless, long and agonizing, smooth and peaceful, abrupt and shocking. None seemed appropriate for a young woman of eighteen.

But then, death had no manners.

The attendant toyed with my sticky bun on the counter. "They don't know what happened. Her little girl tried to wake her up, but she couldn't. They're doing an autopsy."

My heart lurched. Casey had a little girl? And now Casey was dead, and the child an orphan. At least the poor thing had her grandmother. They'd make it through.

"I'm so sorry," I said again, devoid of further words of comfort. I grabbed my sticky bun and coffee and hustled out the door, rushing to get away from death before it could latch on to me.

I walked home without seeing anything but my feet on concrete, then blacktop, then dying brown grass. I went inside. I wanted to push the world away. To crawl into my cot and make everything disappear. To plug my ears and block out the droning automobiles, rumbling trains, and barking dogs that proved life went on even without the dearly departed.

Instead, I leaned against the kitchen counter and ate my sticky bun and drank my coffee. A final swallow, then I tossed my cup and napkin in the trash.

I propped my elbows on the sink to take the pressure off my bad foot, and looked out the kitchen window at the catalpa tree. Its twisted, gnarled branches were like skeleton fingers reaching for me . . . *Help me end the pain, Tish*. The voice echoed in my mind like a remembered dream.

I jerked upright and shook my head.

Grandma was laid to rest. There was no reason to keep bringing her back to life. There was no reason to fear the dead.

Yet at the thought, a prickle crept over my skin. I turned slowly toward the basement door.

17

The old wooden door was the only thing that separated me from the body in my basement. I wanted nothing more than to grab a sledgehammer and smash the cistern to smithereens and prove to myself there was nothing but dirt and stones beneath that lump of white.

But I knew I'd never make it down the steep stairway with my leg in its crippled state. Besides, I didn't even own a sledgehammer.

I pounded a fist on the counter. There was no body in my basement. There was nothing to investigate.

"Leave me alone," I yelled toward the basement. I jumped at the echo of my voice in the empty house.

I grabbed at my temples, hoping to get a handle on my mind. But the more I tried to block it out, the more insistent the image in the concrete became.

A ball of anger lodged in my throat.

I hobbled to the basement door and fumbled with the slide bolt.

I threw the door open. It crashed against the back wall. Plaster dust drifted into an empty stairwell.

"Stop acting like a three-year-old afraid of the dark," I chastised myself. "There's nothing in your basement." A thump sounded behind me in the kitchen. I twirled and screamed, sure I would see the cistern-dweller, wailing like a banshee, hair wild and clothes tattered from the grave.

But it was only David, standing in the middle of the stain-splotched linoleum.

I massaged my neck, that bare place between my shoulders and head that used to be hidden by hair. I could only hope David hadn't heard me talking to myself.

"What are you doing here already?" The words popped out before I could stop them from sounding rude. I had at least nine hours to pull myself together before our scheduled date. How dare he arrive early?

"Sorry to startle you. I came by to drop this off." A key dangled from one hand.

I reached for it. "What's this for?"

He smiled and a dimple formed on one cheek. "It's your house key, actually." He looked around the kitchen. "Are you well? I looked through the window and you seemed distressed. I came in to help, if you needed it."

I blinked hard, trying to imagine what a dork I must have looked like from his angle on the porch. Skinny me, braced at the top of the cellar steps, talking to myself about an empty basement.

"Everything's great." I rocked back on my good heel and swung my arms. "You know how it is. Me and the family ghosts were just working things out."

"Oh." David stared at me. "Is that a new style you've got there?"

On instinct, my hand reached for my head. "Just a couple days old. What do you think?"

"Superb. It really sets off the green of your eyes."

"Thanks." I got that warm fuzzy feeling that came with a well-phrased compliment.

But somewhere in my muddled brain, it finally registered why David had come over. "So. You had my house key. How come?"

He took a step back. "I helped Rick with the water-proofing project last year. I thought I'd lost the key, but I was cleaning out a drawer the other day and there it was. I didn't feel right keeping it."

I tossed the key on the counter. It slid across and jangled into the stainless steel sink. I wondered how many other copies were at large. Did Rick Hershel have one? What about the creepy Jack Fitch? I knew Lloyd the contractor had a copy, since I'd given it to him.

I met David's eyes, soft blue in the reflected daylight. He seemed so handsome . . . so harmless. Someone else must be responsible for the stick-in-the-window stunt. I was holding out hope that David was the genuine article.

"Thanks for bringing it by." I smiled and let down my guard. "I'm really looking forward to tonight."

His eyebrows lifted in what could have been surprise.

"Me too." He shifted his weight. "Uh, six o'clock, right?"

I cut him some slack. He must have had a tough week dealing with Rebecca's divorce bomb. I figured one hour earlier wasn't putting me out too much.

"Six o'clock it is," I said, walking him to the door.

David left and I rushed to call Tammy at the Beauty Boutique for a nail repair job.

"I can fit you in at three." Her voice sounded like she was fighting a cold.

While I waited for the appointment, I headed to the quaint clothing stores scattered downtown, determined to find the perfect outfit. I had in mind something the exact shade of David's eyes.

The air was damp and my injured leg ached to the bone. I Frankenstein-walked my way to Clothing Junction, attracted by the bright sweaters in the window display. I pushed open the door. The warm scent of cinnamon and apples greeted me. Floorboards creaked as I wove through the store to the sales desk on the far side. On the way, I took in the floral swags and wreaths sprinkling the walls, the jewelry and accessories displayed atop each rack, and the clever antique knickknacks showcased in every nook. The overall effect gave me the irresistible urge to buy everything in sight.

Two older women stood behind the counter, talking to each other in hushed tones. They seemed oblivious to my approach. I couldn't help but overhear.

"Arsenic poisoning. Just enough to kill someone with a weak heart, poor dear," said the one with the blonde beehive.

"It's a wonder we aren't all dead," the other biddy answered. "I've drank my share of coffee over there, you know."

I gulped, wondering if the faint bruising on my feet could be caused by arsenic from my Whistle Stop habit.

Biddy Number Two turned and noticed me. Her eyebrows squinched, and I could tell she caught my resemblance to the AWOL Sandra Jones.

"Can I help you?" she asked, all aflutter.

"Hi. I need something remarkable. In blue."

She led me to a rack on the far wall. "We just got in this collection of winter blues. This one is my personal favorite."

She held up a soft cashmere wrap sweater with a satin tie on one side. Elegant. Classy. I pictured myself in it, sitting opposite the dashing David in the Rawlings Hotel dining room. The candlelight would merge the blue of my sweater and the blue of his eyes, and we'd talk about our perfectly meshed future together.

I reached out and touched the sleeve, reveling in the thought of that soft yarn against my skin. I ran my hands down the length of it. An exposed jagged nail tweaked at the surface fuzz. Tonight, of course, I'd have my flamingo nail tips back in pristine condition.

The woman left the sweater in my hands and walked to a nearby rack. "These slacks would really set it off."

The silky black pants were fitted, with no waistband and gently tapering legs.

"Would you like to try them on?" she asked.

"Absolutely," I said, pretending I did this shopping-spree thing all the time. In reality, I never tried stuff on at my usual clothing stores before taking it home and washing it first. Anything could be alive on those second-hand garments.

I stepped into the dressing room and shut the louvered

door behind me. Huge mirrors boxed me in. I couldn't avoid taking a good look at my reflection.

I sighed.

I seemed so hand-me-down. Jeans a size too big and a baggy blouse in original '70s striped fabric. Sure, the combination could pass for the current style, but it just didn't work with my new chic hairdo that said I was sophisticated now. Svelte slacks and a trim sweater would give me that put-together look I craved.

I wrestled off my blouse and pulled on the sweater.

My head popped out the top and I adjusted it into place.

A perfect fit. I ran my hands across every part of the fabric, feeling as if I were special, important, and worth loving.

Wow. I'd have to go shopping more often.

The slacks achieved the same sensation.

I smiled and hugged myself in the mirrors, thrilled at my first introduction to must-have clothing. I would feel so confident tonight. So together. Exactly the effect I hoped to attain.

A long, white tag dangled from one sleeve of the sweater. I hadn't even thought to look at the price.

I flipped the tag over.

I stood for several agonizing seconds, reading and rereading the three digits followed by a decimal point and two zeros.

How could that be? How could this little bit of a sweater cost more than a month's worth of groceries? There was hardly anything to it. Soft fuzzy fabric and a satin bow should only amount to twenty bucks. What crazed individual would pay five times more than a thing was worth? So what if Clothing Junction provided a luxurious and unique shopping experience. Were there really people out there, other than frivolous tourists, that would fork over those kinds of funds just to feel good about themselves?

"How's it fit, dearie?" the biddy called through the slats.

Great fit, exorbitant price, I felt like snapping back.

"It's okay."

I looked at the pile of crumpled, recycled clothing on the floor. Three bucks' worth of stuff, maybe. My whole wardrobe over the past eight years had cost a fraction of what this one outfit would come to today.

Was I worth it? A miser's horde of money sat untouched in my bank account, earmarked for the renovation project. Maybe it wouldn't hurt just this once to treat myself. I'd been through a lifetime of heartaches and hardships. It was time to let go of the past and enjoy the present.

I changed back into my ragtag combination, dismayed at the transformation from princess back to pauper. No wonder the salesladies hadn't paid any attention to me when I walked in the door.

I brought the fantastic duo to the counter, and with a hard swallow, wrote the check.

Beehive Woman gave the document a thorough inspection, glancing first at the lettering, then at me.

"I see you're not related to Sandra Jones," she said.

I waved my hand and flashed a smile. "Heavens, no. But I gather from crowd response that we could be sisters."

"Twins. You could be twins." She squinted at me. "Well, Sandra does have thinner brows. And her eyes are brown, not green, like yours." The woman sighed, fussing and folding my purchase. She tucked it in a burgundy bag with a twine handle. "Sandra was one of our best customers. Shopped here since high school."

"Well, I hope she didn't buy this same outfit. Wouldn't that be tacky?" I clicked my fingertips on the counter hoping the woman would just stick to the task and get me out of here in time for my three o'clock at the Beauty Boutique.

Blonde Beehive gripped the bag, apparently determined I would hear her out. "Sandra hasn't been in here for a good year now. What a shame about her and Martin."

C'mon, c'mon, c'mon, I felt like saying.

"Yeah. I heard she jilted him, poor guy," I said.

"After what he did to her, no one blames her. Wasn't that a mess?"

I leaned forward against the counter, suddenly intrigued by news of Martin Dietz's shortcomings. "Sounds serious. What did he do to her?"

"Well"—the woman's voice lowered to gossip level—"he wanted that big county position. Which one was it, Rita?" She turned to the woman behind her.

"Commissioner," Rita said.

"Yes. Well, he put Sandra in charge of the campaign and she would have won it for him."

"But?" I asked, thanking God Martin Dietz hadn't ended up in county-level government.

"But she decided to run for it herself. And she would have won too."

"What happened?"

"That nasty Mr. Dietz ripped her character to shreds. She left town before the election was over. Haven't seen her since."

The door jangled open behind me, and a cold gust of wind blew in along with a customer.

The woman at the counter clammed up as she glanced past me toward the door. She shoved my bag at me and pasted a smile on her face.

I was sorry to have my investigation cut short, but glad to get to the Beauty Boutique.

I turned to go, and bumped into the broad, solid form of Martin Dietz.

18

Dietz glared down at me, his eyes shot through with jagged blood vessels.

"Ms. Amble," he said with a terse nod. "Just the person I'm looking for." A faint odor of pipe tobacco emanated from his clothing.

"I dispatched your denial letter this morning," Dietz said. His hat moved up and down with his clenching jaw.

At his words, my own teeth clamped together in defiance. Sandra Jones may have been easy prey for a bully like Martin Dietz, but he'd find I wasn't one to trifle with. The more he pushed, the harder I'd fight back.

"The meeting isn't until next week. How can I have been denied already?" I forced the words through taut lips. Behind me, I heard scuttling, and I figured the biddies were running for cover.

Dietz nodded with cruel satisfaction. "I knew your project had a timetable and I didn't want to be the one holding things up. So last night, I called a special meeting of the Historical Committee. Your plan to demolish the cistern was rejected. In fact, they even rejected your plan to wall it in. Seems it's the only one of its kind in Rawlings, and they want to protect it for posterity."

His leer grew more vicious with every detail. "I guess you'll have to give up your basement renovation plans altogether."

My lip started to quiver, whether from impending defeat or sheer terror, I couldn't yet tell.

A snide comeback was formulating in the back of my mind. But I reminded myself that Dietz carried more clout in the community than some nameless newcomer. If possible, I needed to get him over to my team.

I smiled a sweet, submissive smile.

"Wow. Thanks for pushing that request through for me. That really helps solidify things."

His chin tilted and his shoulders dropped into a less-guarded pose. "No problem."

I kept my face neutral as I squeezed past him to the door. I clutched the bag with the fuzzy sweater and silky pants to my chest, grateful I'd finished the transaction before Dietz had shown up.

I hit the cold November air, then turned up the street toward the Beauty Boutique. Martin Dietz might think he had just pulled one over on me, but I'd figure out a way to get my project through, with or without him.

I entered the Beauty Boutique and saw Tammy sitting at her nail station. She waited with slumped shoulders and head resting on her palm. Wads of white tissue peeked through the cracks of her fingers.

"Fighting a cold?" I asked in greeting.

She looked up at me with a blotchy face. She caught a nose drip with the tissue ball. "No. I'm crying my eyes out. A good friend of mine died yesterday."

"Was it Casey from down the street?" I asked.

I thought of Coffee Girl and tried to imagine her and Tammy as friends.

"Yeah." She drew a rasping breath. "Sorry I'm such a mess. Let's get you started."

She wiped tissue along the bottom of her eyes, diminishing the dark circles of mascara that had puddled there. She straightened her shirt, scooted her chair, then invited me with an open hand to sit across from her.

"I'm really sorry," I said, sinking into the floral upholstery. "I understand Casey's death comes as quite a shock."

Tammy opened the bottle of adhesive and painted a layer on my three bare nails.

She shook her head. "Arsenic poisoning. That's the most ludicrous thing I've ever heard. I'm guessing the founding fathers are just using Casey's death to get the village water filter system pushed through."

Tammy pressed my replacement nails, almost bruising my fingertips with her barely controlled anger. I knew how frustrated Tammy must feel. I remember the multitude of villains I held responsible for my mother's death.

The mixer beads in the bottle of Flamingo Pink polish clicked like mini maracas. Tammy unscrewed the top and painted my nails, starting with the new ones.

"Casey was an amazing person. You wouldn't believe the girls she influenced in a positive way at our church's youth group." Tammy painted furiously, talking more to herself than to me. "She didn't deserve to die."

Her brows knit into deep lines. She finished the last nail, then started the process over again. "Maybe she didn't dress the greatest. So what if she had face jewelry. God looks at what's inside. And so should the rest of this town. If it had been someone like Rebecca Ramsey, there'd be a better explanation. Everyone hates Rebecca, but she's somehow more worthy because of her money and class."

Job done, Tammy slammed the nail polish down on the table. She rubbed absently at the crescent-shaped dent left by the bottle. "I'm sorry to go on a rampage. But I can't figure it out. Life can be so unfair."

"I know how you feel." What more could I say?

She looked at me for the first time. "Thanks for listening. Sorry I brought up Rebecca. I know tonight's your big date with David. I don't mean to put a damper on things for you."

"Not at all. I guess it doesn't hurt to know a few things about David's ex-wife before we go out."

"Ex-wife? I didn't think she'd ever get around to divorcing him. Sorry to have been snotty at the supermarket that day. I just wanted to make sure you knew he was tagged. Guess it wasn't necessary."

"He told me last week he'd gotten the papers in the mail."

"Maybe she met someone out in California. Some richer-than-mud millionaire who meets her high standards. I mean, the *Metropolitan Magazine* Woman of the Year deserves better than a computer dweeb husband, right?"

"If you say so." David didn't strike me as a dweeb of any sort. I'd rarely seen a man more handsome than he. As far as manners and character went, both seemed impeccable. And from what I could tell, he made a lucrative living. His drop-dead gorgeous Greek Revival home said all there was on the subject of monetary success. The thing must have cost a fortune to renovate.

Anyway, I couldn't help but be awed by a man who could spearhead a project like that one. The thought processes that supported that kind of vision were rare indeed. I looked forward to dinner tonight when I could get David's insights on my own renovation project.

There would be no time for talk of Rebecca.

I followed Tammy up to the register and paid for my touch-up.

"Thanks for fitting me in on short notice," I said.

"Glad you came. I needed to vent. That's the other thing about you that reminds me of your twin. You're a good listener. I sure miss doing her nails. Toward the end, she could have passed for my therapist."

"I'm surprised to hear you say that," I commented. "I got the impression the other day that you two were rivals from way back."

Tammy looked at her hands resting on the counter. "Yeah. I guess we were. But about six months before she left town, she started helping me with the church youth group. We actually got to be pretty close. And the girls loved her. She used her background as an image consultant to build these girls into confident young women."

She paused. A sad look came into her eyes. "I guess I'm still mad at her. You'd think she could at least drop me an occasional e-mail. Martin may have been the world's biggest jerk to her, but she had friends here. She could have held her head up and weathered his tantrum." She twirled a hand in the air. "There I go again. It's been quite a year. And now Casey."

I nodded in sympathy. "Yep. I've had whole decades like that. It'll get better."

I turned to go, reaching for the door pull.

"Hey," Tammy called to me. "Do you want to come to church with me on Sunday? The girls would love to meet you."

Church. A place I'd successfully avoided for almost twenty years. Hard pews. Excessive singing. Snooty old ladies. Boring sermons. Not a place I felt like dealing with at this point in my life.

"Thanks for the invite," I said. "Sundays are a little too hectic right now. But after the first of the year, I should have things a little more under control."

"I only ask because you're so much like Sandra. It might take the sting out of Casey's death if you were there."

Guilt trips were the foundation of my upbringing. I recognized one a mile away.

"Thank you, but no," I said and hustled out the door. I speed-limped toward home, obsessed with the image of a little white church house crumbling to the very foundation as I walked through its doors.

The bracing wind cleared my mind as I headed home. I stopped at the Fitches' driveway and looked both ways before crossing the road.

I gave a little groan.

There, parked against the curb in front of my house, was a police cruiser. The driver's door showed a number three next to the Village of Rawlings crest. That was the same one Brad had been driving the day he practically arrested me for jaywalking.

I didn't see him in the car, in the yard, or up by the house, and I wondered where he was hiding. My shoulders pulled back automatically as I put up my wall of defenses.

I made it to the front porch without incident and turned the door handle to go in.

"Tish." I heard Brad's call behind me. He waved from Dorothy Fitch's front porch.

I watched with irritation as he gave Dorothy a hug. I refused to let the sweet gesture melt any part of my grudge toward Brad. From where I stood the two looked like Papa Bear and Baby Bear. Without her bulky coat, Dorothy had nothing to her.

Brad sprinted over to my yard. He took the porch steps two at a time. Then he was next to me, filling up a good chunk of vertical space.

"So tonight's your big date, huh?" he asked.

I crossed my arms, giving him the cue to get to the point.

He passed me a white envelope.

I flipped it over. It was addressed to Patricia Amble.

That was me.

The return address listed the Village of Rawlings, Department of Building and Zoning.

That was Martin Dietz.

145

I glared at Brad. "I don't believe this. Dietz told me he'd dispatched a denial letter. I thought he meant U.S. Mail, not private gopher."

Brad's eyes slanted. "Don't shoot the messenger, Ms. Amble. I'm only doing my job."

I rattled the letter at him. "Yeah, well, only in this screwed-up town are the cops in the pocket of the zoning board."

"With good reason. Look at yourself. How do I know you're not going to grab a shotgun and go after Dietz just for upholding a village ordinance?"

"Of course I wouldn't do that. I'm not crazy."

He humphed. "Maybe you're not, but a few years ago, Dickie Boggs went nuts. The zoning board turned down his privacy fence application, and he took it out on the director. A shotgun in the face, right at his desk. It's been village policy ever since to have armed officers be the bearers of bad news."

A shiver snaked up my spine. Everyone in this town was on the edge.

I tucked the letter in the bag with my date clothes. The sight of the light blue fuzzy yarn reminded me that some things were more important than pushing through my cistern-demolition agenda at city hall. Tonight could have longer-term significance. After all, I planned on selling the Victorian next summer. But David and I might find ourselves in a more permanent arrangement. And that meant cooling off over the whole Martin Dietz thing so I didn't drag my rage to dinner.

"Thank you, Officer." I nodded to Brad in dismissal.

"I promise I won't take my aggression out on the honorable Mr. Dietz."

I jerked open the storm door, turned my key in the lock, and scooted inside to lick my wounds.

Fortunately, I couldn't bask in my misery too long. Six o'clock was just a short time away.

19

The clock on the mustard-gold stove read four minutes after six. As I stared at it, the last digit rotated to a five, clicking noisily in the quiet kitchen.

Five minutes wasn't exactly late.

I wandered over to the bathroom to give myself another final inspection, my third in the past fifteen minutes. I had brightened my face with a rosy blush on cheeks, eyes, and forehead. I'd boiled my dried-up old mascara and gotten just enough goo off the applicator to have some lashes. And I'd scraped out the last bit of color from two exhausted lipsticks and mixed the shades together to come up with a fresh, deep orange that looked flattering with my new blue sweater. I'd have to be careful, however, that my Flamingo Pink nails and Mostly Mango lips never crossed paths. If I had known David was going to be late, I'd have had time to shop for a matching shade of lipstick.

I tousled my bangs to give them a little more oomph and thought back to my conversation with David earlier today. I was sure he'd said six o'clock instead of seven. At least I was ready. My fuzzy top and silky slacks fit like gloves over an hourglass figure I'd apparently been blessed with at birth. I sure hadn't done anything to earn it, other than tending toward laziness on the food-preparation side. Of course, renovating homes wasn't exactly a desk job.

I walked back into the kitchen and watched the stove clock flip to 6:15. All the reasons I'd once sworn off relationships were coming back to me. Disappointments, heartaches, and plain boorish behavior seemed too overwhelming to deal with at times. Things stayed nice and simple with just myself to worry about.

I tapped my foot, miffed at myself for falling victim to shattered expectations once again. Outside, the porch creaked. David appeared in the drafty single-pane window of the back door. In his hands was an enormous bouquet of red roses.

I gave a sigh. I was hungry. Eating with David was better than eating alone, even though he'd just broken my first qualifying rule.

"Hi," I said, letting him and the mass of foliage in. "Wow. Flowers." I inhaled a noseful of their syrupy sweet odor.

"Sorry I'm late. Traffic was bad and I stopped to pick these up." He passed me the monstrosity.

"Gosh. Thanks." I smiled at him, wracking my brain for vase ideas. I peeked over the bouquet at David. He wore black dress slacks and a pale pink oxford shirt under his woolen trench coat. How could a guy that dressed so impeccably have such atrocious taste in floral arrangements? I felt like a centenarian who'd just received one flower for every year of life.

I found an empty paint can in the trash bin under the sink and filled it with water. I stuffed the roses in. They flopped in all directions.

I glanced at David. He had a pitiful puppy-dog look in his eyes. I knew I'd better seem more grateful if I ever expected another overt display of affection.

"These are so amazing. If you're not in a hurry, I'll just give them a quick trim." Of course he wasn't in a hurry. He was fifteen minutes late.

I snipped the stems with scissors, careful not to get pricked by a thorn. When they were a more manageable length, I placed each flower in the paint can, counting as I did. Twenty-five. I wondered at the significance of that quantity. Maybe it was the number of minutes we'd spent together. Or the number of words we'd exchanged.

I wrapped a forest green towel around the can to hide the paint-streaked label. I stepped back and smiled. The arrangement had morphed into an elegant cluster of red and green, brightening my kitchen.

I determined to give David the same fresh start. Maybe his habits resembled a disheveled bouquet of roses now. But a little tweaking and trimming, and he'd be in just the right shape to make an excellent lifetime companion.

I was certain of it.

"There. Are you ready? I'm starving." I turned and beamed at him, hoping he'd catch my new appreciation.

"Ready. You look lovely, by the way." He helped me into my jean jacket, which though not very warm, was more presentable than my ragtag ski parka. The poor thing had seen a few too many winters since college.

We stepped into the darkness. The clocks had changed from daylight savings back to regular time a week ago, but I still wasn't used to the sight of stars before supper. Through the bare branches of the catalpa, I could see clouds moving to blot out the display.

"A bit brisk, don't you agree?" David asked. I measured in only a few inches shy of his six foot plus, and I should have had no trouble keeping up with his long-legged stride as we hastened across Main Street. But the pull in my bad nerve seemed worse in the cold, damp air, and I lagged a step behind.

"Brrr. I'm thinking about Fiji for my next project." I pulled my collar up around my chin. Hot sand and bright sunshine would be just the thing right now. We turned and headed down Independence Alley. Our footsteps echoed against the brick and glass of shops that had closed over an hour earlier. Now, what should have been a charming stretch of cobblestone and old-fashioned lampposts felt more like a scene from a Dracula movie.

I moved closer to David.

My arm bumped his as we approached the cheerful facade of the Rawlings Hotel. The place shone like a friendly oasis in a dark desert. Strands of clear lights and green garland spiraled around tall white pillars and spilled from window boxes. Every pane of glass glowed a warm yellow. I could almost hear, floating on the night air, the strains of an old-fashioned piano. I half expected to walk into the circa 1900 building and see ladies and gents in period-appropriate finery singing Christmas carols.

We entered the lobby, which likewise had been transformed into a winter wonderland. A Christmas tree filled one corner. Its branches sparkled with silver and gold ornaments and yards of shiny ribbon.

I stared in unease. Had I known the downtown merchants decorated for Christmas in early November, I would have insisted David take me to some franchise that waited until the last minute to deck the halls. My appetite dwindled in the face of Christmas cheer I'd managed to avoid the past ten years.

I fingered a tiny crystal angel on the tree. Her wings were delicate but strong as she blew her trumpet to the glory of the newborn King.

Pressure built in my temples.

"Mom," I whispered as a tear let go and dripped onto the ornament.

"The table's ready," David said, touching my arm.

I gave a good sniffle and wiped my cheek before turning around.

"Great," I smiled up at him. "I'm dying to find out if the beef Wellington is as yummy as everyone says."

"You won't be disappointed." He led me to a table set for two. A happy little flame danced on the center candle, and I hoped its good attitude would rub off on me. I'd been looking forward to my date with David all week. I couldn't believe I would let bad traffic and a few premature Christmas decorations mar our time together.

I sat in the soft-bottom café chair and laid my ivory

cloth napkin in my lap. No need to look at the menu. Beef Wellington was mandatory after Brad, then David, had recommended it.

David settled in across from me, looking devastatingly handsome in the candlelight. I wondered briefly what Officer Brad was doing this evening. I hoped he'd found something to occupy his time after I'd squashed his big date plans with me. Not really a date, I reminded myself. It was just a "welcome to the neighborhood" kind of thing. Brad had made that very plain.

David had made it just as clear that he was taking me on a real date, from the moment he'd announced his impending divorce to the gargantuan bouquet of roses upon arrival tonight. The down-to-earth Brad probably would have brought me two dozen tomatoes.

David set his menu to one side. I took that as a cue that I could start some conversation. We had a lot of ground to cover before we could get on with our relationship.

"So where do you work, exactly?" I asked. First things first.

He hesitated. "Onyx Technologies, in Southfield."

I knew of Onyx. A tall, black-glassed building at the intersection of Telegraph Road and Eight Mile housed the billion-dollar computer software firm.

"That's a bit of a drive, isn't it?" I asked.

"Around fifty minutes one way if I hit the traffic lights right."

"You must have flexible hours." I remembered grocery shopping with him on a weekday.

"Yes. Very," he said.

"You must enjoy that," I said, a touch of awe in my voice.

"Like I said, I'd dreamed of a career in computers. When Onyx came courting five years ago, I couldn't pass up the opportunity. They set me up with a U.S. work visa and got me out of paying over half my wage in taxes to the British government."

"Do you miss England? Your family?"

He scrunched his chin. "Never had much of a family to miss. Mum died when I was young. Father did the best he could after that, I suppose, but five kids were too much for him. My oldest sister finished the job. I left for University and never went back. How about you?"

I sat silent for a moment, amazed at the similarity of our stories. "My mom died when I was seven. Dad was in and out of town most of the time, then pretty much disappeared from my life altogether around the time I lost Mom. Grandma took over and I did the university thing too." I gave a shrug. "But that only lasted about a year and a half."

David's eyebrows lifted. "Didn't care for your professors, huh?"

"I loved my classes. Just hit a string of bad luck. Gram got sick and I owed her big time for raising me. So I dropped out to care for her. I never got around to going back to school after she died."

The waiter arrived with bottled water. He made a show of breaking the seal on the neck before pouring the contents into two glasses of ice. I breathed an inward sigh of relief for the diversion, hoping David would forget the topic of my grandmother altogether.

David put in our meal request. Then the waiter left, and David and I were alone again.

I leaned forward. "Did you know Casey?"

David stared at me. His brows pulled together. "Casey? You mean the girl from the coffee shop? I've gone in for a cup of tea on occasion, but I wouldn't say I knew her. Not well, anyway."

"Can you believe she's dead? And supposedly from arsenic poisoning." I took a sip from my glass. Cool, refreshing, and arsenic-free.

"It seems impossible. But they're quite good with all that forensic stuff these days. If the coroner said arsenic poisoning, then arsenic it is," David said.

"Personally, I think they ought to dig a little deeper. Do you suppose our neighbor is working on the case?"

David pushed back his chair and crossed his arms. "You mean Officer Walters? You've met him, I take it."

"Sure I know Brad. He introduced himself my first night in town. Quite an introduction too, with the train blaring past." I couldn't help but smile at the memory.

David scowled. "If Officer Walters is on the case, you can be sure they'll never solve it. He's an idiot."

My defenses shot up. Brad might be a blight on my life most of the time, and maybe he had blown off the body-in-the-basement and the stick-in-the-window incidents, but he had also shown thoughtfulness and caring in other matters. David stepped over the line by flinging insults at him.

155

I cleared my throat. "I think highly of Brad. I hope you can be more generous toward him."

David slowly nodded his head. He tipped his chair back on two legs and looked intently at me, eyes glinting. "I'm still getting over the fact that Brad Walters stole my wife. I guess it doesn't surprise me that he's already made the moves on you."

20

My heart dropped into my stomach. I sat flabbergasted, staring at the flickering candle and mulling over David's implications. I didn't care that my Flamingo nails and Mango lips had come in full contact with one another.

Brad and Rebecca?

I caught myself chewing on a fingernail. At least it was fake.

I forced my hands to the table.

Was Brad the reason Rebecca had left David in the first place? But why weren't Brad and Rebecca together now? I thought back to Halloween night, sitting with Brad on my porch. No wonder there had been a softness in the police officer's voice when he spoke of Rebecca. He was still in love with her.

But if that were true, then Brad should be happy that Rebecca was divorcing David. Instead, the news had made him seem sad.

I glanced at David. His eyes looked raw.

He leaned forward and rested one hand on the tablecloth close to me. "I'm sorry I mentioned Rebecca. I promised myself I wouldn't tonight."

His voice sounded raspy.

Compassion bubbled up inside me. "There's no reason to pretend you aren't hurting."

Dinner salads appeared on our place mats. The waiter made a silent escape.

David speared a cherry tomato. "Loving Rebecca was like loving a rainbow. Beautiful, but unattainable. The closer I tried to get, the further she'd slip away. Until there was nothing left between us. Absolutely nothing."

My heart ached for him. "I'm sure you did the best you could. Some people simply can't open themselves up." I dug into my salad.

David gave a half smirk. "It's nice of you to try and see Rebecca's side. But the truth is, she's a coldhearted witch who'd do anything to anybody as long as it meant getting ahead."

I leaned back in my chair, hoping to dodge the beams of anger shooting from David's eyes. From the turn the conversation had taken, I realized it was far too soon for him to be out on a date, unless it was with a licensed therapist.

I dabbed at my lips with my napkin. "Tell me about your renovation project. I'm so envious. Your place is just beautiful."

David's jaw clenched. "I'm glad you like it. It's a monument to the three worst years of my life."

I laughed. "I can relate. Anyone who survives a renovation project can tell a few war stories. Still, you must be pleased that everything turned out so well."

"I believe all expectations were met. If they weren't, the builder would still be there, doing it over until he got it right."

"A perfectionist, I see."

As far as my own projects went, perfection was a goal, not a requirement. I knew all too well how tricky old homes could be. Attempting perfection would drive me to the brink, if I weren't there already.

"I'm no perfectionist," David said. "The renovation was Rebecca's baby. Literally."

I chewed the last of my lettuce as I digested the disappointing news. I had been certain David was the brainchild behind the flawless revival. I had felt such a bond with him, such a kinship because of our common love for old homes. Now to find out Rebecca had handled all the details.

I shifted in my seat. "Wow. She's incredibly talented. I can't hold a candle to that."

"Don't be so sure. Your passion for that place of yours will shine through in the end. Rebecca, on the other hand, renovated the house for the advancement of her career. You don't get a degree in architecture from the University of Michigan and not have a show house to splash across every suburban newspaper's life section."

"Oh. I didn't realize Rebecca was an architect." My self-esteem dropped a mile. How could I compete with that? But there was no room for regrets. If my life hadn't happened the way it had, I would never be renovating homes for a living. Who knew where I'd be today?

I looked at the handsome, hurting man across from me. One thing was certain: I had the same opportunities today that I'd had ten years ago. It was up to me to either grab hold of the good in front of me, or let him slip away and hope I got another chance at love ten years from now.

Skip loneliness. I choose love.

Any kinks could be worked out along the way.

I wanted to drop the whole Rebecca thing. I really did. But curiosity consumed me. "So what's Rebecca doing now? Is she still renovating homes?"

David stared at his water glass. "No. She's out in California, designing skyscrapers at her new firm."

I nodded. California was at least a thousand miles away. That was a good thing. I didn't want Rebecca to be the one rainbow that arced back down to earth to reclaim what she'd tossed away.

My beef Wellington arrived along with David's mutton dish. Steam drifted up from the rich gravy and garlic mashed potatoes. I cut through the pastry pocket and sliced off a piece of beef. I chewed, enthralled with the tender meat.

I swallowed and cut another sliver of beef, reviewing my decision to move to Rawlings. The quaint town made the perfect place to settle down. After David and I got married, we'd live in his Greek Revival, since my Victorian was destined for sale. We'd walk to the Whistle Stop for a cup of morning coffee. We'd sup at the Rawlings Hotel on special occasions. I would go back to school and finish my degree, picking some clever field that allowed more freedom than the average nine-to-fiver.

And we'd have children. Cute little chubby-cheeked, plump-lipped, freckled British cherubs.

"It looks like you're enjoying your meal," David said, startling me out of my pie-in-the-sky line of thinking. No sense going too far down the wedding aisle without first getting the consent of the groom.

"Mmm. Everything's delicious. I can see why you enjoy coming here." I dabbed at my lips and took a sip of water.

"Rebecca spoke to the chef when we first moved to Rawlings and convinced him to incorporate some of my favorite traditional English meals. Needless to say, we were regulars here."

"That's nice." Rebecca's name was starting to grate on me. I wondered if she'd ever sat in the chair I was sitting in. Certainly her perfectly pink nails had coordinated with her barely blush lip color.

"Don't you love how beautifully they've decorated this place?" I asked, steering back to a neutral topic.

"It's exquisite," David agreed. "A few years ago, the whole downtown area was dying. Rebecca helped pull together the local merchants. They started promoting the village in the suburbs. Now it's one of the more attractive and successful historic downtowns in the area."

"Is there anything Rebecca can't do?" I smiled to cover my feeling of inferiority. I'd never be the woman Rebecca was. I couldn't form merchant alliances. I couldn't revive whole downtowns. I couldn't even get my contractor to show up.

I swirled my mashed potatoes into the vegetable medley.

Across from me, David pushed his plate aside, finished with his meal. Obviously, he had less on his mind than I

161

did. I kept chewing and swallowing, determined to finish every delicious bite of food on the fancy china before stress-induced indigestion kicked in.

He checked his watch, then leaned close. "So. What about you, Tish? What's your life story?"

Candlelight danced in his eyes.

I pushed my plate aside and rested my chin in one palm. "You heard most of my story already. After Gram died, I left the area for about three years. When I came back, I moved into her old house and fixed it up. From there, it's the same story, different location."

David smiled. "Never been married? Never been in love?"

"Never been married. Thought I was in love once, back in college. Never talked to the guy, but I would have married him in a heartbeat, if he'd have asked."

"Let me guess. He was in the engineering program."

"How'd you know?" I gave his hand a playful push. The touch shook me. I pulled away and crossed my arms.

Our eyes linked. I tried to steady my breathing, certain he could tell I was practically gasping for air.

"Tish." My name lingered on his tongue. "You are so beautiful. Your smile is so warm. And I can tell you have a very gentle spirit." He shook his head. "Next to you, Rebecca's the Ice Queen."

I tapped my fingers on my arm. He was doing so well until he said her name.

I leaned forward, elbows on the table. "Thanks for the compliment, but I think it's going to be awhile before you get Rebecca out of your system. Let's just keep things platonic for now."

My heart felt like it was ripping in two even as I said it. But David was still getting over Rebecca's departure. I was still recovering from Lloyd & Sons' abandonment. No sense starting things on the rebound. Everyone knew that was a recipe for failure.

"I understand," David replied. He leaned toward me on one elbow. His eyes sparkled with challenge.

I swallowed.

On the other hand, there was nothing like romance to take one's mind off life's problems. So what if David and I didn't end up married? We could at least have a little fun while the world with all its problems kept on spinning.

Unless, of course, it turned out that David had used his key to my house to let himself in, then propped open the basement window with the stick so he could get back in later. And he would only have done that if every word out of his mouth this evening had been a lie.

And it was Rebecca's body buried in my basement.

21

Apprehension slithered down my spine. I shook it off.

How foolish. I was acting like a daffy heroine in one of my gothic novels. Suspect everybody. Trust no one.

Worse, in my case, no crime had even been committed. I was letting a brief flash of superstition, premonition, imagination, or whatever it had been, get to me.

Yet, something about David hit me at the gut level. Maybe his Ice Queen comment blinked like a beacon, warning me how quickly his love could turn to hate. Whatever the case, I wasn't quite ready to go full speed ahead with David in the romance department.

Gut feelings may not be rational, logical, or scientific. But they were still gut feelings. And mine had taken good care of me so far.

Hadn't I known right up front that Officer Brad Walters couldn't be trusted? And tonight I'd been proved right. Brad had seduced David's wife right out from under him. Shame on Brad. I didn't care how nice his tomatoes were, how broad his shoulders, how soft his eyes . . . None of that mattered. My gut had been right.

David locked his gaze on me. I pushed away from the table. "Excuse me, I need to find the ladies' room."

"It's upstairs," David said.

I picked my way through the other diners and fled toward an empty lobby.

I found the steps in an alcove, hidden from the dining room. I paused at the bottom, daunted by the thought of using a restroom separated from the rest of humanity by one entire floor.

Behind me, laughter filtered through the swinging doors that led to the kitchen.

I took a deep breath and ran up the stairs. The effort sent jolts of invigorating pain up my bad leg. Each step creaked and shook as I landed.

I made it to the bathroom, nothing more than a remodeled nook with two stalls. Thankfully there were no ladies present to hear my wheezing as I leaned against striped wallpaper to catch my breath.

I took my time, not sure why I wasn't in a hurry to get back to David.

A few minutes later, I washed up and turned to go. I reached for the door handle.

The knob wrenched out of my grasp as the door flung open.

I squealed and leaped back against the wall.

"Sorry, dear. I didn't mean to frighten you." It was another diner, one of the ladies from the clothing store. She stood in the doorway and looked at me. "That outfit looks lovely on you. Just lovely."

She disappeared into a stall.

I hovered inside the restroom, examining the details of a Monet print. I walked to the sink and checked my makeup. A moment later, the Clothing Junction cashier joined me at the basin. I scooted over to make room.

I caught her eyes in the reflection. "I'm really enjoying this outfit," I said, "although it is a little out of my usual price range." I gave an exaggerated swallow.

"Our clothing is an attitude, really." She smoothed her eyebrows in the mirror. "How much does a person feel she is worth? Twenty dollars or two hundred dollars? Your twin, Sandra Jones, knew she was worth every dollar she invested in herself. Her good taste was undeniable, at least where clothing was concerned."

I gave her a questioning look.

"It's no secret she has terrible taste in men."

I nodded in agreement.

She rubbed her hands vigorously under the water. "Martin Dietz is a cutthroat. Nice women shouldn't get involved with men like him," she said.

The woman grabbed paper toweling from the dispenser and continued. "Sandra had everything going for her. She could have picked anybody to be her suitor. But once Martin Dietz made up his mind that Sandra was what he wanted, the poor dear didn't have a chance. Anyone could tell she'd never get out of that relationship easily."

I pictured the scene between Martin Dietz and Tammy Johnson at the Beauty Boutique. I cringed, hoping Tammy could withstand Dietz's brash advances.

"It's so sad what Dietz did to Sandra." I leaned against the wall.

"I only wish she would have stood up for herself better. If someone gives you a public lambasting, you're at least entitled to a public rebuttal." She shook her head. "But Sandra didn't have it in her. It's best she dropped out of politics. I'm just sorry she let him run her out of town."

"That is too bad." I crossed my arms. "What about Rebecca Ramsey? Did she shop at your store often?"

The woman smoothed the front of her expensive fitted jacket. "Rebecca Ramsey made token purchases all over town. She wanted to stay on good terms with everyone." The sides of her mouth pulled down. "But everyone knows the kind of person she really is." The woman gave me a knowing look. "The kind of woman that nice men should stay away from."

I thought of Officer Brad's attachment to Rebecca, and David's misfortune in having married her in the first place. How could love be so screwed up that all the right people fell in love with all the wrong ones?

"Anyway," she said, toweling off her hands, "I see Martin Dietz already has your number. Be sure you don't cross him."

"Thanks for the warning."

My leg throbbed as I picked my way back downstairs.

I'd gone through a lot of trouble to make everything perfect for tonight. New hairstyle, new nails, new slacks and sweater.

And for what?

David held a multitude of possibilities, but was I ready for him? I couldn't make it through a date without dredging up Basement Lady, Coffee Girl, Officer Brad, and the Ex-Wife.

Not that David didn't have plenty of his own hang-ups to work on. But that's what love was all about, wasn't it? Helping each other through life's hang-ups?

I paused at the bottom of the steps, reluctant to turn the corner, not sure I wanted to face any of the non-decisions I'd made. I stood and listened to the kitchen sounds. The crew worked well together, joking, cooking, and cleaning. After a moment, I turned the corner and settled at the table.

"Dessert, Tish?" David sounded short of breath. His hair and shoulders had little droplets of water on them.

"You look like you got sprinkled by the veggie wash at the supermarket." I smiled and scooted my chair in.

"I stepped onto the porch for some air. First snow of the year tonight." David smoothed his hair and the drops disappeared.

Our waiter wheeled over a tray of gourmet pies and cakes. Normally, the sight of three kinds of cheesecake and several varieties of chocolate layer cake would have me ordering a sample of each. But the stress of the evening had finally caught up. I had no appetite for dessert. All I wanted was to go home, curl up in my cot, and read a creepy romance. My problems always disappeared in light of the screwy lives unfolding on those three hundred or so pages.

"Just coffee for me, please," I said.

David folded his hands on the table. "I would have pegged you for the dessert type. A secret chocolate lover."

"I am. Just not tonight."

"I knew it." David's grin was triumphant. "Anybody

who would make a big deal out of granola versus Sugar Puffs has to be a closet chocoholic."

I gave a weary smile, hoping the waiter would hurry with that coffee.

David and I small-talked through one cup each.

The waiter arrived with the bill.

I jumped up and put my coat on.

"I'll wait in the lobby," I said.

David watched me scoop up my jacket. His look had me thinking I'd forgotten something. I peeked around for gloves or a purse on the floor, but recalled that I'd brought neither.

A few minutes later, David joined me in the lobby.

"Ready?" he asked.

"Ready."

We stepped into a bluster of snowflakes and started down the darkened Independence Alley.

We came out on Main Street and I could see my house just a block away. All the windows were dark. If not for the welcoming beam of the porch light I'd turned on when we left, I wouldn't have wanted to go home.

A few houses over, David's glowed with bright, cheery windows.

"Would you like to stop in for a minute?" David asked through the biting wind.

"Can I take a rain check? I think I'll go take a hot shower and crawl in bed."

"Perhaps another time, then," he said.

I paused on the sidewalk leading to my front steps. "Well, thank you for supper. The beef Wellington was superb, as promised."

David stepped close, looking down at me. His head was covered with fluffy white snowflakes. His three-quarter-length trench nearly touched my jean jacket.

"My privilege," he said.

"And the flowers." I stared at his lips. "Thank you for the flowers."

"Anything for you, Tish." He held my arms and leaned toward me.

Oh, help. I was going to be kissed.

22

Snow billowed into my eyes.

"Gosh, it's cold." I pulled away from his touch and ran toward the porch. "Thanks again. Good night." I threw the words over my shoulder as I sprinted up the steps.

I slammed the door behind me and leaned against it, not sure if I was trying to keep David out or myself in.

Why hadn't I kissed him? What would it have hurt? We'd had an enjoyable night, we had some things in common, we were neighbors. One innocent kiss wouldn't have hurt anything.

I imagined for a moment what it would have felt like, the warmth of his breath on my cheek, the way his nose would rub against mine, how our foreheads would meet for a moment. Then our lips would touch, sending electric sensations across soft skin.

Completely harmless.

Except now I'd never get it out of my mind.

I thought about going after him.

But how stupid would that look? I'd turned down

an invitation to see his house, then ran away from his kiss. If I dashed out into the snow right now and followed him home, would he be happy to see me, or just annoyed?

My level of bravery being what it was, I guessed I would never find out.

I flicked the deadbolt closed and headed toward the bathroom. It wasn't as if I'd turned down a marriage proposal. It was just a kiss.

I hit the light switch on my way through the kitchen. The scent of the twenty-five-rose bouquet reminded me of David's generosity even before I saw it filling up the counter. The petals flashed red as the fluorescent light struggled to come on.

I stopped and studied the scene, picturing the same bouquet in a newly remodeled kitchen. This winter, I'd be tearing out the existing dark, flat-faced cabinet doors and putting in raised-panel light oak to match the home's original woodwork. A workstation with stools would fill the space beneath the back windows. The countertops and floor would be redone in neutral shades, and the whole kitchen would brighten up with new lighting. Tonight, however, the corner by the basement door was pitifully dim. I shot past it and closed myself in the bathroom.

I stood under steaming water and wondered what David was doing. He was probably on his side porch, opening the door, and shutting it tight against the wind. He'd hang his coat neatly on a hanger, take off his shoes and line them in the hall closet. Then he'd make himself a cup of tea and sit on the sofa and look out at the snowflakes, wondering what he'd done wrong tonight.

Why hadn't Tish kissed me, he'd ask himself. He'd run through a million ways he might have messed up. Finally, he'd convince himself that things were hopeless between us.

And he'd never speak to me again.

I paused. Shampoo dripped into my eyes.

Was I ready to have that bridge burned?

No way.

I rinsed off, flicked down the faucet handle, and grabbed my towel. Not even fifteen minutes had passed since he'd gone home. He'd been at least that late picking me up tonight. I could be fashionably tardy for his invitation, as well.

I towel-dried my hair and sprayed it, trying for a cute-n-tangled look. I threw on my usual jeans and T-shirt. David had already seen me at my finest. Time to get back to my true, casual self.

Socks, shoes, and my jean jacket wrapped tight around me, and out the back door I went. Billowing white puffs hit me full in the face as I took the shortcut past the garage over to David's yard.

The turn-of-the-century home between my house and David's acted as the village museum, which explained why it was perpetually empty. Operating hours had been cut back to zero with the summer tourist season long past. I'd taken a tour of the historic home back in July and fallen in love with its total Victorian décor. I also loved the idea that I had one less neighbor in occupancy.

With cedar hedges lining both sides, the museum's backyard repelled any light from the street. I found myself kicking blindly through snow-covered leaf piles and tripping over fallen branches in the snowy blackness. Not very pleasant for my lame leg. A light in David's second-story window served as my beacon.

I squeezed through an opening in the opposite hedge and walked across David's driveway to his back porch. A flurry of snowflakes dimmed the light next to the door.

I knocked.

I jiggled in place as I waited, wishing I'd thought to wear boots. Snow had settled in a thick ring around my ankles and now melted in slow, icy rivulets into my sneakers.

I peeked through the window, shielding my eyes to block the reflection. No lights, no David.

I knocked again, louder this time.

I stepped back. In the glass, my head looked like it had been doused with powdered sugar. My mostly wet hair sat frozen in spiky ringlets around my face.

The wind knifed icy-cold air through my jean jacket. My teeth launched into a continuous chatter.

The thought of standing on the frozen porch another instant gave me the chills. But so did the thought of heading home without warming up first.

Come on, David.

I tested the back door handle. It turned easily.

The door opened a crack.

David had walked into my house without knocking, hadn't he? At least I'd knocked a few times. He was probably upstairs getting into warm jammies and fuzzy slippers. I'd just wait in the back room for a few minutes and thaw out. If he didn't come downstairs by the time my tootsies were toasty, I'd just sneak back out and he'd never even know I'd been here.

The door creaked as I opened it.

Tut, tut, I scolded the absent Rebecca. Squeaky hinges alert buyers to the possibility of other problems throughout the house. It didn't take an architect to figure that one out.

I poked my head inside the dark hall. "Hello?"

No answer.

I stepped in and closed the door behind me. A heavy hush filled the air. I tapped my feet gently to knock the snow off, careful not to make too much noise.

I felt along the wall for a light switch. I found two. I flicked the first and the porch light blinked off. The second one turned on the overhead light in the spacious rear entry hall.

However predisposed I was to disliking Rebecca, I couldn't help but admire her taste. The room looked ready for a photo shoot. Dark walnut paneling lined the lower half of the walls. Matching cubbies and a row of coat hooks filled the far end. Pale ivory-striped wallpaper covered the rest. A floral wreath in burgundy and green provided a focal point upon entry.

David's coat hung askew in one cubby. The red scarf he'd been wearing lay on the floor, almost as if he'd been too rushed to hang it. Next to the scarf were his shoes. Melted snow puddled around them on the polished oak floor.

I panicked. If that mess didn't get wiped up, there was a good chance the finish would be ruined. Then all anyone would see walking into the room would be a big dull patch on an otherwise flawless floor.

I slipped out of my wet shoes and lined them carefully

on the entry rug. I tiptoed through the doorway and found myself in the kitchen.

"David?" I called.

I turned on the overhead light. The room was a chef's dream. A long island wrapped in wood paneling fit down the center. Above it hung a rack of pots and pans, all shiny copper, looking as if they'd never been used. Cabinets and countertops lined two walls. Stainless steel appliances gave the room a clean, sterile appearance. This room alone must have cost a fortune.

The sink piled with dirty dishes was the only eyesore. I stole a few paper towels from the roll on the counter and slunk back to the mudroom.

I wiped up the water and stacked David's shoes neatly on the rug where they could finish drying without doing any damage. Then I opened and closed under-counter cabinets in the kitchen until I found the trash bin.

I pitched in the wad of toweling. It landed in the garbage next to a small red foil envelope, the kind that gets held by that fork thingy in a floral arrangement.

I scrunched up my forehead in thought. My bouquet tonight hadn't come with a little card. Maybe David had written something to me, then changed his mind and threw it away, too shy to share his feelings.

My hand shot out for the envelope.

I pulled back, not wanting to believe that I would actually dig through someone's trash.

Oh, what could it hurt?

A floral greeting wasn't exactly U.S. Mail.

I grabbed for it with two fingers. I straightened, flipping the foil paper over. There was no writing on it. I reached inside and pulled out the card.

Chunky black print jumped out at me: TWENTY-FIVE YEARS. REMEMBER THAT.

Not very romantic. The card had obviously been meant for some other flower arrangement. David certainly hadn't penned those words with me in mind. Perhaps David had received flowers recently himself.

PARKER FLORAL DESIGNS was printed in the upper left corner of the card. That was a shop just down Main Street, one of my favorites. A grapevine arbor arched over the entryway, inviting passersby to step in and check out the knickknacks and doodads. Maybe I'd just have to do that one of these days.

I tucked the card in my jeans pocket, convinced that taking something already thrown away couldn't be considered stealing.

Still, I had to face my dilemma. With no David in sight, I should leave the house. Otherwise, I could be deemed a trespasser. On the other hand, David had offered me a tour. Poking my head into a couple rooms on the first floor before I left couldn't possibly hurt anything. Technically, I was here on invitation. I'd just arrived a little late.

I came to a compromise. I would only peek at one more room. If David hadn't come downstairs by then, I was out the door and back home. With wet shoes off, my feet weren't even cold anymore.

I took the archway to the left and found myself in the dining room. I didn't dare turn on a light. But in the wash from the kitchen, I could see the ceiling was at least ten feet above the floor. The walls were done in dark wainscot and old-fashioned burgundy-on-gold wallpaper. A mammoth table filled the space beneath the chandelier.

Against the opposite wall, a monstrous cabinet loomed, like something from the Addams Family collection. A thin stream of light seeped from behind its doors.

I was drawn toward the beam like a moth to fire.

My hands glowed blue as they reached for starburst-shaped knobs. I pulled the doors open.

A funny-looking desktop computer provided the ambient light. The screen showed a picture of a woman in front of the restored Greek Revival. Her arms were flung wide as if to say, "I did it!" Reams of blonde hair lay gracefully on the collar of a fur swing coat. A short skirt accentuated her miles of legs. She had a flawless smile, a petite nose, and glimmering eyes. In short, she was the most beautiful woman on the planet.

Rebecca, no doubt.

And why not? The woman had talent and spunk. Beauty was a natural accompaniment.

No wonder David was sick to be losing her.

"She looks like an angel, doesn't she?" David's voice came from behind.

I whirled and screamed. I landed with my bottom sitting on the cabinet ledge.

"Please. I didn't mean to scare you," he said.

He wore a wine-colored silky robe over top of loose cotton bottoms. A patch of chest hair peeked out.

"Wow." I stood and brushed off the back of my pants. "I'm so embarrassed. I'm not snooping, honest. I changed my mind about that tour and thought I'd come over after all." I gave a sheepish grin. "I did knock."

His eyes shone bright blue even in the dim light. "Not to worry." He walked toward me. "I see you've found my baby."

"Yes." I tried to plaster down my frizzed-out hair. "I had no idea Rebecca was so beautiful."

He skirted past me and hit the space bar on the keyboard. "I meant my computer."

"Oh." I looked at the flat-screened contraption surrounded by wires and equipment. Rebecca's face was gone, replaced by lines of text.

"Unfortunately, I'll have to give you a rain check on that tour. I received an urgent message just as I walked in this evening." David shrugged, helpless. "Duty calls."

"I hope it's nothing too serious." I straightened, trying not to look as foolish as I felt.

"Nothing that can't be tidied up in a few hours' time. Perhaps you can come back tomorrow afternoon."

"Oh. Absolutely." I fidgeted, sidestepping toward the mudroom. "Again, I'm really sorry to have bothered you. I don't know what came over me."

David stood hands on hips. The collar of his robe stretched open, revealing a surprisingly well-defined chest. Not every computer geek could claim to be as toned as David. I lowered my eyes, embarrassed to even be thinking of him that way.

"No bother," David said. "It's always a pleasure. I'm looking forward to tomorrow."

He advanced toward me. For every step he took, I backed up one, until I felt the hardwood flooring of the kitchen beneath me. I pivoted and almost ran to my shoes. David stood over me in the doorway to the mud-room as I fumbled with wet laces.

From the corner of my eye, I saw him hovering there, watching me. My heart launched into a frenzy at the thought of feisty little pheromones floating my way, making me want to be kissed. I focused on tying my shoes.

When I looked up, I noticed David's fingers tapping almost impatiently on his crossed arms.

I stood. "I can't imagine what you think of me, letting myself in like that. I'm so sorry."

"Stop apologizing. I only wish I could give you that tour this evening." He reached for my hand, bending over it like a knight paying homage. "Alas, I must needs return to my labors."

His crummy Shakespeare imitation made me smile, even as my fingers sizzled in his grip.

"Okay," I said. "I guess I'll see you tomorrow, then."

David's lips touched the skin on the back of my hand, melting it with his hot breath. The noble kiss sent fire through every nerve of my body. He might as well have marked me with a branding iron.

When David lifted his head, I still tingled where his lips had seared me.

His eyes pulled me closer. All resistance was gone. I stepped into his arms, clinging as if I'd never felt a man's touch before.

I leaned into him, soaking up the warmth of his body, the clean scent of his shower soap, the sound of his beating heart.

With his arms linked loosely behind me, life's problems seemed of little consequence.

What did my past matter in the embrace of this man? Any ghosts were laid to rest in light of future happiness.

Who cared if my cellar never got converted to a rec room? I could let it go with David holding me.

So what if Rebecca was beautiful, successful, and made Rawlings what it was today? I, not Rebecca, was in David's arms.

He gave a rasping breath and pushed me away.

"Go home, Tish."

I nodded.

I turned my back to him and stepped into the cold, shutting the door behind me.

23

I stood a moment on the back porch to get my bearings. The wind had lost its bite, though I couldn't be sure if it was due to the dissipating storm outside, or the raging storm within.

I'd accidentally turned off the back porch light earlier during my self-tour. Now I had to pick my way back home in total darkness. There was no way I was going back into that mudroom. Not even to flick a light switch.

I looked toward the streetlights out front and decided to take the long way home. I trudged through the snow, in no hurry to arrive at my destination.

The neighborhood looked enchanted in the snowfall. A few homes already had Christmas lights, even though Thanksgiving was still two weeks away. I looked with envy at Dorothy Fitch's house across the street. Colored lights twinkled on shrubs and eaves.

A curtain in the window moved. I ignored it, chalking it up to Jack Fitch's obsessive habit.

I walked on, tucking my hands in my jacket pockets. I'd never done holiday lights myself. The life I'd chosen required minimal baggage, and holiday decorations were definitely extra weight. Decorating for Christmas was something you did to make a place feel like home. I'd never lived in a house yet that I wanted to make feel that way. I always figured that if it ever became too homey, it would be too hard to leave when it came time to sell.

This was the first year, however, that a twinge of regret pulled at my heart over the matter.

I had no place to call home.

A car lurched over the tracks in my direction. I squinted in the headlights. The vehicle pulled to a stop at the curb.

A squad car.

The passenger-side window rolled down and the interior light came on.

"Tish." It was Officer Brad.

What was he doing? Stalking me? He knew this was my night with David. How tacky could a guy get, tracking me down after my date with another man?

I stopped on the sidewalk, hands on hips, and glared at him.

Maybe he couldn't see my expression in the pale streetlight, or maybe he chose to ignore it.

"How was your night?" His voice carried on the wind.

A blast of snow blew down the collar of my jacket. How rude could Brad get, asking how my date went? I tapped my foot, unwilling to answer.

"Come on. I'm just curious. Did everything go okay?"

Brad probably hoped to hear that I'd had a crummy night. Then he could forever hold over me that I'd turned down a hunky cop for a computer geek.

"I had a wonderful time." I stepped closer to his car. "In fact, I hated to leave. David has such a beautiful place."

Brad didn't have to know that I'd never made it past the dining room.

"Yeah, but does he have a personality?" He looked away, then back to me. "Sorry. That was uncalled for."

"Apology accepted." I leaned against the car, my head practically in the window. "He's got more than personality. He's compassionate and loving and caring . . ." I thought of the blaze brought on by a kiss on the hand.

"Caring enough to walk you home, I see."

I gritted my teeth. "You are way out of line. I wouldn't have let him walk me home even if he'd offered. Which he did, by the way." I threw in the white lie for good measure.

I stepped away from the car and raised my voice proportionately. "Anyway, I don't need anyone walking me home. And I don't need you keeping an eye on me, or snooping, or whatever it is you're doing here. Good night."

I pivoted. Snow piled into my pant leg. I walked up my frozen sidewalk to the front door.

I closed it behind me and stood in the tiny entry, fuming. I kicked off my wet shoes. One hit the wall, marking up the fresh paint. Great. More work later. The stress of the evening threatened to engulf me.

Things had been going great until Brad pulled up. Why couldn't he mind his own business? Jack Fitch was doing a good enough job spying on me. I didn't need Brad Walters trying to scoop me out from under David, just as he had done with Rebecca.

I shivered in my damp socks. There was nothing worse than a big, old drafty Victorian. The house had seemed like a good idea last summer when it was ninety degrees outside. Boy, was I sorry now. I'd been keeping the thermostat at a balmy sixty-five degrees. But tonight it felt all of fifty-five. I wanted to jump in another shower just to get the chill out.

I walked through the parlor toward the kitchen. Every step sent a shiver up my spine, and it wasn't coming from my bad leg. By the time I got to the dining room, I realized the draft was more than just wind whipping through old windows and siding.

I looked at the thermostat on the dining room wall.

Fifty-seven degrees.

Brrr.

I tapped it, hoping the little pointer was just stuck.

Nope.

Something must be wrong with the furnace.

Nice timing. The weatherman called for a three-day November squall, and I didn't have heat. I pictured the mess I'd have on my hands if the pipes in my gravity system froze up.

I twisted the controls and hoped to hear the sound of the furnace cycling on.

Nothing.

The problem could be basic, like giving the thing a good, swift kick. Or, it could be more of a nightmare, like needing a new boiler.

Either way, I'd have to go down and take a look at it, just in case I had only to hit the reset button or flip a switch.

I didn't relish the idea of tackling the basement steps with my bum leg. Sure, I'd been hobbling around just fine all day, but now I was tired.

I yawned. Too late for all that tonight.

I would simply put on a few extra layers and curl up in my sleeping bag tonight. Tomorrow, there would be plenty of sunshine down in the basement so I could see what I was doing. And my leg would be rested up to handle the task. If I couldn't figure out the problem in the morning, at least it would be business hours so I could call somebody.

I slipped into my shorts-and-T-shirt pajamas and pulled sweats and a sweatshirt over top. I put on fat wool socks, as well, just in case the temperature dipped dramatically during the night. I climbed into my down-filled sleeping bag, snuggled into my pillow, and tried to drift off.

What must have been only a few hours later, I jerked awake. The blast of a train sounded in the distance. The rumble must have woken me.

I looked around the room, bathed in light from the street lamps.

I could see my breath. The temperature in the house had dropped into the danger zone. I tucked my nose into the nylon covers, in hopes of avoiding the icy air.

Then I remembered my dream.

Grandma, again. She lay in bed, dying. In her hand was a red foil envelope. She turned it over and over.

"Let it lie, Tish, let it lie," she whispered.

I remember a feeling of helpless rage washing over me in my dream as Grandma stopped breathing. Then

186

she was sinking into the cistern. Her features turned to stone as she plunged into the concrete. I was kneeling next to her, clawing at the cement, trying to bring her back. But all I did was break off my artificial nails, one by one, until they looked like pale pink rose petals sprinkled on a grave.

Safe on my cot, I almost laughed out loud at the image. That just went to show how foolish dreams could be. There was nothing pale about my fake nails. They were as neon as a color could get.

I fanned out my fingers, just to confirm that my nail color was really as obnoxious as I'd remembered. The Flamingo Pink almost glowed in the dark.

One of my fake nails was missing. I wondered if I'd lost it at the restaurant, David's place, my house, or somewhere in between.

I curled my hands into balls and tucked them back under the covers. A girl could get frostbite if she wasn't careful.

By now, I had launched into an uncontrollable shiver that started at my toes and worked its way up to the muscles in my neck. I lay shaking for a few minutes before admitting defeat. There was no way I would get back to sleep in this freezer. As much as I wanted to avoid it, I had to go check the furnace, if only to give it a good kick. I threw back the covers and put my stocking feet on the carpet.

I put on my ski parka and shoes, then flicked on every light along the way to the kitchen to face the cellar door.

I stopped on the linoleum in the alcove between the kitchen and the bathroom. I stared at the oak-paneled door in front of me, suddenly hot under my layers of clothes.

I slid back the bolt.

I reached for the doorknob and gripped it. The freezing metal burned against my skin. I half hoped I would be stuck there, my sweaty hand frozen to the knob like a tongue stuck to the monkey bars, rather than having to go downstairs.

I listened.

Just the steady hum of the refrigerator and howl of the wind outside.

I turned the knob.

24

The door creaked open into the stairwell, then thumped and stopped against the wall.

I looked down. The steps dissolved into blackness.

The stove clock clicked and rotated. 4:00 a.m.

Night was mostly over.

Another five hours and it would be bright as day down there.

I turned toward the kitchen sink. I could almost see pipes bulging, ready to burst from the ice inside them.

Another five hours might be too late.

I turned on the basement light.

I took a deep breath to steady myself, then stepped down.

My foot took forever to touch the wooden riser. I stepped again. An eternity passed.

I listened as the stove clock made another rotation.

No other sounds.

I swallowed, gathering up the minuscule crumbs of courage scattered through my veins.

Then I bounded down the steps. My bad leg hit the

cement first, sending an extra oomph of pain shooting through my body from the memory of the last time I'd been down here. I squinted in the direction of the cistern.

The semicircle of rocks looked pretty much the same as the last time I'd gotten a peek at it.

Except tonight, the collage of colored stone seemed somewhat attractive. The light from the bare bulb hit one of the pinkish-toned rocks and brought out a shimmer like diamonds, and for a moment I could almost see the stone wall integrated into a classy entertainment center of some sort, complete with a mounted plasma TV.

Hmm. Plan C.

With Plan C in action, I could have my rec room and not mess with demolishing the cistern or walling it in.

Not that I was worried there was a body behind those lovely stones, of course. Simply because Plan C made my life easier than if I decided to take on Martin Dietz and his board of Nazis. I could turn the original historic detail of the home into a major selling point.

There. Dietz wasn't such a bad guy after all.

I bent to look at the furnace, no longer afraid to be alone in the basement on a cold, dark night. A couple wires, some dials, a few knobs. It all looked Greek to me. I tapped and twisted, hoping for a fiery resurrection.

I knelt down and looked in the tiny glass window close to the floor.

Yep. The pilot was still lit.

I held my fingers close to the flickering flame, soaking up its precious warmth as I considered my next course of action.

If I had any friends, I could call one of them and finish the night out at their place.

I thought of the not-so-long list of people I'd met in Rawlings. The first name that came to mind was the too-hot-to-keep-my-hands-off computer geek, David. Calling David for help in the middle of the night was absolutely out of the question.

Then there was the everything-by-the-book Officer Brad.

I shook my head at the appalling thought. I'd have to be mostly dead before I accepted help from a man in blue.

Dorothy Fitch across the street presented a decent possibility. But then I'd be under the same roof as Jack the Ripper. No, thank you.

Tammy at the Beauty Boutique came to mind. I'd figured out she wasn't hounding after David. That made Tammy, with her welcoming smile, the most logical choice of those to call. Sure, it was four in the morning. But she was a gracious, giving person. She wouldn't mind a middle-of-the-night jingle from a desperate customer.

I sighed, feeling all alone in the empty basement. I couldn't call Tammy. She'd just lost Coffee Girl, which meant she was probably emotionally exhausted and didn't need the extra stress right now.

There had to be someone else.

I thought of Verna, my old cellmate. She'd be there for me. Too bad she was still serving time.

I stared into the tiny flame, remembering my first day with her.

"So how'd you land yourself behind bars?" My new

roomy was a large woman, with arms as big around as my thighs. She sat in the corner, slouched down, legs sprawling.

"Um," I said, "I'm kind of here by accident."

"Me too. I accidentally got caught." She gave a throaty guffaw. "At least that lying, scheming, no-good man of mine is dead. That wasn't no accident." She laughed again.

"You killed your husband?" My voice had a mousy squeak to it.

"If you'd have been me, you'd have done it too. Don't kid yourself. If you're here, you have it in you."

I shook my head, horrified at the thought of this woman shooting or knifing or beating a man to death, and accusing me of being able to do the same. "No. It's not in me."

Her features looked small in her rotund face. She leaned forward, squinting. "Deny it and it'll poison your mind like a viper. You'll end up in the loony wing." She rocked her head back and forth and made a funny face. Her tongue slithered out like a snake's.

I stood at the cell gate and stared at the chunky cross-eyed convict. First I smiled. Then I laughed.

"We'll get along just fine," she said. "You just tell me what you need. Verna will take care of you."

The pilot light on the furnace came back into focus. My hands were toasty, but my knees had frozen from crouching on the cold basement floor. I worked them back and forth, then attempted to stand up. I grabbed the edge of the furnace and made it to my feet.

I dusted off my jeans and considered the problem at

hand. It looked like the only way I would get any more z's tonight would be in a hotel.

I gave the furnace a final, frustrated kick. Unfortunately, I used my bad leg to do it. I crouched in pain and tried to catch my breath.

A tear coursed down my cheek. I would not let this furnace thing get the best of me.

I lifted my head with new resolve.

Across the basement, the shimmery pink stone caught my eye. It looked so pretty from where I stood. Curiosity compelled me to take a closer look.

I glanced around and checked out the far reaches of the cellar. No boogeymen in sight. I worked my way toward the basement wall on my left, then kept the hard rocks to my back as I sidestepped closer and closer to the cistern.

I could feel something electric in the air. I heard a buzzing in my ears. But there was no turning back as I drew nearer and nearer to the glimmering stone.

Ten feet to go.

My breath quickened as I stared at the rock in front of me.

Five feet.

I stopped and leaned forward, peering at the shiny surface. A salty odor stood out from the usual musty scent.

I squinted. This close up, the stone looked wet.

I dared myself to touch it, to prove to myself that what I perceived as fresh blood was really just the stone's natural gleam. Hadn't my eyes tricked me when I looked inside the cistern the first time? There had been no body, just lumpy cement.

And now, on the shiny pink surface of that rock, there was no blood. It was just the dim light hitting the century-old quartz at the right angle.

I lifted my arm, shifting it ever closer to the stone. The buzzing in my ears grew louder.

I ignored it.

My finger reached out and touched the rock.

25

I rested my finger against the stone, a shock of cold raced to my heart.

I drew my finger down the rippled surface. It slid easily in whatever slimy liquid covered the rock.

Not blood. It couldn't be blood.

I flipped my finger over and checked the color.

Blood.

I gasped and pressed my back against the wall. Sharp stones poked into my spine.

The sound of harsh breathing echoed through the basement.

It was my own.

I stood frozen against the wall, afraid to move a muscle, afraid to be noticed by whatever blood-loving creature had left this mess.

I waited what must have been five minutes, just listening.

Total silence.

I prayed for the sound of the furnace to spur me into action. My fingers became numb in the cold. My breath puffed like fog around me.

Stuck in the headlights. That's what Grandma would have called it. She'd tell me that not making any move was still making a move. I was just more likely to get squashed by an oncoming truck if I just stood here.

Move, Tish.

I inched toward the staircase, keeping an eye on the cistern. My foot pushed off on the bottom step, and I kept going straight to the top. I pulled the door shut and locked it with the deadbolt. If the viper was still down there, it wouldn't escape through the kitchen door.

I rubbed my hands together and blew on them. The moist air fell short of warming my fingers.

The clock on the stove clicked and I turned to look. 4:20. My instinct was to call the police. But after the mockery I'd received last time I'd asked for help, I felt like skipping it. Still, did I have a choice?

I shivered and lurched my way back to my bedroom. I dug through the pile of clothes on the floor and found my cell phone. I hit the power button and dialed 9-1-1.

"Central dispatch," said a woman's voice.

"Hi." I gulped, not sure what to say. "Um, there's blood in my basement and I don't know why. Can somebody come down and take a look?" I felt childish with my request.

"Are you injured?"

"No, I'm fine. I just don't know why there's blood down there."

"What's your name, ma'am?"

"Tish Amble."

There was a moment of silence at the other end.

"Miss Amble, have you been drinking at all?"

"No."

"Have you taken any drugs?"

"Excuse me?"

"Where did you see the blood, Miss Amble?"

"In my basement. Over on the cistern wall."

"Please hold while I dispatch an officer to assist you."

The line went silent. I sat on my cot and waited.

"Miss Amble?" The dispatcher was back on line. "Officer Walters will be arriving shortly."

I ended the call and cradled my forehead in my palms.

It seemed Officer Brad was on duty 24/7.

Within minutes, lights flashed against the bedroom wall, and I knew without turning that Brad had pulled in the drive. Living a mere two blocks from the cop shop had its rewards.

I patted down my hair and opened the front door.

Brad stepped in.

"Going somewhere?" He looked my outerwear up and down.

"Just to the basement to fix my furnace." I turned and started walking toward the kitchen. "That's when I saw the blood."

I could almost feel him rolling his eyes behind me. Another hallucination from the queen of paranoia, he must be thinking.

Humph. I wasn't hallucinating this time.

I stopped at the top of the cellar steps and crossed my arms. "There you go." I nodded toward the steps. "The blood is over on the cistern."

"Come down and show me."

"I am not going down there. Don't you have a partner or something? What if the perpetrator is still in the basement?"

"I'm a trained professional. I'll make sure you don't get hurt."

I patted my bad leg. "I got hurt last time I went down there with you. I'm not making the same mistake twice."

"The reason you got hurt last time is because you were consumed with fear. You should have seen your face. There's nothing to be afraid of. I'll be with you."

"You don't understand. Whether you believe me or not, there is blood in my basement. I'm not about to put myself in danger because you think I'm imagining things."

"I never said you were imagining things. As your neighbor and friend, I'd like to see you get over your fears. And the only way to do that is to confront them. Admit it. Once you looked in the cistern and saw there was no body in there, you felt better."

My jaw clenched. He had no idea what I'd been through since I'd seen that image in the concrete.

"You're right." I leaned against the wall. "There's no body in the cistern. I feel great about it. But I'm still not going down there."

He snorted, shook his head, then descended the stairs.

I paced the kitchen and waited for him to emerge from the cellar with some explanation for the bloody wall.

The squawking of a police radio drifted up the steps. Obviously, Brad had found whatever I'd been lucky enough to miss.

He thumped up the stairs and came over to me, glowering, his eyes filled with accusation.

At his look, I scrambled backward, cornered by the window and the kitchen counter.

"You were right. I was wrong," he said through gritted teeth.

"What do you mean?" I bit my lip.

"There is a body in your cistern."

Horror coursed through my veins. "Is it Rebecca's?"

I didn't want to know the answer, but after last night's date with David, I'd been chewing on the awful possibility that it was Rebecca who called to me from the cistern.

"Rebecca? Have you seen Rebecca?" His expression turned from anger to surprise.

"Of course not. She's buried in the basement."

Brad grabbed my arms. "Tish. Get a grip. Rebecca's in California. Martin Dietz is in your basement."

My head lolled to one side. Only Brad's strength kept me from falling over.

"Why is Martin Dietz in my basement?" My words slurred.

"That's what you need to tell me."

I shook my head, dazed. "I have no idea. Maybe he was inspecting the cistern and fell."

Brad helped me slide to the floor.

"You two had an issue regarding the cistern, didn't you?" he asked.

An issue. That was a nice way of putting it. "Yeah. I wanted to knock it down, he wanted to keep it up."

"And he threatened you if you removed it?"

"I guess he threatened. He's the zoning czar. He doesn't have to let anybody do anything."

"Isn't it true that his denial interfered with your renovation and resale plans?"

"Well, yeah, but that doesn't mean I'd . . ." I halted midsentence. "I don't like your tone. Are you accusing me of killing Martin Dietz?"

"The man is dead in your basement. You had the motive, the opportunity—"

"I didn't kill him." Defending myself against his accusation was futile. Anything I said could and would be held against me. Just like last time. I struggled to lift myself off the floor.

Thuds and thumps sounded from the front of the house, and moments later, my kitchen was filled with donut dunkers.

The largest of the crew found his way over to me while the rest disappeared into the basement.

"Miss Amble, I'm Chief Doyle. Has Officer Walters explained to you your Miranda rights?"

Exasperation bubbled like lava in my guts. "I told you, I didn't kill anyone." I glared at Brad.

"You have the right to remain silent . . ." The chief droned through the list as if I'd never heard it before.

I stared numbly. Not again. I couldn't face going through it again.

I was jostled and nudged. Next thing I knew I was sitting in the backseat of a police cruiser.

26

I was questioned, swabbed, fingerprinted, and booked.

The attorney assigned to me, a young guy named Moranski, knew less about the process than I did. I coached him along out of pity, but by midmorning, I realized a shortened version of his name might suit him better.

At least I had a warm place to spend the next couple nights, even if the lingering odor of vomit revealed that my cell did double-duty as the drunk tank.

Outside, the wind blew. Every few minutes, a gust blasted its way through the caulk around the high window. I lay on the hard bench beneath it. The cold air drifted down and settled around me. If I got convicted of Dietz's murder, my life was as good as over. I'd already languished away three years. With a murder rap, I could write off the next twenty-five, minimum.

On the bright side, maybe I'd get to be cellmates with Verna again. And this time around, I'd agree with her about the injustice of the justice system and the inhumanity of humanity.

I curled up in a ball to keep warm. At least I'd already been wearing my coat when Officer Brad threw me out in the storm at four o'clock this morning. Too bad he hadn't had the courtesy to provide me with a blanket after questioning today.

I stewed for a couple hours, beating myself up for even giving a rip that there was blood on the rocks of my cistern. So what? It's a basement. There's bound to be undesirable slime in anyone's cellar. And considering that there was already a body under the concrete, what was another one on top of it? The scent of a decaying body would blend right in with the general odor of mildew. And if my furnace hadn't gone out, I never would have gone down in the basement. Spring would have been a much better time to deal with the murder of Martin Dietz.

I didn't like the guy anyway.

The door to my cell clanked and a female deputy came in. "If you got someone who'll put up a hundred grand, you can go home."

Look lady, I felt like saying, I couldn't even track down a friend to help me with my furnace, so what makes you think I can find one to fork over a hundred g's?

She looked at me with something like pity or compassion on her face. "You get one phone call."

She stood aside to let me go through.

I stayed on the bench thinking for a minute.

I had the cash sitting in my bank account, but every penny of it was reserved for renovations. If I dug into it for bail, I wouldn't be able to finish the job on schedule. And I'd be stuck in Rawlings for at least another year. Maybe even forever. There had to be someone out there who could put up the money. I was good for it. It's not like I could leave town with my Victorian unfinished.

The only face that came to mind was Tammy Johnson's from Beauty Boutique. She'd invited me to church, hadn't she? It was time she put her fortune where her faith was. If she refused to help me post bail, I'd know she was just another one of those Sunday Soldiers.

I followed the deputy. She handed me a phone book. I looked up Tammy's home phone number.

The line rang. An answering machine picked up.

"Hi. This is Tammy. I can't take your call. Please leave a message at the tone. Thanks!" Her voice sounded perky as ever, but I knew that in real life she was probably wiped out from grieving over Casey.

The machine beeped, waiting for a message.

"Um, hi, Tammy." I leaned against the dirty white wall, adding my fingerprints to those of other desperate callers. "This is Tish Amble. You know, the one who reminds you of your good friend Sandra? I'm at the county jail and I need your help. Can you please come down as soon as you get this message? Please?"

The other end was silent. Then a beep sounded as time ran out.

I hung up the phone.

"She'll get here," the deputy said in a gentle voice.

I squeezed my eyes and bit my lip, waiting until I gained control of my emotions before I looked at her.

"Thanks, but she barely even knows me. I guess I can only hope."

I waited in the cell. Supper came. I ate the familiar, flavorless fare. Daylight faded to dusk.

Maybe Tammy had gone out of town.

Maybe she hated me and wasn't coming.

Maybe she figured anyone who'd killed her admirer deserved to be alone in a cold, dank cell.

I cradled my head in my arms. The cell started to spin around me. I could feel myself sinking into blackness.

Despair.

I lay down on the bench. Sleep would help the time pass.

The door clanked.

"You have a visitor." It was the female officer.

I sat up, groggy. I must have dozed off.

"What time is it?" I asked.

"Almost ten." She stood aside to let me through.

I sat in the interview room. Tammy came in and took the chair across the table from me. Her face was puffy and red. Her hair had lost its body and hung loosely to her shoulders. Runoff from her mascara blackened the bags beneath her eyes.

Her chin had a sharp slant. "I was at Casey's service when I heard about Martin. I didn't want to come here tonight. Brad talked me into seeing you."

"Tammy. I'm so sorry. I know you've had a rough week. But I really need your help."

She pushed back in her chair. Her eyes glinted and her voice took on a bitter edge. "Rough is an understatement."

I opened my palms, pleading. "I didn't kill Dietz. But

204

I can't find out who did if I'm stuck in a jail cell. I need someone to post bail."

She crossed her arms. "I just can't believe you'd kill Martin over a stupid cistern."

"Exactly, Tammy. It was a stupid cistern. Nothing to kill over. But somebody felt they had a very good reason to kill him. Help me so we can find out who. And why."

"You're the obvious candidate. He was found in your basement."

"I also had three people swear I was at the Rawlings Hotel at the time of the murder. You invited me to church, remember? Give me a chance."

"Just because I'm a Christian doesn't mean I'm willing to aid and abet criminals."

I dropped my voice to a whisper. "You know I'm innocent, Tammy. Would a Christian leave an innocent woman in jail?"

With as many guilt trips as my grandmother had put me on over the years, I knew how to dish one out.

Tammy looked down and sighed. "Even if you're innocent, there's nothing I can do. I'm broke and then some. I'm holding on haircut to haircut. I don't know how much longer things can last."

Her sob story hit me. It was hard being single, trying to make ends meet, and still wake up with a smile in the morning.

It looked like I'd have to use my own seed money to get out of jail quick, and hope the arraignment could be scheduled soon. Otherwise, I'd find myself in a financial crunch that would drag out the renovations indefinitely.

And I didn't need anything stopping me from selling the Victorian full price come June.

I told her where to find my personal checkbook, and how to get the cash and post bail. Nothing could be done until the banks opened on Monday, so I geared up for a solitary couple of nights.

27

I woke up Sunday morning wondering how it would have felt to be getting dressed for church about now. What if I had taken Tammy up on her offer the other day and said, "Sure, I'd love to go to church with you and meet your teens and help them get over the death of Casey. I miss God. I can't wait to talk to Him again"?

Maybe if I had, I wouldn't be sitting in jail. Martin Dietz would still be alive. The murderer would have refrained from bonking Dietz's head on the rocks and pitching him into the cistern. All because God would have been pleased with me.

But God wasn't pleased with me.

And Martin Dietz was dead.

I toyed with possible suspects. Not David. He was at dinner with me. Not Dorothy. She was too small to heave that lug up and over the edge. Of course, her son Jack could have done it. Tammy herself might even be a suspect. Didn't it always come back to a scorned lover?

But why my basement? Why the cistern?

Revenge.

207

That could be the motive. A year ago, Dietz buried a body in the cistern, and someone just found out what he'd done. Insane with grief, that someone clonked Dietz and evened the score.

That led me back to my original question.

Who was buried in my cistern?

I had plenty of time to run the various scenarios while I waited for Monday.

When Monday finally rolled around, Tammy did her part and posted bail, and with my prompting, Mr. Moron managed to get me out of police custody by late afternoon. The hearing was scheduled for mid-January, meaning my basement renovation would have to be delayed until I got my bail cash back.

Officer Brad escorted me home, trusting me enough to give me the front seat. The sky held solid gray clouds, making nightfall seem only moments away. Friday night's snow had melted, but the wind still whipped in fury.

All I could think about was the mess I'd have when my pipes thawed out. Sitting in custody for two and a half days, I couldn't exactly dial up my plumbing and heating professional.

Brad parked the cruiser and opened his door. I jumped out mine and headed up the front porch steps, leaving him to eat my dust.

I turned and gave him an aloof, irritated wave. He mounted the steps anyway.

"Thanks for the fantastic date," I said. "I imagine we'll be seeing a bunch more of each other before it's all over."

He closed his eyes for a second as if praying for strength. "Don't take it out on me, Tish. I was just doing my job."

"Yeah, well, when you come back to get me, call first so I can pack a weekend bag. My teeth feel like they have a layer of algae on them."

"Don't worry, you're off my list of suspects for now."

"What do you mean?"

"Time of death was sometime around seven o'clock Friday night. The bartender and waiter at the Rawlings Hotel vouched for you."

"Then why did you say I'm off your list 'for now'?"

"The neighbor across the street says she saw you and Dietz enter the house together a little before seven that night. That's why the prosecutor wouldn't drop charges."

"There was a blizzard going on Friday night. How could Dorothy have seen anyone going into my house? I could barely find my way home."

"Mrs. Fitch is part of our neighborhood watch program. Believe me, her information is generally right on. She remembers makes of cars, license plate numbers, facial features, clothing, height. She's the best there is, so her testimony will probably be given a lot of weight in this case."

"Well, we wouldn't want the fact that I'm innocent to get in the way of Dorothy's perfect record." I pushed open the front door, ready to slam it in Brad's face.

"Hey. I have a friend who's a heating contractor. I had him come over Saturday morning and get your furnace going. Hope you don't mind."

I drew in a sharp breath. Brad had my furnace fixed?

The hard shell around my heart fractured like cracking ice. Guilt oozed out of the fissure. After all the spite I'd shown Brad over the past few weeks, I didn't deserve such an act of kindness.

I crossed my arms. "I guess it's the least you could do after arresting me for murder." I hated my words. Why couldn't I have simply said thank you?

"He'll send you the bill." Brad strode down the steps and got in his cruiser.

I stood in the cold watching him go.

My foot nudged a frozen lump on the front porch. I kicked at it mindlessly before I looked down to see what it was. A newspaper. I peeled it off the decking and brought it in.

I walked into my bedroom, shoulders slumping, and dropped the newspaper in the corner. I didn't even subscribe to the local news.

I sighed. Brad might be a cop, but he was probably the most decent guy I'd ever met. If I would just stop being such a jerk to him, we could probably be friends. But who had time for friends? I had to finish this renovation project before I ran out of cash or got run out of town. June or jail was just around the corner.

I took off my coat and pitched it in the pile on the floor, thankful the house was warm again. Break-ins, breakdowns, jail breaks. Too much came against me. I didn't know how to handle the barrage. If I had a bed, I'd crawl under it. Instead, I sat on my cot and leaned my head in my arms.

When I looked up, the newspaper caught my eye. It

had unfurled where it landed. A picture of my house splashed the front page. I picked it up. A sick feeling spread across my stomach. I read the murder story. Martin Dietz's name appeared three times. Mine showed up eleven. Jason Blane, whoever that was, ripped me to shreds. He'd dug up details of my life that I hadn't even known and couldn't possibly be true. The guy begged for a libel suit.

But even if I won a million in damages, the damage was already done. Not a jury in the land would set me free after that kind of publicity. The doorbell rang. I hadn't showered in three days, my hair spiked up on one side, my teeth were pale green, and I could feel a pimple growing on the side of my nose.

The doorbell rang again.

"Go away," I yelled halfheartedly.

The intruder pounded on the front door.

I jumped up. "Go away."

Dorothy Fitch's ratty hairdo peeked through the glass of the door. Somebody else stood behind her, but with the waning light, I couldn't see who.

I sighed and rolled my eyes. That busybody was the last person I felt like talking to right now. But Grandma would tell me to put on a smile and open the door.

I did.

My smile disappeared when I saw the love seat. The overstuffed styling sported unsightly navy-blue-and-burgundy plaid upholstery. I hoped Dorothy and her helper wouldn't be upset when I sent it right back home with them.

Dorothy stood on the top step in her bulky quilted coat.

She squirmed to keep a grip on the awkward corner. A middle-aged man with Down's syndrome held up the other end. Dorothy's son Jack, I assumed. Confronted with his personal challenge, I was suddenly ashamed to have made a monster of him in my mind.

Though the piece of furniture must have weighed a ton, it remained suspended between Dorothy and Jack while I gawked.

I snapped out of my trance. "Gee. Put that down and come in, won't you?"

"It's for you." Jack smiled and pushed on his end impatiently.

Dorothy edged toward the door, her face red from straining. I had no choice but to hold the door open with one hand and grab an end of the love seat with the other.

The three of us stuffed the piece through the doorway and settled it against the wall by the staircase. The rolled arms and arched back filled the space perfectly.

"Thank you," I said. I didn't mention that I'd have to take the thing out the back door piece by piece in black garbage bags.

"Came to talk," Dorothy said, taking off her coat. "Knew we'd have to bring our own chair."

I sighed. "I don't mean to be rude, but I've had quite a weekend. What I really hoped to do was get some sleep."

"Can't blame you." Dorothy sank into the soft cushions. Jack sat down next to her. I stood there, almost drooling at the idea of a comfortable seat. The hard bench I'd been sentenced to the past three days hadn't done my back any good, and my own bumpy, narrow cot wasn't much better.

"Thing is," Dorothy said, "I feel real bad about what happened and wanted to make it up to you somehow. Brought the love seat I promised, for starters."

"That wasn't necessary. Really." I crossed my arms, hoping they'd take the hint and leave.

"Wanted Jack to meet you." She turned toward her son. "See, Jack, this is the lady who lives here now. Tish Amble. You sure she's who you saw Friday night?"

"I saw her."

"Was she with someone?"

"I saw her with Officer Brad."

I laughed in relief. "Yes, about nine o'clock Friday. I was walking out front. Brad pulled over and talked to me." I left out the part about being at David's.

"Before that, Jack. You saw her before that too, right? Going in the house with Mr. Dietz?"

I lodged my protest. "I was at dinner. He couldn't have seen me."

"Hush," Dorothy waved me off and watched Jack.

"I saw the lady who lived here."

"Jack, this is the lady who lives here. Is this who you saw?"

"I saw the lady who lived here."

Dorothy sighed. "You saw Miss Amble walk in this house with Mr. Dietz Friday night?"

Jack put on a stubborn chin. "I saw the lady who lived here. She went in with Mr. Dietz."

"Do you remember Jan Hershel? She used to live here, Jack. Is that who you saw?" Dorothy asked.

He squeezed his forehead in concentration and shook his head.

Dorothy patted him on the shoulder. "Okay. Okay, Jack."

Jack turned his face away, pouting.

Dorothy lowered her voice. "Think his memory is starting to go."

Jack turned on her in a rage. "I remember, Ma. I remember."

He pushed up from his seat and fumed out. The front door slammed behind him, rattling the windows.

Dorothy flinched. "Pretty sure he's got memory loss. Can happen early for Down's syndrome adults. Premature aging, you know. Sometimes they end up with Alzheimer's by forty."

"Officer Brad said it was you that saw me going into the house with Dietz. But you're telling me it was Jack who supposedly saw me?"

"Jack said it was the lady who lived here. Asked him over and over, but he always said the same thing. I just assumed he meant you. Maybe he meant someone who lived in the neighborhood. Guess I owe you an apology."

"So it's Jack that's never wrong, not you." Dorothy couldn't miss the edge to my voice.

She looked up, eyes pleading. "Have to say it was me. The police wouldn't listen if it was Jack who told them."

"How do you know?"

"Don't want my Jack talking to the police. Got too many problems as it is."

Dorothy patted the cushion next to her on the love seat.

I sank down beside her and crossed my legs. I leaned my head into the softness behind me. I breathed in, enjoying the moment.

"You won't tell, will you, dear?" Dorothy sounded distressed.

I lifted my head. "If it comes down to me going to jail or you losing your reputation as the perfect spy, you bet I'm going to tell."

Her hands twisted in her lap. "I'll say it was too snowy and I can't be sure who I saw. Jack can't talk to the police. It's not a good idea."

"But Jack may know who the killer is. I'm sure if he talks, the police will understand. No one will blame you." I wasn't at all sure of that, but Dorothy had to be persuaded to tell the truth. My freedom was on the line.

She clawed at my arm. "My Jack's all I have left." She sat back, her eyes toward the ceiling. "Had four children once, you know. The oldest died when he was just eleven years old. Right there on the railroad tracks. Thought he could beat the train."

My hand flew to my mouth.

"I'm so sorry," I mumbled through my fingers.

"Jenny died when she was twenty-three. Cindy was twenty-seven and pregnant when she passed away."

My eyes must have been the size of saucers.

"Cancer took them. Not as strong as me, I guess." Her expression glazed over.

I looked again at her patchy hair and opaque skin,

215

startled to realize that Dorothy herself was a cancer survivor.

"You see why Jack's everything to me, don't you? When he was born, everyone said he was a burden to bear. But God knew I was going to be alone. And He gave me Jack to keep me company."

I touched the back of her hand. "Let's just see what happens. I can't promise to keep your secret, but I'll hold off telling as long as I can. Who knows? Maybe they'll find the real murderer and it won't matter."

She gave a single nod of her head and stared at the carpet.

Her dejected look did its job. How could I tattle on the only surviving son of a woman whose children were genetically cursed? "All right. I won't say anything."

She gave a relieved sigh.

"But, in exchange, I want some honest answers to a few questions that have been bothering me."

"Answer what I can," Dorothy said.

"Great." I settled into one comfy corner of the love seat, hoping to be there for a good, long stretch. "I want you to tell me everything you know about Martin Dietz."

28

"Not one to gossip," Dorothy said. She shifted in her seat. "All I know is what I see and hear for myself. Don't pay no mind to rumors."

"I understand. I'm not looking for rumors. I'm looking for facts. Did Dietz have family? Friends?" I leaned toward Dorothy on the love seat, eager for information that might clear my name.

"Heard he's got family over in Jackson. That's where the funeral is, the paper said. Far as friends go, I don't think there's a soul in town that liked the man. Even Sandra eventually saw through him. Everyone else just paid him due homage."

"How long did Sandra and Martin know each other?"

"Can't say for sure. They'd been dating quite awhile before he popped the question. Saw the ring when she first got it. She'd been over to the Ramseys'. Showed me on her way home."

"Sandra knew Rebecca and David Ramsey?"

"Small town, dear. For a good number of years, they

were pretty tight. Sandra loved watching the renovations. David teased that she was Martin's spy."

Dorothy rubbed her eye with a bony knuckle. "Then long about a year ago last April, Sandra quit hanging around the jet setters that had made her career, the Ramseys included."

I remembered Tammy saying Sandra had helped with the church youth group. I assumed that activity took up Sandra's former big-shooter schmooze time.

"And let me guess," I said. "That's when she broke up with Martin."

"She didn't want to call it off. Said she just wanted to get her life together. Martin harassed her for trying to change. Mocked her for wanting to do the right thing. When she jumped in the race for commissioner against him, that's when he showed his true colors. She held her head up as long as she could. But he intimidated and embarrassed her in front of everyone. She had to throw in the towel." Dorothy shook her head. "Never thought she'd just up and leave like that, though."

"How was Martin after she left?"

"Think she broke his heart. He bad-mouthed her every chance he could, promising she'd never be able to come back to Rawlings. But men only do that when they've got their hearts broken. Don't know why he thought he could be mean to her and she'd stick with him. A woman can only take so much."

Control freak. That was Dietz. Sandra was okay as long as she toed the line, but do something for herself, and she was toast. Maybe all that bad-mouthing Dietz did was designed to wrap a smoke screen around the facts.

Sandra Jones was dead in my basement. And Martin Dietz put her there. I was almost sure of it.

That got me back to the important question: who killed Martin Dietz?

It had to be someone who knew and loved Sandra. Someone loyal to her memory. Someone who knew what Dietz had done and was just waiting for the right time to take revenge. Waiting for the day when some schleppy renovator chick could take the rap.

I leaned toward Dorothy, feeling as if the answers were somehow mingled with the ganglia in her brain and all I had to do was ask the right questions. "Tell me about the waterproofing project last year. What part did Martin Dietz play in that?"

"He had to approve it. Saw him there a couple times while it was going on. He was always one to keep a close eye on things."

"Did you ever see him down there after business hours? You know, a time maybe when he shouldn't have been?"

Dorothy looked at the floor in front of her. "Can't think of one."

"What about Jack? Do you think he might know of a time?"

"Might, I suppose." She glanced up quickly. "But he doesn't like to talk to strangers. I'll ask him for you."

Yeah, right. By the way he'd plopped his bottom into the love seat, Jack had wanted to stay and visit.

Dorothy stood. "Promised you soup, didn't I?" She headed to the front door. "Best get to it."

I wasn't done digging for clues, but I didn't want to push her. I'd hit a nerve somehow asking about Jack.

"Thank you for the love seat," I said as she walked out.

Half an hour ago, I'd been ready to burn the plaid atrocity. But having cuddled up in it, I was hooked on its sink-down-to-my-toes comfort. I stood back and looked. The shape softened the angles of the open stairwell. Between the love seat and new paint job, the parlor seemed cozy. And free was always better than renting.

I curled into the curved arm, almost giddy to own a stick of real furniture.

I closed my eyes. Lucky for me there were Officer Brads in the world. Instead of freezing, I was toasty in my usually drafty Victorian.

I must have dozed off.

Clang, clang, clang. Prison guards were opening and closing my cell door. Behind me, Verna was telling me how to make coffee. "Three scoops in the top. But don't you use that nasty water." I was only half listening to her. Mostly I was wondering why the guards kept banging the door. "Am I in, or am I out?" I asked.

"You're in," the guard said and stuck his face up to the bars. It was David.

I stumbled backward to get away from him and fell across Verna. But it wasn't Verna anymore. It was a dead, decaying body.

Teeth without lips smiled up at me. "I'm waiting, Tish."

I screamed myself awake, scrambling upright on the love seat. My heart pounded.

Night had fallen while I'd napped. Streetlights sent a dim glow to the parlor. I stood and groped my way to the kitchen.

I turned on the light and waited for the fluorescent bulb to reach full intensity. I eased toward the kitchen sink and looked over at the cellar door. Yellow police tape draped across it, most likely forgotten after the brief and unrevealing investigation. CRIME SCENE, the black letters warned.

I could only hope that Martin Dietz had made amends with his Maker. I didn't need another ghost wandering the halls. As it was, his death was enough of a curse. A picture of my house plastered all the area papers, along with details of the murder in the basement. I crossed my fingers that no one would recognize the Victorian once I transformed it with a fresh coat of paint come spring.

I opened the fridge and scrounged around.

An onion bagel and some low-fat cream cheese fit the bill.

I leaned against the counter as I ate and thought about breaking through the police tape. If I had a speck of courage, I would throw a private grave-digging party and have the case wrapped up in thirty minutes or less. And without Dietz around to stop me, no one could comment on the excavation of my cistern.

I brushed a crumb off my lip. I was stuck in limbo between knowing the right thing to do and having the gumption to actually do it.

And it wasn't like I had anybody to come to my rescue. Officer Brad probably choked down a chuckle every time he remembered the body I thought was in my cistern. And I couldn't invite a police officer to join me in wrecking a crime scene, even if it was already abandoned.

David remained a possibility. But I shuddered to imagine his reaction if I asked him to help exhume a body. He might think I was a little on the loony side now, but after that, he'd be convinced I'd lost my marbles.

That left Jack Fitch as the most likely White Knight in the neighborhood. I could tell him I just wanted to redo the concrete job in the cistern. No offense, Jack, it's just too bumpy. Can't you help me take out the old concrete and smooth in some new? And if we happen to find a body under there, oh well. You never know what you'll uncover in these old homes.

I scraped the bottom of the cream cheese container with my last chunk of bagel. There was always the off chance that my basement was devoid of a body. No Sandra. No Rebecca. No Jan in residence. Just plain soil under that chunk of mortar.

I swallowed a lump of dough.

I was betting on a body. Of course, with Dietz getting so carelessly clunked in my cellar, I might end up back in the slammer.

A *thunk* came from outside the back window. My heart did a double flip-flop.

I froze against the counter, then pitched the cream cheese container in the trash and dusted off my hands.

29

I tiptoed to the window and peeked through the glass, shielding my eyes to block the glare. I could vaguely see movement almost directly below me at the basement window over the cistern.

I squinted and craned for a better view. Could be a dog.

I bit my lip. Or the person who did in Dietz.

My heart kicked into overdrive. Oh, for a pair of outdoor floodlights.

I heard scratching, like someone prying at the window casing.

I slunk toward my bedroom, avoiding the squeaky spots on the floor. I dug through my jean jacket for my cell phone and dialed Brad's home number. I'd had enough of the criminal justice system to last the rest of my life. I sure didn't want any more officials at my door. But maybe, if Brad was off duty, he could come by just as a friend and nab whoever was outside peeling my paint.

"Hello?"

I almost sagged to the floor in relief. He was home.

"Brad. Hi. It's Tish. Um, I think there's someone behind my house, and I was hoping you would take a look for me. Unofficially, of course."

There was a beat of silence.

"Sure, Tish. I'll be right there."

Ten minutes or more passed. I heard a knock at the back door.

I opened it to find Brad standing with Jack Fitch.

"I found your visitor." Brad glanced at Jack.

"Jack?" I said his name in a high-pitched squeak. "What were you doing back there?"

"I didn't get to finish. Have to finish."

I shook my head, bewildered, and looked at Brad. "Finish what?"

Brad touched my elbow and spoke to me in a low voice. "Can I talk to you alone for a minute?"

I glanced at Jack. He seemed consumed with his cuticles.

I shrugged. "Sure. Come on in."

Both men entered. Jack stood in the kitchen while I led Brad to the new love seat. We sat down at the same time. I scrunched back into my own corner as far as I could go. Our knees angled toward each other, almost touching.

Brad blew out a breath and looked at the fireplace. "Jack has a bit of a compulsion. He likes to finish what he starts." He smiled and looked at me. "A lot of people are like that. But with Jack, it's really hard for him to let go of the waterproofing project he helped with last year. He wasn't there when the crew finished, and he worries that it got left undone."

"Did you bring him down there and show it to him?"

"Yeah. He's seen it. But he always insists it isn't finished and he has to finish the job."

"Okay. So he was trying to get in my basement just now to finish a year-old project that's already done?" No wonder Dorothy had flinched at my mention of ghosts that day on the porch. She figured Jack was doing the haunting.

Brad tapped his fingertips together. "Something like that. This has happened before. I talked to Dorothy about it last week. She was supposed to keep an eye on him."

My eyebrow lifted. "You talked with her about it last week?" I remembered Brad hugging Dorothy on her front porch that one day. He must have been speaking to her about it then.

I bounced my fingers on my thigh. "You mean, the stick-in-the-window thing, that was Jack?"

"Most likely."

"Why didn't you tell me?"

"To protect Jack's privacy." He leaned toward me. His voice softened. "Listen, no harm has been done. Jack's no killer. He was at home with Dorothy when Dietz was murdered. And now that you're aware of the situation, you can be on the lookout. It's hard enough for Dorothy. Please don't make it worse just because you're mad at me."

"Mad because you respect Jack's privacy but not my own? Imagine that." I crossed my arms.

It had taken Brad all of thirty seconds to spread the rumor of my background in October. I hated double standards. My look must have said it all.

225

"Whoa, Tish. I'm doing my job as a peacekeeper. Dietz's murder in your basement couldn't exactly be kept under wraps."

"I'm not talking about Dietz. I'm talking about my grandmother."

Brad's brow shot up. "I didn't release that information."

Pressure built up behind my eyes. "Maybe not just now. But you knew about it last month. How could you go around telling everyone?"

His forehead creased. Brown eyes stared into mine. "You're wrong. I read about it in the paper this weekend, along with everyone else."

"You looked me up in the police computer and saw my rap sheet."

"No. I didn't."

"You already knew my name. The second day I was here."

"I saw Dorothy the next morning. She'd talked to the realtor and knew your last name. That's all. The only reason the story's out now is because some reporter did his homework."

"I wish I could believe you." I almost choked on the lump in my throat.

"Why don't you?"

"Because you're a cop."

"And that makes me a liar?"

"Let's just say I have a basic mistrust of anyone in authority."

"And why is that?"

I wanted to slap him for asking so many questions.

"Because I spent three years behind bars and found out that jerks run the system."

Brad looked off toward the window. "A uniform doesn't make someone good. It doesn't make someone bad. It's just a uniform. People are human everywhere you go."

"Well, some people have an obligation to be better than human."

"Does that include you?"

My hands yearned to strangle him. "I'm not exactly in a position of power. If I mess up, I'm not wrecking other people's lives."

"What about your grandmother's?"

I stared at him a second, shocked that he could even make the implication. His needle came a little too close to popping my balloon.

I jumped up and stumbled toward the kitchen. "How are you doing in here, Jack?"

He stood at the water dispenser, holding down the lever. Water dripped to the floor.

"Hey, buddy." I smiled and headed his way with a towel. "Someone's going to slip in that puddle."

He took the towel and wiped up the spill. "I like this. It's better than the small bottles."

"Cheaper too." I swung my arms. "So, Jack. I heard you did a great job down in the basement. Who else worked on it with you?"

I felt Brad's aura enter the room. I glanced over my shoulder. He leaned against the doorframe, arms crossed, listening.

Jack put up a thumb and a finger. "There was Mr. Lloyd and his son Josh."

That was old news. I knew about Lloyd & Sons' participation back in July when I started canvassing for a contractor.

Jack put up another finger. "You know David. I saw you with him the other night."

I remembered my surprise to learn that David Ramsey had earned a key to my house from his efforts on the project. It was hard to picture him wearing work clothes and wielding a sledgehammer.

"There was Mr. Hershel. He used to live here." Jack added a finger to his count.

I'd only met Rick Hershel briefly, but from what Dorothy said, Rick was having a hard time letting go of the Victorian himself.

Another finger made a full hand. "And I helped," Jack said. "I carried buckets of cement down the steps. I dumped it in the holes."

"You did a great job."

Incredible. It was hard to picture myself actually living in a neighborhood where people would work together like they had on this one waterproofing project. When I was growing up, Grandma always complained that no one would lift a finger to help her out. Of course, she'd never admit she needed help.

Rawlings had that good-neighbor element that so many towns lacked. Then again, a year after the project, one man was dead, bashed by one of these so-called neighbors. And there was the possibility that another body was beneath the surface of a waterproofing project gone bad.

I poured myself a cup of water and took a sip. "So,

Jack, do you remember seeing Mr. Dietz in the basement?" I glanced over my shoulder to see what Brad was up to. His stony features hadn't moved.

"I saw him sometimes. He came down to talk to Mr. Hershel. He got in a fight with Mr. Lloyd one day."

"A fight, huh? What was it about?"

"Mr. Lloyd wasn't doing it right. He wanted to dig a hole for the water to run into. Mr. Dietz said no, he had to put in a pump. The hole could be outside, not inside. Mr. Lloyd said, 'What do you think that cistern is there for anyway?' Mr. Dietz said he better not catch him digging holes in the basement unless he was hooking up a pump. The job better get done right, or Mr. Dietz would make sure Mr. Lloyd lost his license."

I could almost picture the scene between the two men. Tall, gray-haired Lloyd versus stocky, bald-headed Dietz. One bare basement bulb reflecting off their sweaty brows. Gentlemen, take your corners.

"Sounds like Mr. Dietz was really mad." I imagined veins popping from his temples, ready to burst.

"He yelled really loud. Jan came down to see what was wrong. She told Mr. Dietz to get out, but he wouldn't go. Said he wasn't done inspecting the project. She went back upstairs and called Officer Brad." Jack nodded toward the off-duty Brad.

I turned, intrigued. "So, you broke up the neighborhood brawl?"

"Dietz was gone before I got here. Jan was pretty upset, but Rebecca and Dorothy came over and helped her calm down. As usual, Sandra came by later and smoothed everything over for Dietz."

"Of the four women you mentioned, three of them aren't around anymore." My unspoken question hung in the air.

Brad nodded once. "Rough year. Three relationships down the tubes."

I pursed my lips. "You don't sound very sorry for the trouble you caused."

Brad raised an eyebrow. "What trouble was that?"

"Please. Don't pretend you weren't all over Rebecca Ramsey."

Brad squinted. "I don't know where you got that information, but it's incorrect." His voice took on a ragged quality. "There was never anything between Rebecca and me."

I blinked, wondering whom I should believe. David, who swore Brad was after his wife. Or Brad, standing there close to tears, seeming to wish there'd been something more between him and Rebecca than merely friendship.

And maybe there had been.

I moved a step closer and squinted at him. "How does Rebecca like California? Hot enough for her?"

Brad gazed down at me. "We don't correspond."

"Well, maybe now that David's out of her picture, she'll be back in touch."

"Highly unlikely." Brad closed the gap between us. "Am I missing something? You called me. So why do I feel like you're annoyed I'm here?"

I stood my ground. "I'm not annoyed. I'm ready for bed." I ruffled my fingers through my hair. "Thanks for coming by."

I turned toward my other visitor, who toyed with the nozzle on the water jug. "You want a to-go cup, Jack?" I looked at Brad. I wanted in the worst way to be polite to him. But somehow, manners would signal a truce. And I wasn't ready for that. I pushed Brad and Jack out the door using only eyebrows, crossed arms, and tapping fingers.

30

I ran a hot shower, hoping to calm my nerves and get some sleep. But later, as I lay on my cot, I couldn't banish the day's events.

The whole town knew about my grandmother. And they all thought I killed Martin Dietz.

My self-preservation instinct told me to never leave the house again. Order my groceries in, finish the renovations, and get out of town fast.

But the rebel in me said, Hold your head up. Don't let anybody run you out of Rawlings.

Tonight I sided with the rebel. But who knew? Maybe tomorrow I'd go along with the preservationist.

A train whistle blew in the distance. The faint rumble grew louder and louder until the whole house shook from the vibration of fully loaded boxcars flying past on narrow steel rails.

I imagined I lay in a hole in the cistern, damp sand and lumpy pebbles beneath me. A layer of wet, slimy cement mix covered me, getting thicker and thicker as it hardened. Yet with each lurch of the train, the cement settled around my body, filling in every tiny crack and crevice, until my face, hands, and foot protruded from the grave like a plaster cast. Whoever had poured the concrete mix on top of me hadn't counted on tremors from the tracks doing such a great leveling job. I needed another layer of cement to cover my features, so anyone looking down at me couldn't see me screaming and clawing and fighting for my life. I wasn't finished.

I sat up on my cot. Beads of sweat dampened my forehead. That's what Jack kept saying. The job wasn't finished.

I swung my feet to the floor.

Did Jack have something to do with the murders? Or was I being paranoid? Even Brad seemed to know a little more about neighborhood events than he let on. He shouldn't even be on the Dietz case. He was too embroiled in the whole affair to be impartial.

Who was Brad protecting in this mess? Just Jack? Or was Rebecca a part of it?

I rubbed my temples. With my mind moving as fast as the train outside, I'd never get any sleep. I stood. The warning bells outside quit dinging, and the rumble of boxcars faded into the distance.

I was wide awake. I might as well get something accomplished. I grabbed my paint supplies from a corner of the parlor.

The front stairs creaked and groaned as I made my way to the second story.

I flicked on the light to the bedroom directly at the top of the steps. The room had an odd shape where it angled in for the staircase. It looked like a square with one corner cut off. One window looked out to the side yard, right into the branches of the maple tree. The other looked out onto the balcony. The walls were in decent condition—nothing a little spackle couldn't cure. The Hershels had been kind enough to strip the thick bands of woodwork down to a light pine color. I spent the next half hour taping the trim so I could edge around it with a fresh coat of paint.

But taping was a mindless job. Thoughts of murder, bodies, and motives had plenty of room to roam. I'd already narrowed down the identity of the body in my basement to three possibilities. Unfortunately, by midnight, the list of suspects topped ten and continued to grow. Even the biddies from the clothing store weren't immune from my late-night scrutiny.

Motives ran the gamut from love scorned to money owed to rumors spread. And still nothing made sense.

I had to get this thing figured out. Then maybe the authorities would take my body-in-the-basement theory seriously. And I could be cleared of Dietz's murder.

I poured paint into an old cottage cheese container and started cutting in. I wondered what David must think of me now that the story of my grandmother was out. Would he avoid me like the plague? Would he plague me with accusations? I couldn't blame him if he reacted just as everyone else had over the years. Like I was worthless because of what I'd done. Who wanted to hang out with someone capable of murder?

I wished I could go back ten years and redo Grandma's last days. I'd been too eager to please. I should have said no. I should have had standards, morals, ethics, something that would have prompted me to do the right thing instead of the easy thing. I should have had compassion. I should have had a backbone. I should have known better. I should have been more patient. I should have had more faith.

I dipped the brush in the paint and tackled another section of wall. But why stop with Grandma? I carried an equal load of guilt for Martin Dietz's murder. I should have seen it coming. I should have tried to stop it. I should have known arguing with Dietz was a waste of time. I should have gone along with him and not made him mad. I should have installed a security system so people couldn't sneak around in my basement when I wasn't home.

I could bury myself in should-haves. Or I could figure out what made this small town tick like a bomb about to explode, and try to stop it.

I yawned. It had to be almost 1:00 a.m. My body ached, my brain ached, my heart ached. I wrapped my brush in cellophane. I'd come back up tomorrow to finish the job.

The baseboard pipes clunked as the furnace kicked on. I glanced out at the hallway. Blackness. I stretched plastic wrap over the paint, half-expecting to see Jacob Marley standing in the doorway of the room. With my favorite tappy hammer, I sealed the lid on the paint can. I wiped a glob of ivory on my pass-me-around pants.

The neighborhood seemed eerily quiet tonight. No midnight train, no cars bouncing over the tracks. Even the wind had died. It was as if the hot water pipes and I were the only two noisy elements in the universe.

I cupped hands around my eyes and peeked outside.

A foggy halo circled the streetlight in front of my house. Without the snow, the town had gone back to looking like Halloween. Spooky, and silent as the grave. And I was the main caretaker of the graveyard.

The skin on the back of neck my prickled. Beneath me, two flights of steps down, lay a body. I was almost sure of it.

I jolted down the steps, shaking the walls around me as I beelined to my bedroom and slammed the door.

My sleeping bag became a sanctuary. In its warm safety, I finally drifted to sleep, ghosts and guilts and guys flitting through my mind.

A week went by as I hunkered down in the house, my brushes and rollers my only friends. Dorothy had come by a couple of times and brought soup. I wouldn't answer the door. She left the pot on the porch, and I snuck out to get it after she'd left. I never heard from my buddies at the cop shop. Officer Brad may have dropped by once or twice, I don't know. I ignored any knocking I heard when his cruiser was parked out front. He never barged in to arrest me, so apparently, the local loon squad had some other culprit in mind for the Dietz murder. Even so, that didn't erase the fact that I'd been fingered for the crime. And you couldn't brainwash a whole town into forgetting the details that had surfaced throughout the ordeal.

Becoming a hermit for the week definitely lowered my stress level about the Dietz/Grandma accusations. I pretended that nobody really paid attention to gossip and rumors anyway. I gave everyone in the Village of Rawl-

236

ings the benefit of the doubt when it came to holding a grudge against a truly harmless, albeit too-daffy-for-her-own-good Renovator Chick.

But today, the cans of nuts, the dried fruit, the cereal, and the slightly moldy bread had run out. I was Old Mother Hubbard. And I was hungry.

Deucey gulped twice, then fired up after the long vacation. I backed her out of the garage and turned on to Main Street.

The second block past the tracks, a sign caught my eye: Parker Floral Designs. I hit the brakes, earning a blast of the horn from the driver behind me. Traffic cleared and I maneuvered Deucey into a parking spot made for the compact cars of a new generation. There was barely room to squeeze my knees past the bumpers as I made my way to the sidewalk and into the quaint flower shop.

Eucalyptus seemed to be the mainstay of every arrangement in the shop. Its mellow odor greeted me at the door and stuck with me to the back counter.

"May I help you?" a middle-aged woman asked. Short brown curls bounced with her animated walk. She rounded the end of the counter and nearly tackled me with her perkiness.

I stepped back. "I got a flower arrangement a couple weeks ago from a secret admirer. I was hoping you could help me figure out who it is."

The woman gave a look of disapproval. "We value the privacy of our clients. If the individual wanted you to know his identity, he would certainly have revealed himself to you on the card."

I had no idea floral arrangements were protected by the Privacy Act. Take two. "Actually, it's more complicated than that. I'm dating a guy who got me some flowers. But I think they were really flowers that he got from somebody else. I just wanted to make sure he really got the flowers for me." I took a big breath. "I absolutely hate hand-me-down roses."

Her eyelids peeled back in a look of horror. "That would be understandable. How do you know they came from Parker's?"

I fished in my jeans pocket, relieved the woman couldn't know they hadn't been washed since the night I'd snuck over to David's. I pulled out the card and envelope and handed it to her.

She studied the chunky black lettering.

TWENTY-FIVE YEARS. REMEMBER THAT.

"Not very romantic. From the letter formation, I'd say a woman wrote this. Did this come with your bouquet?"

"Not exactly. I found it later. I'm sure it wasn't meant for me. I guess that's why I'm a little upset. Can you find out who originally purchased them?"

"I'll see what I can do. You said you got the arrangement a couple weeks ago?"

"Yes. There were twenty-five red roses. I counted."

"Hmm. Twenty-five. Just like on the note. Sounds like somebody was sending a definite message. That's what flowers are for, you know. Let's take a look."

She tapped at the computer on the counter, entering data faster than I could think.

"Were they delivered to you?"

"No. Picked up by David Ramsey."

The woman's fingers came to a dead stop. She looked at me through curly bangs, never lifting her head.

"I see. You must be Patricia Amble, just down the street."

I held my head up. "Yep." The word may have come out a little snotty, but I had my pride.

Her chest rose and fell in quick little gasps. She was nervous. Scared to death, even. Here she was, stuck alone with a woman on a possible killing spree.

"Here it is," she stammered. "Twenty-five red roses. Tea roses, to be exact, which appropriately stand for remembrance. Wired through central ordering. No information on the sender. To be picked up by David Ramsey, 306 South Main."

She pushed away from the counter, putting distance between us. "There you go. Hope that helped."

"Thanks." I watched her squirm a minute. Then I left and climbed in my car.

I pulled into traffic and drove to the supermarket. The flower lady's attitude was no big deal. Reputation wise, I'd gone from being the twin of Dietz's reject to being a slayer of old people and maybe even the zoning lord. Definitely a lateral move.

I shopped at full speed, dumping items into my cart without checking prices or expiration dates. Never once did I look into a pair of eyes. Even the checkout girl got the brush-off.

I bolted out the door, positive I could sense haughty looks and vicious whispers on my tail.

I wanted to climb up the nearest lamppost and scream down at those arrogant people, "Don't you know how hard it was? You would have done the same thing if you had been me!"

But what was the point in defending myself? Everyone sat in judgment over me. I could scream 'til I was blue in the face, and nobody would ever understand why I'd done what I had. If only they'd been there. If only they'd been me. Then they would know how hard a decision it was. Then they'd quit condemning me for what I'd done. Because they would have done the same thing.

31

I parked in the garage and pulled the door down. I never wanted to go out again. Starting right now, I would be a hermit for the rest of my life. I didn't want to deal with people, look at people, get mad at people, or fall in love with people. I just wanted them all to go away. Leave me alone. Disappear.

I rounded the back of the house and jerked to a stop.

Brad. Standing on my back porch.

He stared. I stared. Apparently, neither wanted to be first to break the silence.

My foot tapped.

I caved. "Are you here to arrest me?"

I knew from his winter coat and blue jeans that he wasn't on duty, but the brat in me wouldn't be polite.

From where I stood, Brad's eyes looked all shiny or watery or something.

"I stopped by a couple of times this week. Why don't you answer the door?" His breath made white puffs in the frosty mid-morning air. One hand rested on his hip, one leg stretched in front of the other.

I clenched my jaw. I wasn't obligated to answer. I could simply brush past him and lock the door behind me.

I started for the porch, intent on doing just that. The sidewalk had a crackly white design from the frost. The porch steps felt slick under my tennies from the same sparkling layer.

Brad's brown leather boots entered my circle of vision and I steered to the left. The boots cut me off. I stopped.

Against my better judgment, I ratcheted my neck up a few notches and met his eyes. "Move."

He stood his ground.

"Move, please."

He reached for my arm. "Are you okay? I just want to know."

I pulled away. "Of course I'm okay. I'm always okay. Now let me in."

"Here, I'll hold that for you."

I handed him my groceries.

He stepped aside and I unlocked the door.

"I can take that now," I said, reaching for the sack of food.

He swooped it out of my reach. "Let someone help you once in a while."

My hands landed on my hips. "You've gone over and above the call of duty in that department. Thank you for all the unasked-for assistance. I think I can handle my own groceries."

He made no move to relinquish them.

"I'm sure you can. Listen, Tish. You're a beautiful young woman. I hate to see you shut up in this house day after day. You should be out having fun. Living life."

My nose squeaked as I drew in several seething breaths. "My life is none of your business. I happen to renovate houses for a living. That means I'm shut up at home day after day. Occupational hazard."

"I think you take it to the extreme. Especially after the whole Dietz thing."

I cocked a loaded finger at him. "You have no idea what the 'Dietz thing' has done to my life. I can't go grocery shopping without people staring and whispering about my past mistakes. Why would I give them more opportunities to point fingers?"

I looked at my weapon and tucked it in my pocket.

"People might talk about you for a while, but pretty soon you'll be old news. Don't let them get to you. You're entitled to a life, you know."

"Am I? I think most people would disagree. Eye for an eye, tooth for a tooth. A life for a life."

"You did your time. You paid the price. Now grab hold of your second chance and make it count."

"You make it sound as if I'm some kind of loser, like I'm not doing anything worthwhile with my life. I disagree. Entire neighborhoods benefit from my efforts. Historic homes are saved from utter ruin. What I do is important to communities."

"Don't you ever want to get married? Have a couple of kids? I have a hard time seeing how that's going to happen with you hiding out in there."

My head felt like it would explode. My heart skipped a

couple beats. I forgot to breathe. Then everything rushed out at once. Loud.

"Give me my groceries and get out of here. There is nothing wrong with my life. How dare you come over here and imply that there is! You better focus on fixing your own flaws before you start nitpicking mine."

I may have come off a bit demon-possessed. I didn't care. I was right and he was dead wrong.

I wrenched the bag of groceries out of his grip, ran inside, and slammed the door. Tears started to flow. By the time I unloaded the perishables, my sleeve was a gooey mess.

Brad had no business butting into my life. Maybe I did want to get married one day. Maybe I did want to have a kid or two. But all that was on hold now. The one man I cared about lived two houses down and hadn't even tried to see me this past week. Then I find out the stupid roses he had given me were hand-me-downs from some vindictive female.

I looked at the drooping arrangement that still graced my countertop. Twenty-five dead red tea roses. David didn't have to worry. I'd remember.

With all my whimpering and sniffling, I barely heard the knock on the door. I peeked through the glass.

Brad just couldn't figure it out. I didn't need him. I didn't want him. I was fine. He could just go away and leave me alone.

I opened the door and stood there without saying anything.

"Can I come in?" His voice was all raspy.

"What do you want?"

"I just want to know you're okay."

"I already told you I'm fine."

"Lie to yourself all you want. Don't waste your breath lying to me."

I probably turned three shades of purple before I pushed the door closed. Brad's hand got in the way. One rock-solid arm kept the latch from catching.

"Talk to me, Tish."

"I have nothing to say."

"Come on. Let's go somewhere, get a cup of coffee, and talk."

"I can't. I'm taking a quick lunch break and getting back to work."

"Let me buy you lunch."

"I just bought fresh turkey. I don't want it to go to waste."

"Eat it tomorrow. Come on. There's a restaurant up-town you'd really like."

Uptown? I didn't know Rawlings had such a place. "I don't know. I'm already behind schedule."

"Great. Then I'll have you back here in an hour."

The second I relaxed pressure on the door, Brad pushed it open. He took my hand and led me onto the porch, closing the door behind us.

"I'll drive," he said. I pulled my hand from his grasp and followed obediently on the outside, grudgingly on the inside.

We cut through my side yard to the walk that led past Brad's house. The crisp air cleared my stuffy head. I sniffed, and realized I hadn't even looked in the mirror or freshened up before going back out in public. With all the crying I'd been doing, I must look like a two-by-four had connected with my face. Brad hadn't seemed to notice, so maybe my eyes weren't as puffy as they felt.

We angled down his driveway. Just past the back door was his one-car detached garage. Too small to add any value to the property. If he were smart, he'd build a two-car attached in its place. That would give the home half a chance of ever selling.

He lifted the overhead door by hand, reminding me that I, too, lacked an automatic opener. I'd have to shop around Flint for a bargain brand one of these days.

The clouds parted and the winter sun glinted off the hood of the most hunky metallic gray SUV I'd ever seen. With barely an inch to spare, the vehicle filled the door with its silver grill and monochrome bumper. Dual head-lamps were protected by clear glass, giving the front end a clean, hi-tech look.

"Wow. Is that yours?" I couldn't keep the awe from my voice.

"Yep. Hop in."

I squeezed past the bumper and opened the passenger-side door. The smell of leather greeted me. I sank down in cool luxury. The door closed with a pleasant *thunk*. Next to me, Brad turned the key. The engine turned over, then faded to a bare purr. He pulled out and turned right onto Railroad Street.

"You left your garage open," I said, knowing I'd never enjoy lunch if I had to worry about his tools the whole time we were gone.

"No one will bother it. I'm a cop, remember?"

How could I forget that fact? I couldn't believe Brad

talked me into lunch. We came to a stop at the intersection. I glanced over at my Victorian. My head jerked. David stood on my back porch, watching the SUV as Brad turned onto Main Street.

"Oh." My hands pressed against the glass as David disappeared from view. He must have come to see me. I felt an urge to jump out the door and race to him. Yeah, and I could kiss his feet too, and thank him for finally noticing I was alive.

Brad must have sensed my inner struggle. "Do you want me to go back?" he asked. His voice sounded strained.

"No. Thanks." I hadn't thought about David when I'd agreed to Brad's invitation. If David really had watched Rebecca slip away into Brad's clutches, how did he feel watching me ride off next to Brad now?

I tried to relax. I looked into the shop windows as we drove, glad I could enjoy the view for once. I couldn't worry about David's reaction. Besides, I was probably giving myself too much credit. I turned to Brad. "So how long have you lived in this godforsaken town?"

He chuckled. "There's nothing forsaken about this place. Believe me. God pays close attention to Rawlings." Brad stopped for a traffic light. "Maybe you can't tell at first glance, but if you look closely, you'll see all kinds of miracles happening."

Up ahead, a youth in baggy clothes strode across with the signal. He shook his fist at the car in front of us for encroaching on the crosswalk. "I must need a magnifying glass, then. All I've seen so far is murder and mayhem."

Brad cracked a smile. "It's all in your perspective."

I put on a look of surprise. "You mean Martin Dietz

didn't really die? I didn't get booked for the crime? I didn't spend three days in the slammer?" I humphed. "You're living in some kind of fairy-tale world."

The light changed and Brad drove ahead. "You're not seeing the good that's coming out of all the crud."

"What good?" The car closed in around me, like a tent collapsing.

"Well, you got your furnace fixed, didn't you?"

My hand tightened its grip on the door handle. "That's pretty minor when you look at what I had to live through."

"Not at all. You had a warm place to sleep and your pipes didn't burst while you were gone. It could have been pretty ugly this time of year, you know."

I wondered how bad it would hurt to jump out of a moving vehicle. "Like I said, thanks." I crossed my arms and glared at the dashboard.

"I bet you had a lot of good happen in your life, and you just never realized it."

"Yeah, right. My mom died when I was seven. Where's the good in that?"

"You went to live with your grandmother and got to know her."

Brad just couldn't take a hint. I swung to face him. "Yeah, and I got to go to prison when she died. Where's the good in that?"

"You decided to fix up houses for a living when you got out."

"And what's so good about that?"

"You came to Rawlings."

"Please. I'm beginning to think that's the biggest mistake I ever made."

"No it's not. You met me."

I drew a sharp breath and looked out the window. Brad couldn't mean what I thought he meant. He was merely being cute with a pompous comment.

He couldn't possibly be serious. Brad and me? No way.

32

The SUV pulled into a vacant space in front of the same strip mall that housed Goodman's Grocery. I'd never noticed the café before. A rectangular lighted sign said Sam's Coney in red letters. A hot dog wearing a diner hat and holding a cane danced beside the words.

"How often did you say you ate here?" I had a hard time imagining I'd find any reasonably healthy items on Sam's menu. It was bad enough I splurged on pastries at the Whistle Stop. I didn't need to clog my arteries with dancing hot dogs.

"Couple times a week." Brad opened his door. "Come on. I want you to meet someone."

I followed him past the plain brick façade and into a dimly lit interior. Square tables cluttered the center of the room, each one accented with a tiny white vase and a fake red carnation with a sprig of pine needles. Someone's interpretation of Christmas decorations, I supposed. A row of red-upholstered booths lined the perimeter. Stark white walls held art that commemorated dead movie stars.

The title on one poster caught my eye. Boulevard of

BROKEN DREAMS. I stared at the drawing. Elvis Presley, Marilyn Monroe, and Humphrey Bogart were among those that huddled at the far end of a diner bar. I swallowed, surprised to find myself fighting back tears and battling a lump in my throat. With a few brushstrokes, the artist could add my mother, grandmother, and one day me to the scene. Boulevard of Broken Dreams. Yep. I lived there.

"What do you see?" Brad asked.

I shook my head and cleared my tears. "Nothing. Sorry about that."

He put an arm loosely on my shoulder and looked at the rendering. "That's all of us, Tish. We've all got dreams we've set aside or given up on. It's part of life. You get a new dream and keep moving ahead."

"I thought you went to school to be a cop, not a psychologist."

"Same difference. It's all about what makes people tick." He dropped his hold and moved toward the counter. "Let's sit over here."

We sat on retro red stools. He ordered a Coke. I ordered the diet version.

"Tell Sam we're here, would you please?" Brad said to the waitress. She scurried off to the kitchen.

"To answer your question," he said with a smile, "I've lived in Rawlings all my life. The house I live in now belonged to my grandmother. She died when I hit my early twenties. I moved in and fixed it up over the years."

So Brad lived in a family heirloom. That explained his lousy choice of location. "You've never wanted to leave Rawlings? You know, shake its dust off your feet and move on?"

251

"I owe a big debt to my hometown. It's why I am who I am today. I love giving back to the area a little bit of what it gave me."

"You must have had a good childhood experience to say that. Most people can't wait to get out of Dodge."

"Too many roots. Here's one of them now." Brad stood for the arrival of a stunning, tall brunette wearing a tight T-shirt with the diner's logo across the chest. She leaned over the counter, held Brad's cheeks between her hands, and kissed him on one eye.

"Hey, bro," she said with a grin.

Brad pretended to wipe spit out of his eye. "Sam. I want you to meet my neighbor, Tish Amble."

She extended her hand and gave me an unwavering gaze. "Nice to meet you, Tish. I'm Samantha Walters, Brad's adorable little sister."

Samantha's adjectives for herself fell far short of an accurate description. I came up with *beautiful*, *leggy*, *lippy*, *sexy*, *funny*. *Adorable* and *little* never made the list.

Her grip felt firm but not stifling. I liked her. "Hi."

"So what can I get you two for lunch?" She pulled a pen and pad out of her apron pocket.

"I'll have the usual, please," Brad said.

I hated to think of the fat content in something called "the usual."

"I'll have a tossed salad, ranch dressing on the side, and a cup of the chicken noodle." Sometimes you had to show by example the right way to eat, regardless of how hungry you really were.

"Comin' up." Samantha sashayed to the kitchen, leaving Brad and me in awkward silence.

"So . . . is she the Sam from the sign?" I asked.

"Sort of. This was my dad's diner. Believe it or not, when I was in high school, I used to flip burgers and dogs back there on the grill."

I smiled at the picture he brought to mind.

"When Dad died, Sam Junior there took over the restaurant."

"How does she do it? Didn't she have plans of her own?" I thought of my own plans that had been forever boggled by my grandmother's illness and eventual death.

"I've never seen anybody happier. She runs the diner, plays in a band, writes songs. She has more friends than King Solomon had gold. Life always looks good to her no matter what she's going through."

I swallowed. "I could sure use some of her outlook. Does she sell that here in the diner?"

Brad grinned. "No, but she could probably tell you where to get some."

I felt my face turn red.

"Church," Brad said quickly. "She goes to a really great church. I go to the same one, actually. Maybe you'd like to come with me Sunday?"

I shook my head. "Thanks, but no. I'm taking a spiritual hiatus. I have a lot of healing to do before I can head back to organized religion."

"Then you're taking a church hiatus. Nobody gets off the hook on the spiritual part. That's just a part of being alive. You're on a journey whether you want to be or not."

"However you want to put it."

Sam dropped our drinks in front of us and disappeared. I unwrapped the straw and started slurping, hoping to put an end to the discussion.

I watched Brad take the paper off his straw. I liked his hands. Wide across the palm with long, agile fingers.

Neither Walters sibling wore a wedding band, a quirky fact for two so attractive people. "How is it that you two have managed to stay single? Or were you married before?" I asked.

Brad looked in my eyes. "I've waited a lot of years to find the right bride." He looked away. "Sam was married when she was young, but got dealt a dud. She hung in there longer than any of us thought she should. I think she's still getting over the sting. But I have to say, I've never known anybody as happy to be single as Sam."

Seeing Brad's brotherly devotion to his little sis, I struggled with David's accusations against him. How could this sweet, sister-loving guy be a big-time philanderer?

Of course, no one could, by simply looking at me, say, "There goes a grandma killer." Unless they'd read about it in the papers.

Secrets. Everybody had them. Mine happened to be tough to keep.

But like Brad, some people out there excelled at keeping secrets. Such as the person who murdered Dietz and Cellar Dweller.

"So where do you call home, Tish?" Brad's voice interrupted my brooding.

"Um . . ." His question stumped me. "I spent most of my youth in Walled Lake with Gram. But I guess if I think about it, home's up north, where I was born."

"Up north. Like Traverse City?" Brad asked.

I bit my tongue. I got really irritated with people who thought Michigan ended at the Straits of Mackinac.

"No. Up north, like Escanaba," I said.

Brad raised his eyebrows. "An Upper Peninsula Girl, huh?"

I geared up for the insults I'd grown accustomed to hearing whenever I mentioned my place of origin. Sure, the U.P. had its problems. But so did the rest of the world.

Brad cleared his throat. "I went to the academy with a guy from Gladstone. Mike Segerstrom. What a great sense of humor. He's a state cop in Manistique now." He shook his head. "Man, is it beautiful up there. I spent a couple weeks fishing with Mike after graduation."

I sighed in relief. No insults. "I barely remember it," I said. "I was only seven when I moved downstate."

I closed my eyes and saw gentle waves licking a rocky shore. Heard leaves fluttering in a playful breeze. Smelled fresh earth and pine needles. Felt hot sand running through my fingers. All memories of a happy childhood, before Mead Quarry rose up that night and swallowed my mother.

"Maybe I'll take you back there one day." Brad nudged my shoulder and smiled impishly.

"Maybe." I looked toward the kitchen, avoiding Brad's eyes.

I didn't like the way he got to me. I shouldn't want to know more about him. Or want to have lunch with him again. Or even feel comfortable around him.

But there was something about Brad that ate away

my defenses, made me trust where I shouldn't, made me hope where I mustn't.

Sam glided to the counter and set our meals in front of us. Hot steam from the soup hit my nose and I grabbed for a napkin. I looked over at Brad's fare. A Coney dog and a bowl of the chicken noodle. Not bad looking, actually.

I watched Brad take a bite out of the juicy chili-n-cheese-covered dog smothered with onions. I dipped a fork into my salad, spearing a chunk of lettuce. Brad chewed the spicy-scented Coney. I crunched away on iceberg.

Brad spotted me staring.

"Want a bite?" He pushed his basket toward me.

"Maybe just a little one." Using my fork, I sliced off a piece. Nothing had ever tasted so good. "Mmmm" was all I could manage.

"You haven't lived 'til you've had Sam's Coney Deluxe." Brad took another bite.

"Sounds like a radio ad. But I think you're right." I dabbed at the spot of mustard on a corner of my mouth.

"Sam," Brad called.

She came around the corner.

"Yeah?"

"Get Tish a Coney Deluxe, please."

I waved my hands in protest. "No. No, really. One bite was enough."

"One bite is never enough," Brad said.

Sam looked me up and down. "You look like you can afford it. One Coney Deluxe coming up."

256

Brad had me laughing all the way through the second Coney. Sam joined in with her blithe jokes and bright smile. I'd never felt so warm inside. Must have been the chili beans. And all those onions.

At one o'clock sharp, Brad took me back to the house and dropped me off at the back door. Staring out the kitchen window, I rubbed my arms to warm up and watched Brad drive off. The Victorian had never felt so lonely.

33

I closed my eyes and let my dreams run free around me. A pot of chili simmering on the stove. Brad at the kitchen island I'd be putting in next month, reading the paper, a cup of steaming hot coffee in his hand. Kid Number One, with reams of dark spiral curls framing her round four-year-old face, sitting next to him, filling in the lines of her princess coloring book. Kid Number Two beating on the tray of his high chair, babbling for more crackers. My heart swelled at the imagined scene.

I rubbed a tear from my cheek. A beautiful dream. Nothing more.

Yet for some reason, Brad led me to believe it could come true.

I gave in to the burst of maternal energy that lunch with him had somehow unleashed. By six that night I had finished another upstairs bedroom. The two little dream kids now had a place to call their own. By the time I finished everything, Brad and I could lodge four cuddly whippersnappers each in their own bedrooms.

258

I washed the paintbrushes in the sink, content. Everything seemed to fit together. My life had unfurled like a mural, with Rawlings the final chapter. Right here in this house I'd spend my days loving my husband, raising my family, and entertaining friends.

Life would be perfect, for the first time ever.

I looked up from the suds at a figure crossing in the dark outside my kitchen window.

David.

I squeezed my eyes closed and sighed. What would I say to him?

What could I say to him? Sorry, David, your worst nightmare has come true. One bite of Brad's Coney Deluxe and now I'm hopelessly in love with him.

Hearing myself think the words snapped me out of my intoxicating drama. In love with Brad? In love with a churchgoing, iron-pumping police officer? It didn't even sound like me. In fact, it was almost the exact opposite of what I'd planned for myself.

David knocked. I wiped my hands on a crusty paint rag and opened the door.

"Hi." I couldn't think of anything more brilliant to say.

"Tish. I missed you this afternoon." Remorse, or maybe accusation, sounded in his voice.

"Oh, that." I waved it off. "I just went for a quick bite to eat."

"Then you and Brad aren't . . ." He paused and raised his eyebrows.

"What? An item?" I giggled. "Good heavens, no."

"Can I come in? Do you mind?"

"Oh, gosh, of course." I stepped aside.

David walked over to the watercooler and poured a cup. "Would you care for any?"

"No. Thank you. Listen—" I fidgeted, uncomfortable with his familiarity in my kitchen—"why don't we walk over to the coffee shop? We can talk there."

He set his cup on the counter, its pure-as-a-mountain-spring contents untouched. Two long paces and he stood over me, barely a foot away. His body radiated heat. I blew at my bangs to cool my forehead.

"How long have we known each other, Tish?" His voice came low and soft. I nearly keeled backward.

"The cumulative total?" A whisper was all I could manage. "About three hours."

David smiled, unshaken. He reached for my hand and pulled me six inches closer. "I think we know each other better than you think. We both want the same thing from life. Someone to love, a measure of happiness, maybe a child or two."

My outer vision blurred until David's face became the only thing in focus. The only thing in the room. The only thing in my life.

He slid his hands upward until they cupped my cheeks. Heat from his palms added to the impossible burning in my head.

"Tish. What I'm saying is, I want you to marry me. We'll be happy together, I swear." He pulled me to him. His heart beat in my ear.

I held on, drowning in the warmth of his body. I let myself go under for the third time, never wanting to come up for a breath of air, never wanting to end this moment of surrender.

His lips burned against my neck. I closed my eyes, feeling close to death from sensory overload.

"Marry me, Tish." His lips touched mine. I clung to him, ignoring his question, ignoring nudges from the practical Tish who tried talking sense into me.

But Miss Practical wouldn't shut up. "David." I peeled myself away from him. "I can't. I mean, I'll have to think about it."

His ragged breathing filled the kitchen. "Right. Right. Sorry." He pushed me an arm's length away, but kept hold of my shoulders. "Of course you have to think about it. It's a big step. Take a week to mull it over. Just know that I love you, Tish."

He brushed his lips against my forehead, cleared his throat, and went for the door.

I stood in place ten minutes after he left, wondering what had just happened. My first marriage proposal and I said I'll have to think about it? The guy wasn't perfect, but he wasn't exactly a loser. I could do worse.

But could I do better?

I chewed on a fingernail, glad it was my own, and paced a square around the room. "Better" was all in one's perspective. It came down to what I wanted in a man. Did I want the computer geek–engineer type with an amazing historic home and silky bathrobe? Or a Joe Schmo–cop type with a fixer-upper and sweatpants? Or somebody else altogether?

I couldn't think. Why did David give me only a week to mull it over? Why not a year? What was his rush? If he thought he'd be getting the cooking, cleaning, domestic type, he'd probably be disappointed. It was one thing to imagine being a mom and wife, but another thing to actually be one. What was my example, after all? My mom ran into a snag or two in her life and took the easy way out. And Grandma. The woman could inflict pain on everyone around her but had no tolerance for it herself.

I couldn't trust myself to do the right things or act the right way in a relationship. If I failed, perhaps I'd fall into despair. Then what would stop me from carrying out the family tradition? I couldn't bear to do that to people I loved.

The only guarantee would be to remain single and childless the rest of my life.

I stopped at the bushel of wilted roses.

But what if I said yes to David and everything turned out all right? What if we had lots of wonderful years together? Things always worked out in my gothic romance novels. Arranged marriages, forced unions, all began with a measure of loathing. Maybe the couples weren't on fire for each other at the beginning, but deep love and respect always grew over the years.

Besides, with David's financial backing, I could finish the Victorian. The profit from the sale would help get our marriage off to a good start. We would even be able to afford to have kids right away.

I plucked the bouquet of roses from the paint can and laid it on the counter. I took the red ribbon and tied it around the stems. Then I hung the whole batch to dry, upside down from a nail over my kitchen window.

I knew how to make the best of things. I'd been doing it all my life. And David could definitely be the best of things.

Tomorrow I would tell him yes. Yes, I loved him. Yes, I would marry him. Yes, we would be happy together.

I finished cleaning up my paint mess, lost in a swirl of contentment.

Brad would be surprised at the announcement. Disappointed, even. I hoped the news wouldn't come between our budding friendship. I thought of his beautiful, smiling sister, and I hoped she and I could still become friends one day.

I wondered about Tammy. How would she react? Would she be upset that David was off the market almost as soon as he'd gotten back on?

I thought about Dorothy across the street. She wouldn't be pleased. She'd be certain I could do better than a member of the jet-set crowd, as she'd called David. She'd have been thrilled if I'd told her Brad would be my groom.

But I couldn't worry about what everyone else thought. I was entitled to my own life, as Brad had pointed out. And my own life meant my own choices.

Tonight, I chose David, and all the happiness that choice would bring me.

I drifted asleep on my cot, dreaming of wedding decorations and dresses and invitation styles and cake patterns and bridesmaids and guests.

34

The next morning, I spent extra time on my hair. A sample bottle of perfume, found abandoned in the bottom of my duffle, got a workout. I even put on my pretty blue sweater with the silky bow.

I downed a container of yogurt, dusted the lint off my coat, and took the front sidewalk over to David's.

The morning was cold and crisp. A light snow had fallen during the night. Fresh prints left by my tennis shoes along the sidewalk dispelled any secrecy I might have hoped for surrounding my mission. I watched for Brad's cruiser, sure he would show up to try to baffle my plans.

But I made it to David's back door without any interference. I paused to rehearse my lines, then lifted my hand and knocked.

I fidgeted while I waited, jumping up and down to stay warm. No answering sounds met my ears. I sighed and rolled my eyes. David's house was such a tomb. My knocking probably hadn't made it past the mudroom door.

I looked toward the garage. I couldn't tell from all the tire tracks if David was home or out. The path of footprints worn from the porch to the garage and back was as unrevealing.

I knocked again. Still no answer.

Should I go home and try back later?

Nah. I was his bride-to-be, for heaven's sake. If he could propose marriage, I guess we knew each other well enough for me to walk in and see if he was home.

I turned the handle and entered. I slipped my shoes off next to a pair of boots on the rug. A pair of women's boots. A pair of size 7 black leather women's boots with fur lining and a designer label.

Oh. Okay.

Hmm.

I squeezed my eyes shut, determined not to cry. Maybe now wasn't a good time to barge in and accept David's marriage proposal. But it was certainly a good time to meet the competition. And maybe slap David for getting my hopes up at all. Or at least bawl him out for toying with my heart, when all along he was two-timing me. That put him and Brad on equal footing. Both were detestable when it came to women and honor.

I headed around the corner and into the dining room. There were no occupants, but my eyes glommed onto the computer, perched like a blue-eyed Cyclops atop the massive armoire. The printer spewed paper piece by piece into a tidy pile.

I walked to it and turned the top page over.

Mortgage document of some kind. I'd seen a million of them. I picked up the pile and flipped through.

265

Great interest rate. No prepayment penalty and no balloon.

Wow. I'd have loved terms like that on my place.

Sugar Cane International Bank. Never heard of it. The address showed someplace in the Virgin Islands.

I looked back at page one. The documents were assigned to Tammy Johnson of 675 Maple Street, Rawlings, Michigan. My hair stylist. The papers refinanced her home for almost two hundred thousand dollars. I had a hard time believing anything on Maple Street went for that amount.

More paper came through on the printer. I peeked at the appraisal that followed, which backed up the re-fi price. I skimmed the comparable homes used for the final determination of value. One of them was my Victorian. But the sales price shown on the appraisal was almost double the amount I'd actually paid.

Somebody was scamming somebody.

I looked at the computer screen. Squares blinked sequentially in a center rectangle. *Printing* . . . , said the text.

I wished I knew something about computers.

My heart sounded like cannons in my ears. I glanced over my shoulder at the empty room. Future fiancée or not, I was stepping into dangerous snooping territory. I already didn't like what I'd found. Looking further might only cement the situation.

A manila folder lay on the desk. I angled it to read the label. IMM, it said in sloppy ballpoint pen. I flipped it open with shaking hands.

The top page was on U.S. Citizenship and Immigration Services letterhead, complete with the crest of the

U.S. Department of Homeland Security. I scanned the contents, forgetting to breathe.

> . . . due to the October 31 severance date from your corporate sponsor . . .
> . . . Divorce Decree dated October 15 . . .
> . . . failure to comply with naturalization requirements . . .
> . . . must depart the country as of December 31 or face deportation . . .

I slammed the folder shut like the lid of Pandora's box.

Deportation? No wonder David had only given me a week to think about marriage. Maybe I had an ulterior motive for hooking up with him. But his ulterior motive for hooking up with me bordered on usury.

The floor squeaked behind me. I let out a scream of surprise and twirled to face David and Tammy, standing in the archway to the parlor.

Tammy had been crying again. Tears of black mascara trickled down her cheeks. She wiped them away as I watched.

I waited for David to yell at me for snooping, but he only smiled and walked toward me. He gently plucked the manila folder from my hands and set it back on the desk.

"Good morning," he said and kissed my cheek.

Tammy watched the exchange without a twinge or a blink. Maybe I had the whole two-timing thing wrong.

She was first to break the silence.

"David is looking over some paperwork for me. I hope we didn't startle you."

"Well, gosh," I said, putting a hand over my chest, "I

guess getting caught with one hand in the cookie jar did shake me up a little."

David closed the doors on the armoire. "How about a cup of coffee?" He led the way to the kitchen.

Tammy and I got stuck at the door, undecided as to which of us should go through first. I hung back and let her go ahead, more like a hostess than a guest, I figured. I wasn't yet ready to give up my claim on David.

David dug around through the cupboards looking for the coffee paraphernalia. I got frustrated watching him, so I jumped in to help him track down the supplies and properly load the machine.

I grabbed the filters from him and set to work. Within minutes, we were sipping delicious hot coffee from expensive pottery.

I asked David the question that hung in the air. "So, what paperwork are you looking over?"

He took a slow swallow of coffee.

Tammy rushed to fill in the silence. "I'm getting a home loan to tide me over."

"Tide you over until when?" I asked. "What's going to change that'll make being over-mortgaged a good thing?" Surely she knew the dangers of being upside down in a home loan.

Her jaw clenched. "I'm discussing my options with David, thank you."

"I don't know who did that appraisal, but the numbers are all wrong. They show that my house sold for twice as much as it actually did. That's a pretty big error. And while it pushes up the value on your place, I can't see you ever catching up if you go to sell one day. I don't care what kind of rates Sugar Cane offers you, it's still a bad move."

Total silence met my sound advice.

"How long were you here, Tish?" David asked. "I didn't hear you knock."

I looked at the floor. "A little too long, I guess." I caught Tammy's eye. "I just hate to see you get stuck in a panic that you can't get out of."

"Thanks for the advice." She sipped her coffee and leaned against the counter.

"Okay. I've got to go." I set down my mug and charged toward the mudroom.

David followed me and watched me tie my shoes. He could probably tell from my mood that this was no time to spew excuses all over me. I jerked my laces tight. I could almost hear the list—"I was going to tell you about my job . . . I always meant to go to citizenship class . . . I hope you don't think I'd only marry you to stay in the states . . ." Blah, blah, blah.

Out of the corner of my eye, I saw David shifting his feet.

"Was there something you came here to tell me?" His voice sounded hopeful. Maybe there really was more to his proposal than just an easy way to remain in the country.

I met his eyes. "No. I just came over to say hi."

Chicken. I'd botched the perfect opportunity to confront him about my suspicions. He could have explained that he loved me deeply and planned to ask my hand in marriage very soon anyway. The letter from Immigration merely made it a more urgent matter than he'd intended.

We stared at each other for a minute. Then I dove out the back door.

I steamed home, dwelling on my cruel turn of fate. Getting married to stay in the country. I guess David wasn't the first person to have to do it. Still, I'd hoped for something more romantic to launch my new life with him.

I just couldn't see lining up the kids one day and hearing David explain to them in his sexy English accent, "I love your mother's beautiful eyes, soft lips, and keen wit, but what I really love is . . . America."

I kicked a twisting path through the snow. The second I walked in my front door, I dialed Lloyd's number, just in case I didn't already have a big enough headache.

He didn't answer. The connection flipped to his voice-mail.

"Hi, this is Lloyd . . ."

I started talking at the beep. "Hi. Tish Amble here. Don't know if you heard about Martin Dietz, but I'm going to make another try at getting my cistern removal approved. Still available in January? I hope so. I'm pretty sure I can get this thing through. Call me."

It occurred to me while out kicking snow that there was now a vacant seat on the Historical Committee, a seat I intended to fill. And the first thing I'd change would be the rule that prevented my cistern from coming down.

I might have to leave the house and meet some people. But it would all be worthwhile. The cistern would be gone, my basement would be finished. And I'd be kissing Rawlings goodbye through the rearview mirror, with proceeds from a full sale price weighing down my trunk.

Of course, the whole plan depended on somebody other than me sitting in jail come January.

35

No sense wasting time. I walked down to the village office and requested the necessary forms to run for the latest vacancy on the Historical Committee.

The clerk looked at me with wide eyes. "Aren't you Tish Amble?"

I smiled. At least I had a reputation of my own now. Move over Sandra Jones.

"Yes, I am. How do you do?" I offered her my hand across the polished wood. Might as well start politicking.

She jutted out her chin. "You know, I can see where you might be upset that Mr. Dietz wouldn't approve your project. I didn't like the guy much, either. But to murder him and then run for his seat? That's just wrong."

For a moment I was speechless. It hadn't occurred to me how the general public might view my drive for justice. To have it laid out so bluntly by the Collating Queen knocked the wind right out of me. But I wasn't about to let her know that.

"Innocent until proven guilty," I said. I snatched the forms off the counter, twirled, and sped home.

I snuggled into my love seat and read through the application. I had until mid-January before the special election took place. That meant I had to get 51 percent of the voting population to choose me over the next guy.

If there was a next guy. How many people wanted Dietz's slot, anyway? I mean, the man was murdered.

The thought dampened my enthusiasm, but only momentarily.

I was no Martin Dietz. I had personality and pizzazz. I'd been on the receiving end of an ordinance violation more than my fair share of the time, and I could dole out sympathy and solutions to applicants. And if anyone valued the historic quality of a home, I did. I'd spent my adulthood bringing the structurally dead back to life. And I did it with style.

I stared at the shaggy carpet, anxious for the spring day I could haul the rug and its inhabitants to the curb. The key to my political success would be getting the right sponsor. Someone who had a lot of pull with the citizens of Rawlings. Someone who could introduce me to the movers and shakers of this Podunksville.

Someone like Officer Brad. He had connections within the village hierarchy, among the average Joes, and in the church community. With his backing, I might just get the seat. Then it was bye-bye cistern and bye-bye Rawlings, with cash to spare.

I'd start by inviting Brad to an organizational brunch at the Rawlings Hotel. Then I'd pop the question.

As I dialed Brad's home number, it occurred to me

that I might have to break down and get a landline. With all the phone-calling and schmoozing I'd have to do, it would probably be cheaper in the long run than relying only on my cell.

Brad's phone rang. I ran my hand along the soft fabric of the love seat and sighed. It seemed my stay in Rawlings would be riddled with broken rules. Still, one piece of furniture and a telephone line hardly constituted a permanent residence.

As long as I didn't get too attached, I'd be okay.

Brad's answering machine kicked on.

"Uh, Brad," I said, wishing I'd prepared my spiel. "It's Tish." I paused. "Amble," I added, as if he wouldn't recognize my voice. "You know how Martin Dietz is dead now and there's an opening on the Historical Committee?" I started to sweat. That was bad. Very bad. "Well, I'm hoping to be the newest member. I think you can help me get my way. I mean, get the position." Oh, boy. This was all on tape. "Anyway, please call me back."

I pressed the END button and cradled my head.

Puh-leeze. Had I really said those words into a recording device? Maybe I could plead the fifth and the tape would be disallowed at trial.

While waiting for return calls, I started to yank the floor-to-ceiling cabinetry from the kitchen wall. Once finished, the area would host a generous pass-through countertop to the dining room. Then the two rooms would have a combined feeling, like in contemporary homes.

Outside, daylight had disappeared. My stomach reminded me that I'd forgotten to eat. Chiseling at ancient joints, twisting screws, and pulling rusty nails had given far more entertainment than preparing a balanced meal. Still, food had its place, and my body seemed determined to have its way on that point.

I chopped the black spots off one of Brad's tomatoes, cut up the fruit, and laid the slices on a piece of bread. I covered the whole thing with co-jack and stuck it under the broiler until strings of melted cheese dangled toward the oven floor.

I sat on my love seat and savored the simple but healthy meal, catching orange threads before they hit the upholstery.

I dusted the crumbs off my lap and looked at my hands. Short nails, scuffed and scratched skin, and blistery palms. Not exactly wedding-day material.

I sighed. David had to pass a few more tests before I could say yes to any eternal arrangements. I wasn't exactly desperate yet.

And I didn't plan to fall into that category. Ever.

There was no need to panic and do anything hasty or irreversible just because the whim struck.

I cleaned up the kitchen project and got some early z's. I woke up fresh the next morning, ready to hit the campaign trail.

I set out to canvass my neighborhood. I lived in the historic district, after all. What better place to start my drive for equal rights for historic-home owners in America? I brought my cell phone along, hoping I'd hear back from Lloyd, Brad, or both.

An old beater was parked next door at the village museum.

I might as well get the museum people on my side. I walked up the freshly shoveled steps of the ornate turn-of-the-century home.

I poked my head in the beveled-glass door.

"Hello," I called.

An older gentleman dressed in baggy olive slacks and a plaid shirt scuffed toward me across the creaking oak floor.

"Not open," he said.

"I'm Tish Amble. I live next door." I walked in and stuck out my hand in greeting.

He ignored the gesture. "We're closed until spring, young lady."

I ignored the reprimand. "I'm running for the opening on the Historical Committee." I decided to leave Martin Dietz's name out of it this time. "Owners of historic homes need to respect the original intent of a structure, it's true. But they shouldn't have to sacrifice all the comforts and benefits that new-home owners enjoy. This is America. We should be able to determine for ourselves what's best left alone and what can be gracefully altered to accommodate today's lifestyles."

"Martin turned you down on something, didn't he?" The old man grinned. "You just needed to negotiate better. Take this place, for instance. Had to put in a bathroom on the first floor to satisfy public sanitation requirements. Martin said no, a first-floor john would alter the historic accuracy of the place. It looked like there wasn't going to be a town museum. So a bunch of us got together and decided Martin needed a new riding lawn mower. Next time it came up for a vote, we got our bathroom."

"You bribed a city official?" My jaw dropped.

"Not a bribe. A thank-you gift. For his future support." The man walked me to a room at the back of the house.

"Ain't she beautiful?" He smiled and rubbed a hand along the door trim.

The restroom looked original to the home, with a pull-cord, raised-tank toilet and tiny pedestal sink.

"Wow. You did a great job." I started to get excited about the removal of my cistern. My new basement rec room would look all spiffy in polished oak and smooth off-white drywall, and have enough space to accommodate a modern family's social life.

I turned to the old guy. "The election's in January. I promise you won't have to get me a snowblower if you want to update the kitchen."

He nodded. "So what idea of yours did Martin take offense to?"

"I made the mistake of asking if I could remove the cistern."

"Sounds like an expensive job." He rubbed his chin. "I'm thinking that might have cost you a new dishwasher. 'Course you saved all kinds of money by killing him first, eh?" He cackled like an old hag.

I pursed my lips. "Please vote for me in January. I promise to be fair." I started out the door.

"You might be in jail come January." His voice died out as I hit the front sidewalk. I'm glad he could laugh about it. I failed to see the humor.

I headed to the next house, determined to complete my five-resident goal.

David's house. I hesitated before heading up the driveway to the side door. I'd spent entirely too much time here in the past several days. Today, if he didn't open the door himself, I sure wasn't going to open it. There was no way I'd enter uninvited again.

The back door hung open about an inch. Gusts of snow blew into the gap.

Great.

I knocked on the doorjamb and listened. No answer.

I was not going in there.

I pushed the door wider and called into the shadows. "Hello? David?"

No response. I refused to step over the threshold. To be nice, I closed the door against the weather. I shivered on the porch, contemplating my next step. Multiple tracks led out to the garage. Maybe that's where I'd find David. My shoes squeaked in the light snow. I opened the paned-glass door of the detached garage and stuck my head in.

"David? Anybody here?" I hadn't really expected an answer.

The dim winter sun barely reached through the high, tiny windows. I felt around for a light switch. I found it and clicked it on.

Two cars took up the parking spaces. David's red coupe, and some silver hot-rod variety. I wondered why on earth he needed two cars, especially now that he was single again.

I couldn't resist a peek inside the sports car. Everything looked leather and shiny and very expensive. The shifter filled the space between the only two seats. The vehicle could hardly be comfortable, sitting so low to the ground.

David probably wouldn't mind if I just sat in it a minute and tested it out. I glanced up. The coast was clear. Quietly, I pulled the handle and opened the door. I slid onto the smooth cushion of the driver's seat. I could almost feel the power that pulsed under the hood, waiting to be let out in one pedal-to-the-metal ride. But it wouldn't be me driving. The law already hoped to nab me for murder. I wasn't about to provide a second reason.

I leaned over as I got out. My eye caught a blemish on an otherwise clean floorboard. I reached over and picked up a flesh-colored object. It was a fake fingernail, painted in Rebecca's favorite Barely Blush shade. This must have been her vehicle.

If I were a newly promoted bigwig at a super-goliath architecture firm in L.A., wouldn't I want my cute little California hot-rod with me? I'd leave my silver baby behind only over my dead body.

I tucked the nail into my pocket and got out of the car.

I checked out the far reaches of the garage for any interesting gadgets. The fake nail in my pocket gave my fingers something to fiddle with.

Lawn implements in one corner, a shovel and some concrete-encrusted buckets in another. I took a closer look. These must be the pails Jack Fitch had hauled up and down the staircase during the waterproofing project last year. Jack had seemed so proud to help.

A row of cabinets lined the far wall. Padlocks kept the contents secure for all but the one closest to the door. The chain and lock were off and sitting on a nearby bench. The cabinet door hung open a few inches.

Curiosity may have killed the cat, but I was no feline. In fact, I had a right to see what David kept locked up. Knowledge of one's potential life partner was integral to the decision-making process.

I crept toward the cabinet and pulled open the door.

Folders. Boxes and boxes of manila folders.

My breath quickened. To look, or not to look?

Definitely look.

I pulled a file at random.

PYLE, ELEANOR, the tag read. I flipped through the bank statements inside. Monthly withdrawals of five hundred dollars were highlighted in yellow. I flipped it shut and filed it as close to its original location as I could.

I reached up a shelf and pulled another file.

Fate. Destiny. Irony.

Whatever was responsible, I held Martin Dietz's file in my hand. A slew of questions popped to mind. Why did David have a file on Martin Dietz? Something to do with work, maybe?

There was only one way to find out.

36

I opened to the top document. A tax return from last year, showing thousand of dollars in losses. Yeah, I bet Martin Dietz didn't claim his "gifts" from the town folk, either. The refund he received would have bought several riding mowers.

Next was a mortgage document from Sugar Cane International. I glanced at the comparable homes and final value of Dietz's Oak Street residence, willing to bet the whole thing was fudged. I could see average homes in Rawlings going for prices like Dietz's in about two years when urban sprawl arrived. But not yet. Not today.

Beneath the mortgage was a life insurance policy. The amount made me choke. The document listed Sandra Jones as the beneficiary. Now there was one lucky woman. Obviously Dietz hadn't thought to change his papers after their breakup.

I flipped to the next item. Another life insurance policy, identical to the first. This time, Rebecca Ramsey was listed as beneficiary, with David Ramsey as contingent. Why on earth would Dietz have the Ramseys listed in his policy, even if he and Sandra were on the outs?

I thought of the body in my cistern.

Up at the house, the back door slammed shut. My head jerked toward the sound.

Footsteps crunched in the direction of the garage.

I stuffed the file back into the top box as best I could, but something got in the way. I could only jam Dietz's file about three-quarters in. It protuded from the box like a blinking neon light.

If David caught me in here, I hated to think what could happen. There was a good possibility that he'd killed Rebecca to keep her from claiming Dietz's insurance money. Now he could claim the money for himself.

I looked around in alarm. The garage had no clutter to hide behind. I dove for the sports car, rolling under it to keep out of sight.

From my shadowy nook, I watched David walk in carrying a tan cardboard box that matched the other file boxes. He set it on the bottom shelf of the cabinet, then started to close the doors.

He looked toward the top shelf and hesitated.

Dietz's file.

David reached up and took the box down. He inspected the out-of-whack file. He took a slow look around the garage.

I held my breath, certain that my heartbeat was as loud to him as it was to me.

He straightened the file and put the box back in its place. He shut the cabinet doors, ran the chain through the pulls, and fastened the padlock.

He walked to the door, took a long backward glance into the garage, then shut the door soundly.

I gulped for air. I promised myself never to snoop again. David was not marriage material. I didn't care what explanation he gave for the files he kept on local residents. Now was a good time to find out that good looks and good manners couldn't outdo ethics and morals.

My lip quivered as I crawled out from beneath the car. I stopped at the entrance, peeking through the glass at the bleak morning. If I took off across the yard, David was sure to see me. He'd know I'd been in here. He'd seen the Dietz file and he'd know that I knew. There was no back way out of this place, unless I wanted to risk breaking my neck falling out the high windows along the rear of the garage. That is, if I could fit through the narrow openings in the first place.

I fingered the fingernail in my pocket. Poor Rebecca. Killed for a half-million dollars. Human life was worth far more than that. Of course, many had died for far less. David must have been working out his plan slowly and patiently. First he'd killed Rebecca and pretended she'd gone off to California. He was a computer expert, wasn't he? Any correspondence from Rebecca, including the divorce papers, were scams, meant to keep anyone from suspecting that she had never made it out of town. Then, nearly a year later, he'd offed Martin Dietz, ready to collect the reward money for a game well played.

He probably already had a set of falsified documents ready for the day he sucked the life right out of me like a vampire, and left me dead somewhere. I was a perfect candidate for his sick diversion. No friends, no family. I'd disappear as if I'd never existed. No one would even know. No one would even care. Of course, if I took the fall for Dietz's murder, so much the better.

I leaned against the garage wall and assessed my situation. The best action would be to sneak out the door, hang a hard left, and hide out behind the garage. I could wait a few minutes to make sure the coast was clear, then run behind the museum's garage over to my own yard.

Chances of anybody seeing me would be slim. Of course, if Jack Fitch was on duty, he'd wonder why I was acting like a criminal.

I twisted the handle and peeked out the garage door. I didn't see anyone, but the glare of daylight on David's windows kept me from knowing if he was watching.

I ducked out the door around to the back of the garage. I leaned against the siding and caught my breath. My plan had one glaring flaw. Maybe David wouldn't notice the set of solo prints heading toward his back door from the street. And he sure wouldn't notice my prints mixed in with the tracks he'd beaten between the house and the garage. But how could he miss the trail of size 10 boots announcing to anybody with eyeballs that someone had run behind the garage?

But, hey, snow didn't hang around long this time of year. Maybe it would melt by noon. I tiptoed as fast as I could over to the back of the museum garage. My pants got snarled in some dormant raspberry bushes. Apparently the staff of museum volunteers never took the time to clip the rear of the property.

I tripped over a rusty shovel and landed on my backside.

The shock of the snow against bare fingers held me motionless a moment. As soon as I caught my breath, I struggled toward safety. But the stringy thorns tangled around me, cutting my hands and burying prickers in my clothing. With every attempt to stand, the tentacles snarled more tightly around me. I ripped myself free. Blood dripped from my hands. Miles of scratches lay hidden beneath my jeans.

Out in the open again, I ran past my garage and straight into the house. I bolted the door behind me.

I stood at the sink and let warm water flow over my mangled hands. The thorns had left deep scratches that were now raised white lines. I toweled dry, then gingerly pulled from my skin whatever glasslike prickers I could detect. I must have missed a dozen. Every movement seemed to drive one or more deeper into my flesh.

I tried pulling thorns from my jeans, but gave up. I'd have to change them altogether and start fresh. I started toward my bedroom when I saw a head pass the side window.

My heart did a belly flop in my chest. It was David, striding up the back steps. I dove past the kitchen door, out of sight in the dining room. David tried the knob, then pounded on the door.

If he got in here, I would be dead. I had no weapon, no way to defend myself.

"Tish. Let me in." David sounded half off his rocker.

I crept through to the parlor, consumed with fear. He'd get in eventually. I had to get out.

I dashed out the front door and across the street. I knocked on Dorothy's front door.

"It's Tish. Let me in." Please be home. Please. Please.

Jack opened the door. I shoved past him and headed toward a couch in the corner of the enclosed front porch.

"Thanks, Jack."

"Tish. What's up?" Jack shut the door behind me.

I stared across the street at my house, watching for David to cross the yard and go back home, but I couldn't see the back porch from my seat at the Fitches.

"Jack. Hey. I'm just getting a head start on my campaign for the vacant seat on the Historical Committee. Is your mom around?" A raspberry thorn worked its way into my thigh. I scratched at it.

"Yeah. I'll tell her you're here."

While Jack was gone, I kept an eye on my house. Still no sign of David. Maybe he got inside. Maybe he was flinging my cot and dirty clothes around in my bedroom, looking for stuff. I squinted, trying to see any movement through the glare. Nothing.

At least I didn't have anything to hide. The only thing that might incriminate me was the floral card I'd plucked from his trash. But it was safely hidden in the pocket of my other jeans. I doubted he'd look for something small enough to fit in pants pockets. He probably figured I'd swiped something useful, like a file with incriminating evidence.

And why I hadn't grabbed Dietz's file was beyond me. Everything I needed to exonerate myself for Dietz's murder was in that file. It might be circumstantial, but it

286

could definitely lead to David's conviction. Especially once they uncovered Rebecca's body in my cellar.

Dorothy walked in. I barely glanced at her, afraid to take my eyes off the Victorian.

"Tish. Nice of you to stop in." She sat on the opposite end of the sofa. "Jack tells me you want to fill Martin's place on the Historical Committee."

I smiled in her direction, still looking out the window. "Yes. I think it's a shame we historic-home owners have to be confined to old-fashioned applications for our homes." I spotted David going down my back porch steps. He rounded the back of the house. "Take my cistern, for example. Its use is completely outdated. Nobody needs storage for rainwater anymore." I saw David cut between my house and the museum house. Phew. He was going home. I looked at Dorothy. "That cistern is a danger to the homeowner. I'd hate to see a little kid get trapped back there. Maybe get hurt and not be found for a while. I ought to be allowed to remove it."

"Have you thought about walling it in?" Dorothy asked.

I took a deep breath. "Absolutely not. It needs to come out. That's the only option."

"So you're becoming a member of the committee so you can get your project through?"

"There's nothing wrong with that. I'm happy to help others, as well. We can find a balance between historic preservation and comfortable, modern living."

"Don't suppose my opinion counts for much, but I'd say you're better off leaving that cistern alone. Old houses can get mighty particular if you start cutting them up."

I waved off the comment. "I don't believe in that stuff. Houses are inanimate objects. The only life they have is what we give them in our own imagination."

I adjusted the denim around my thigh, dislodging a thorn. "You mentioned that the Ramseys and Martin Dietz were close at one time," I said. "How close was close?"

Dorothy sighed. "Birds of a feather. Dogs in a pack. Fleas in a circus. Every one of them expert at getting what they want and using each other to do it." She shook her head. "Just glad Sandra got away from all that."

There had to be more to the Main Street Triangle than met the eye. Life insurance policies, fake appraisals, fudged tax returns. I had the feeling I'd merely scratched the surface.

I was only sorry to see Tammy Johnson getting involved. There were more than her finances at stake if she got too wrapped up with David and his services.

"So," I said, getting to my feet, "please vote for me in January."

"Stay for soup, Tish. There's chicken noodle on the stove," Dorothy said.

I had no place better to go. Home wasn't an option right now. I had no idea what course of action to take as far as David went. If I called the cops, I'd be blowing stuff out of proportion again. They'd need a warrant and hence, good cause. Which my word alone didn't seem to provide.

As much as I hated the thought, the only proof I could get on David that would put him behind bars required an excavating party. Me and a hammer and chisel.

Tonight. I'd do it tonight. No more guessing, wondering, lost sleep, or nightmares.

Tonight I'd know.

37

"I'd love to stay." I looked at Dorothy standing across from me in her living room. "Soup sounds good."

We went into the kitchen together. A lace runner hid the Formica tabletop. Baskets stuffed with unopened mail, multicolored hankies, seasonal napkins, and various fingernail and letter-opening accessories littered the dining area.

I stepped toward a wall of photographs. Judging by the quality and hairstyles, the pictures had been taken in the '70s. Two girls and one boy. The boy had a big-toothed smile and sticky-out ears. He was no more than eleven. He must be the one that got killed on the tracks.

I wondered how Dorothy could have stayed put in this house with a tragedy like that happening so close to home. Every day when she heard the train go by, she must think about that little cutie playing chicken with a metal monster. And losing.

I swallowed with a tight throat.

The two girls had at least made it to their high school graduations. Both wore the same powder-blue sweater. Their hair was pulled back in buns. They wore sweet but sorrowful expressions on Farmer's Daughter faces. A few more framed photos documented boyfriends and husbands in laughing embraces. Then nothing. No grandbabies in bibs, on bikes, or in Grandma's lap. Just nothing. End of the line. End of the family.

I searched the wall again. "Where did you hang Jack's pictures?"

Dorothy stared at the wall of pictures. "Look at them. They're all dead. Adored them, raised them, hung their pictures on the wall, and they died. But not my Jack. Never wanted pictures of him on the wall." She tapped her temple. "Keeping him up here."

Tears coursed down my cheeks. I couldn't stop the flow. My whole body shook, and next thing I knew, Dorothy cradled my head against her shoulder. She sat me in a chair and let me cry. I sobbed a trash can full of tissues before I could control myself again.

"Don't fuss on my account," Dorothy said. "Loved those kids. But they were God's to do with as he pleased. Now all of them are safe in heaven."

I sat up and wiped my nose. "How do you do it? How can you keep going after everything that has happened to you?"

"Take it one day at a time. Get up. Put on my shoes. Say a prayer. Eat. Work. Live another day. Go to bed. Then do it again."

"But how do you handle all the thoughts and emotions? Sometimes it's too much for me. And I've barely lost anything compared to you."

"Every day you tell yourself that God loves you. He's

going to take care of you. He'll take everything that's wrong and make it right. And when your time's up, he'll take you." She wiped a teardrop from my face. "Woke up alive today, didn't you? Then put your shoes on and get to living."

I sniffled. "But what about a person who didn't wake up alive today? What if they're dead . . . and it's not their fault?"

"Can't do anything for them."

"But what if they're dead because of something I did?"

"Get it right with God. Then get on with life."

If only it were that simple. How many times had I tried to get it right with God, only to crawl away and hide in shame?

Dorothy set a bowl of soup in front of me. The hot broth started my nose running again, but somehow made me feel better. When I'd scooped up the last spoonful, I thanked her for her hospitality and let myself out.

I paused on her porch, not really feeling like hitting the campaign trail, but too scared to go home. I walked along a wet sidewalk to the house next door, and directly across the street from David's.

I stood on the front stoop of a completely modernized circa 1920s home. Cream vinyl siding erased any architectural details the home had once worn. Boring concrete steps took the place of a covered porch that had previously graced the home. The only evidence of the former porch was a plain swath of white trim halfway up the facade. Houses like this one were the whole reason

292

the Historical Committee existed. The brutal mutilation of historic architecture had to be halted.

I rang the doorbell, then turned to watch for signs of activity across the street at David's.

No answer.

I walked to the next house. The brown shake-and-brick two-story was the blight of the neighborhood. I stepped over a muddy pothole in the driveway on my way to the back door, which apparently was the only way to gain entrance. I swerved around a girl's banana bike and picked my way up crumbled concrete steps. The storm door was missing its glass, so I reached through to knock on the dented metal exterior door.

"Yeah?" said the woman who opened the door. She had long, thin hair on her forty-something head. I knew by the guarded look in her eyes that my coifed hairstyle and trim figure posed some imagined threat to her oversized sweatshirt and baggy jeans.

I introduced myself.

A smile crept over her face. "I'm Kay. Come on in. I've been wanting to meet you. Anybody with the guts to kill a guy like Martin Dietz deserves a toast. How about a glass of homemade rhubarb wine?"

I stepped over the threshold, not sure if I was brave enough to venture off the entry rug onto the gouged and grungy linoleum. The stench of last night's greasy dinner lingered.

"No, thank you. I don't drink," I said. I'd watched my grandfather drink himself to death by the time I was ten years old and never had the inclination to touch the stuff myself. Maybe fear of becoming a drunk like him

293

kept me on the straight and narrow. Goodness knows, I'd be comatose in my cot right now if I drank to deal with life's problems, like Gramps had.

I cleared my throat. "I'm running for the vacancy on the Historical Committee. I'd like your vote."

I looked around the kitchen, which other than '70s appliances and flooring hadn't changed since the home was constructed. "When you're ready to update, I'll help you find a balance between historic preservation and modern living." Kay didn't need to know that by the time that day rolled around, I'd probably be long gone.

"Never could afford to update. Not with Dietz's infernal fees. Two months of cleaning houses just to cover the application. That didn't include whatever gadget I'd have to bribe him with, either."

"I'm surprised his corruption was so widely known." I shook my head. "Couldn't the authorities do anything about it?"

"Dietz knew everything about everybody. He had enough dirt to keep half the town broke buying his silence. Especially the authorities. Believe me, if you hadn't gone and killed him, somebody else would have."

"Well, let's just say I didn't kill him. Who do you think would have been next in line to do the job?"

Kay humphed. "Take your pick. Sandra Jones would be top on my list. But, like I say, if it hadn't been you, it could've been anybody."

"Sandra had already broken up with him. Why would she want to kill him?"

"It was what Dietz did to her in the elections that should have got him killed. I know I couldn't have controlled myself if it had been me. Dietz stood there in front of a thousand people in the county park and called Sandra a backstabbing Mary Magdalene. Said she was in church on Sundays but in league with Satan the rest of the week. I don't know about you, Tish, but that goes beyond name-calling."

"I see what you mean." From what I'd heard, Sandra was doing amazing things with the youth in Rawlings. Going against Dietz didn't make her a bad Christian. Dietz was the jerk. Too bad Sandra let him get to her. She should have stuck it out and won the election. That would have been the best revenge.

"He sunk himself anyway," Kay said. "No one wants to hear all that fire and brimstone stuff. Thank goodness the other candidate took the slot. I'd hate to think what this county would be like today if Dietz were in charge."

"So you'll vote for me in January?" I asked.

"Sure," Kay said. "Are they going to hold the meetings down at the jail?" She gave a hearty laugh.

I smiled on my way out the door. I couldn't blame anyone for taunting me about Dietz. It helped that their laughter only made me more determined to nab the real killer.

I gave a quick look to make sure no police were watching, then walked kitty-corner across the street to my house. David couldn't help but see me if he was watching. I shook off the clammy feeling that crept up my spine.

Once at home, I scarfed down some cottage cheese. Running a campaign sure worked up an appetite. While the food did its job, I thought about the info I'd gathered along the trail. Dietz had enemies. Lots and lots of enemies. But only one man would greatly profit from his death.

David.

Without another thought, I headed for my toolbox on the counter, grabbed a flashlight and a hammer, and picked out the heaviest chisel. I'd unearth Rebecca and show her to the authorities along with Dietz's will from David's garage.

Motive and opportunity. David had them both when it came to killing Martin Dietz. Hadn't his hair been damp when I got back from the bathroom that night at the Rawlings Hotel? He could have had time to meet Dietz here, kill him, and get back to the table by the time I returned. The hotel was only a block away if you took the shortcut.

I gripped my tools and took a determined breath. I wouldn't be taking the fall for anyone this time.

38

I twisted the knob that led to the cellar and pushed the door open. I stood silent at the top of the steps.

No voice called. No presence pulled at me.

I flicked the switch, adding a yellow glow to gray late-morning light. I ducked under the single strand of police tape and stepped down into the dimness, ready to do what I should have done weeks ago.

The air grew colder as I reached the basement floor. Prickles ran over my skin.

I hadn't been down here since the night my furnace had gone out. I could make out a shoe tread here and there on the dirty concrete, left over from the investigators. No doubt some of the tracks belonged to Officer Brad.

I drew near the cistern. Dietz's blood still encrusted the rock.

I shuffled closer to the stony crescent. I set the hammer and chisel on the flat ledge above, then started my climb up the face of rocks. I made it to the top and slung my knee over, clinging with one hand while I turned on the flashlight with the other.

I aimed the light into the hole, where daylight from the adjacent window couldn't reach. I don't know what I had expected. Maybe a body. Maybe the outline of a body. But all I saw was a dark patch on lumpy white concrete. The stain of Dietz's blood.

I slid down the interior and grabbed my tools off the ledge.

My feet felt tingly, as if I'd accidentally stepped on a grave at the cemetery.

"Sorry, Rebecca," I whispered. There was no way to avoid walking on the body beneath me. The cistern simply wasn't big enough.

I set the tools down, then crouched on the cement, trying to remember the angle her body had lain when I'd seen it so clearly that day in October.

I ran the flashlight over the lumps. One bulge caught my attention. I squinted, trying to picture a splayed palm or a clenched fist beneath the surface.

I set the flashlight on the concrete and picked up the hammer. I angled the chisel and gave it a tap. I jumped at the sound of metal on metal. From the corner of my eye, I caught movement and jerked around.

I fell backward, gasping and half laughing at myself for being afraid of my own shadow, projected by the flashlight onto the cistern wall.

I angled the light away from the ledge and into the corner. That way I wouldn't think someone was peering over the top at me every time I lifted the hammer.

I rubbed at the floor. The chisel had left only a small indentation in the cement. I sighed. This was a bigger job than I'd imagined.

298

I tapped away, eager to get the task done, but not so eager to do something I'd regret, like clip off a finger—either mine or Rebecca's.

I blew back my bangs and hit the chisel again. The things I'd been reduced to. Here I was grave robbing instead of home designing.

I gave the chisel a mighty whack, then blew back the dust to check my progress. I'd been working around ten minutes already, but there were only a few cement chips to show for it.

I turned my back to the ledge and tried a new angle. If there were something under the cement, I'd bump into it eventually.

I chipped away, wondering if maybe the real trouble with my life had started when I'd finally rebelled against my grandmother. "Honor your father and mother," the Bible said. I supposed that meant grandmothers too, when she was the one raising you. Maybe my life would have gone better if I'd done things her way.

That fateful night my senior year popped to mind. I had left work around six thirty, sick to my stomach at the thought of facing my grandmother. Rush hour in Walled Lake ended right about the time I got into my rust-bucket gold Granada. It was a waste to get on the roads before half past six, since they were packed with traffic trying to navigate the winding, narrow passages that led between the numerous lakes in the area.

I pulled into the yard of our tiny lakeside bungalow. The slam of my car door echoed in the still of early evening. A neighbor dog barked. I looked up at the few stars that penetrated the glow of suburbia and fought the knot that twisted my guts. I couldn't put it off forever. I had to tell her.

We sat down to our usual four-course supper.

"Wish you could get home early once in a while. My arthritis is acting up, and that salad didn't chop itself, you know."

I stared past Grandma at the collection of salt-and-pepper shakers from around the world. Gram herself had never left Walled Lake, but her globe-trotting friends always remembered her in their travels.

"What's for supper tomorrow? I'll help you chop it up tonight," I said.

"We'll probably just have leftovers. I'm too tired to be cooking like this all the time." She plopped food on our plates.

"I can bring something home from the store," I said. "You know you don't have to cook all the time. It's just us two. And I can fix myself something, Gram. I'm big now." I smiled, but the nerves in my stomach pulled tight as I geared up to tell her the news.

I told her. She sat silent for a moment. Scary silent. I chewed and swallowed, waiting for a response. I didn't have to wait long.

"You're not running off to any university. You're staying here and taking classes at the community college." Grandma slammed her fork like a gavel on the supper table.

"Gram, you know it's what I've always wanted. And it's paid for. I'd have to work twice as hard for half the education if I went locally."

"Your mother went to community college and turned

300

out just fine." Gram gripped both sides of her plate. I knew from her taut lips and gleaming eyes that she'd fight until I gave in.

"Mom was married at twenty years old. To a guy who left. Maybe she should have set her goals a little higher," I said.

Gram's face contorted and she rose from her seat, leaning over the table toward me. "Don't you say those things. Your mother was a good girl. She never did anything wrong." She poked a finger to her chest. "She always listened to me."

I took a bite of my acorn squash. "Mom's dead, Gram. She killed herself. Remember? Is that how you want me to end up?"

"That's how you'll end up if you go to that university. What do you think happens to girls there? They're used up and lied to. There's drugs and sex and alcohol. Is that how you want to start your life? You want to know those people? You want to associate with those people?" Grandma's arms quivered as she pressed against the table.

"Those same people are everywhere, Gram." My voice softened. "I know you worry about me, but I'm not like that. I'm not going to be in that crowd."

"Tisher," Gram said, using her pet name for me. Her eyes teared up. She sat back in her chair and covered her face. "You've got a good job already. You know everybody here. Why do this?"

"I don't want to be a checkout girl at the Foodliner the rest of my life, Gram. This is my chance to do something big. Change the world."

"You don't know how the world is. You don't know how bad it can be."

"Then maybe it's time I found out."

"They'll ruin you. You'll think they're your friends, but they want you to die. And they'll help you do it."

I crouched by her chair and buried my head against her arm, patting her back. "No, Gram, no. I'll be okay. I'm not afraid. What do you always tell me? God's watching over me."

She grabbed my hand and squeezed hard. "I'll help you stay on God's good side. I couldn't bear to lose you too." Tears coursed down her face.

"Shh. You're not going to lose me. I'll always be here for you."

"Then you're not going?" Gram looked up, victory in her eyes.

"I'm going." I kept my voice firm. "Lansing is only an hour away. I'll come home every chance I get. You know I can't pass up your stuffed peppers." I smiled to ease the blow.

"God's going to punish you," she whispered.

39

The hammer hit the side of my hand. I flinched and sat up on the hard concrete floor, sucking the skin to stop the sting. In my side vision, the light from the basement window dimmed momentarily, as if someone had just walked past.

I froze, listening. The thump of feet up the back steps blended with the pounding of my heart. What if it was David, coming back to finish me off? I was already in the grave. All he had to do was conk me in the head like he had Martin Dietz, throw a little concrete on top, and no one would be the wiser.

I didn't want to make it that easy for him.

A knock sounded on the back door.

Maybe it wasn't David. I couldn't imagine him being so courteous after my intrusion earlier today.

I picked my way out of the cistern and jumped off the ledge onto the basement floor. A twinge in my ankle reminded me of my lingering injury. I hurried upstairs despite a throbbing ache, brushing the concrete dust from my knees along the way. If the murderer figured out I was excavating last year's kill, I'd be joining Rebecca permanently in the cistern.

I turned the corner at the top of the steps and gulped to see Officer Brad, in uniform, standing at the back door.

My shoulders sagged. I'd been so close to proving my body-in-the-basement theory. If only Brad had come a couple hours later. Instead, I'd be carted off to jail just a few wallops shy of proof that I hadn't killed Martin Dietz.

I slumped across the kitchen and opened the door.

Brad looked great in police blue. Everything shone right down to his boots.

"I'll just grab my toothbrush," I said and turned to go.

"Wait. Why?" The gravelly sound of his voice grabbed at my heartstrings. Pressure built in my temples as I tried not to cry for what might have been, what could have been.

"Aren't you picking me up?"

"Did you need to go somewhere?"

"No. I thought you were taking me back to jail."

"Oh. That. No. I was just doing my rounds and wanted to check in on you. Make sure you were safe." He smiled. "No more dead bodies or leg injuries. That kind of stuff."

I stared at the lines in the corners of his eyes. "I'm okay. I guess."

My heart raced. Maybe Brad could help me. Maybe if I told him what I'd found in David's garage, he'd believe me that Rebecca was buried in my basement.

"Do you want to come in a minute?" I asked.

He shifted his weight. "Sure. I'd like to see that everything's secure." He came in the kitchen. "After all, if you didn't kill Dietz, someone else did. And I'd hate for you to be the next victim."

"Thanks. I'd rather not be the next victim. Care for some water?" I loved my dispensing unit. No worries about arsenic poisoning for me.

Brad walked to the machine and helped himself to a cup. He took a sip, then scrunched up his nose. "Smells a little funny. I think I like the tap better."

"Just be careful. You don't want death by heavy metal. That's what arsenic is, you know."

He pitched his water in the sink and filled his cup from the faucet. He took a swig. "That's better."

"Whatever." I sipped my tasteless, odorless, filtered beverage, wondering what he had up his nose.

We talked about the snowstorm the weatherman called for while I avoided his eyes.

He set his cup down. "I'm going to take a quick look around." He headed for the cellar.

"Oh, no." I waved my hands and raced toward him. "No, you don't need to check anything. That door stays locked." I grabbed his arm, immediately sorry to have touched him. I put my hands in my jeans pockets.

"Okay. I'll just check around outside." Brad headed toward the back door.

"Great. I'll go with you." I slipped on my coat and followed him into the yard. The air was icy, a welcome change from the heat inside.

Brad walked around the front first.

"So have you heard from Rebecca lately?" I asked in a casual voice.

Brad stopped his inspection and looked at me. "I told you, we don't correspond."

I waved my hand. "I just wondered if there was any juicy gossip now that the divorce is final."

His jaw clenched. "You would know more about that than me." He turned the corner onto the driveway, checking out the upstairs windows.

"I was talking to Dorothy the other day, and she made it sound like you and Rebecca were pretty close." Not entirely accurate, but Brad could call my bluff.

Brad smirked. "Rebecca liked me close, all right. Every chance she had, she'd call the station for assistance. And request me by name."

"Oh."

"Yeah. The chief thought it was pretty funny. I caught a lot of flack from the guys. No one was under the illusion that she actually had feelings for me."

"No one but you?" I whispered.

Brad stared at the ground. "I knew better. I really did. But I guess when a woman throws herself at you like that, you can lie to yourself to make it seem like more than it really is."

"Did you love her?"

"I guess I loved what she could be. She's beautiful, smart, talented. But her heart is . . . I don't know. Warped or something." He gave a sheepish smile. "It's foolish to try to fix people, isn't it?"

"Yeah. I guess it is."

"Anyway, Rebecca's gone. Only God can fix her now."

His words shook me for a minute. "Oh, you mean gone to L.A.," I said.

He squinted at me. "What did you think I meant?"

I gave a nervous giggle. "Oh, nothing." I rubbed my arms against the chill.

We got to the back corner of the house. "Look," I said pointing to a circle of gravel. "That's the dry well they put in last year." The dry well consisted of a three-foot-diameter by seven-foot-deep hole filled with gravel. All the drain tile on the exterior of the house, as well as the new sump pump, emptied into the well, preventing the basement from flooding again.

"I know. I worked on the project, remember?" Brad said.

"You worked on it? I thought you were just called in to baby-sit when Dietz went ballistic."

"I did my share of hard labor. Rick and Jan were good neighbors. I didn't mind helping out around this place when I could."

"Really? How come Jack didn't mention it?"

"Because he's Jack. Besides, he was probably embarrassed. Half the time I was called out to David and Rebecca's renovation project was because Jack was hanging around Rebecca and she wanted him out of there. Jack probably blames me that he didn't get very far with her." Brad grinned.

"How far did you get with her?" Yeah, I was jealous in a juvenile way.

"Far enough to ask her to go to church with me."

"Did she?"

"Turned me down flat. Once she quit laughing."

"Ouch."

"Yeah, ouch. But that's good. I shouldn't have been

going that route. Some people you just stay away from. I should have been like Joseph running from Potiphar's wife. Instead, I got all wrapped up in trying to convert her. But if she wants to be dead, that's not my problem."

I took a step backward. "What do you mean, 'dead'?"

"Spiritually dead. Sorry, too much Christianese." He ran a hand through his hair. "What I mean is, she thinks she's in control of things . . . and she's not. It's only a matter of time before she crash-lands."

From everything Brad said, I figured Rebecca had already crash-landed—in the cistern. Her husband David had done a stellar job pretending Rebecca was still alive. But there was no doubt in my mind she was stone-cold dead.

40

Brad left, apparently satisfied I wasn't harboring any more dead bodies on the premises. I stood under the catalpa and watched him cut through the yard on his way back home. I blew back my bangs, relieved he hadn't checked out the cistern during his inspection. I'd left my hammer, chisel, and flashlight in there. Brad would have no doubts regarding my activity. He'd be calling 9-1-1 for help putting me in a straitjacket.

I gasped a quick breath. I couldn't remember turning the flashlight off. Batteries were too expensive to treat callously.

I hoofed it back down to the cellar. A yellow beam hit the far wall of the cistern. I huffed over the ledge and dropped behind the stone wall.

I knelt and checked my progress. Barely a dent showed in the floor. I'd have to think less and chisel more if I were going to liberate Rebecca.

I picked up my tools and pecked away at the endless white. Maybe I'd get down an inch or two and find only more cement. Maybe I'd find plain dirt. Maybe there was no body.

I'd know soon enough.

Strands of hair got trapped in my lips as I concentrated on my chore, reminding me that I'd have to visit Tammy at the Beauty Boutique again soon.

I'd taken a ten-year hiatus from powdering and primping. It felt good to be treating myself special again. Mom would be proud of any interest I took in my personal appearance. She'd gone through a lot of trouble dressing me up when I was a kid.

It hurt to remember.

"Try this one, Tish." Mom held up a pale blue dress that my seven-year-old self couldn't resist. I grabbed at it, beaming.

"I'll be as pretty as you," I told her, modeling the spring dress in the department store mirror.

"You're always pretty." She knelt down close to me.

"Yes, but on Easter, I feel pretty." I spun around. The skirt opened like an umbrella around me.

Mom stepped back and gave a nod. I could tell by the smile on her face that I made her happy. She liked being my mom. We didn't care that my dad never came around. We were happy, just the two of us.

A tear dropped onto my wrist. I set the hammer down and wiped my face. I was such a baby. How many years had it been? Twenty-six? I should be over it by now.

I took a deep breath and smashed the chisel with the hammer. A chunk of cement went flying.

But I hadn't felt pretty that Easter.

"You're not wearing blue to your mother's funeral," Grandma said, pulling me down the aisle of yet another store. Spring hadn't been a good time to find sad colors.

Grandma had to buy me a white sailor dress. Only the trim was black.

I hated it.

After the priest was done talking, I snuck up to the front and stared at my mother. They told me she was dead, but I was happy to see her anyway. I had been staying with Grandma, and I didn't know where Mom was that whole week. Grandma wouldn't tell me. Just said Mom had to fix some things before I could see her again.

I don't know if she got to fix things or not. I think she must have died first, because things sure felt broken.

I held on to the edge of her casket. I was glad the fabric inside was silky. She liked silky stuff. Mom was dressed in a pretty pink blouse with ruffles down the front. I wished I had my blue ruffled dress on instead of the sailor dress. Then we would have been matchies.

Mom's face had a pushed-in spot on the forehead. Someone tried to make it look better, but I could tell it must have hurt bad. I reached out to touch it.

"Patricia Louise Amble," Grandma said behind me. "Come away from there. Let somebody else get a turn." My arm hurt when she pulled me away. She sat me in a corner by a smelly bunch of flowers. People I didn't know walked past my mother. They shook their heads and whispered. Sometimes they looked over at me and shook their heads and whispered some more. I played with the black scarf on my sailor dress and pretended I didn't notice.

"What's my darlin' doing here all alone?" My grandpa came and sat next to me on the metal chairs.

I giggled. "Grandpa, your breath smells like beer."

311

"You sound just like your mother, darlin'." His eyes were red and watery, and I knew he felt sad just like me. He smoothed down my hair and I felt prettier for a minute.

Grandma came down our row. "There you are, you old drunk. You're supposed to be at the door, thanking people for coming."

Grandpa winked at me. He stood to attention. "Aye, aye, Captain." He marched like a soldier across the room.

Grandma slapped at him. "Stop that. You're embarrassing me."

"Aye, aye, Captain," Grandpa said and kept marching.

I laughed until tears ran down my cheeks.

In the cellar, a smile crept over my face at the memory. I held the hammer suspended, not wanting to shatter the vision.

Good old Grandpa. What had I done all these years without him?

The faint ringing of the doorbell floated down the staircase.

I stiffened, debating whether or not to answer it.

If I didn't, there was a good chance whoever it was would come in anyway. Nobody paid attention to closed doors in this town.

I set down my tools, clicked off the flashlight, and climbed out of my cubby. By the time I got to the front of the house, I was breathing hard.

I pulled open the door.

"Oh, hi," I said. A vaguely familiar-looking man in a brown leather bomber jacket and blue jeans stood there.

He nodded. "It's been awhile. Do you remember me? I'm Rick Hershel. I used to live here."

My eyebrows went up. "You look different with your beard shaved off." Should I ask him in? Should I throw him out?

He smiled. "Yeah. Things were a little crazy last summer. Life's starting to come back together now."

I nodded in sympathy, leaning against the doorframe so he couldn't push his way through. I didn't want him thinking he had any rights to my house. He'd signed it over to me. From the dust balls in the attic to the body in the basement, the whole place was mine.

I waited for Rick to speak.

He shifted his weight back and forth, clasping and unclasping his hands. What was he so nervous about?

He cleared his throat. "You probably remember that I wasn't too happy to sell this place."

Cry me a river, Rick, I thought. I ain't giving it back.

"I heard something like that," I said.

"Well, a couple of people told me you're fixing it up pretty nice. I thought maybe I could get a tour."

I crossed my arms. "It's not done." Sorry, Rick. No mercy.

He gave a laugh. "Oh, no, that's no problem. I just wanted to see how far you got."

"Not very."

His smile vanished. "I would really appreciate a tour."

"I'm sorry, there's nothing to see." I reached for the door and started to close it.

He held up his palms, as if pleading. "You don't understand. I feel really guilty for leaving a couple things un-

313

done. I was hoping I could take a look around and see where I could help out."

"I'm not hiring right now." Of course, I might change my tune if I didn't get a call back from Lloyd in the near future.

"No. I'm not looking for money. Seriously. I'm going crazy because I didn't have time to finish some of the projects. If you let me help out a little, I would sleep a lot better at night."

Free labor. One of those things in life that was too good to be true. I couldn't help but wonder about his ulterior motive.

"Which projects concern you the most?" I asked, just in case he was a godsend.

He hesitated. "Look. I don't want you to think that I'm going to camp out here and fix up the house for free. There were a few details that I'd like to finish up. You know, like waterproofing the basement. I wrote on the seller's disclosure that we had completed the project, but it's only mostly done. If I don't finish it, then come spring you'll be taking me to court. I don't need that. Believe me."

I had to agree. With all the hype the waterproofing project had gotten, I'd be miffed when March arrived if there was even a hint of water in my basement. The whole rec room idea depended on the walls downstairs being absolutely watertight.

"What's left to be done?" I asked.

"I can show you."

I swallowed, thinking of my tools in the cistern. How would I explain that situation?

"You know, today really isn't a good day. Can you come by tomorrow around the same time?" I said.

He gave a slow nod. "Sure. Tomorrow it is." He turned to go, but stopped himself. "By the way," he said over his shoulder, "if you're ever interested in selling this place, let me know."

"Sure thing."

I watched him get into his brown coupe and drive off. Odd that scruples should be catching up to him at this late date. Of course, I knew firsthand the power of a guilty conscience. Either right the wrong or go crazy thinking about it. At least Rick had the opportunity to make things right. Some of us had to settle for going crazy.

I locked the front door, determined that if the doorbell rang again, I'd ignore it. I put myself on a twenty-four-hour deadline. If I didn't unearth a body by this time tomorrow, I'd hand the basement over to Rick and tell him to finish the waterproofing project.

But if I did unearth a body . . . water in my basement would seem a minor problem.

41

Dorothy's soup and my mid-morning snack had quit working. The stove clock read 12:45. I was famished. And the only thing that could fill the giant hole in my stomach was a greasy, juicy Coney from Sam's.

I locked the back door and jumped in Deucey for the trip uptown. As I bounced across the tracks, I caught David in the rearview mirror pulling out of his driveway and onto Main Street behind me.

I pressed the accelerator hoping to make it through the intersection at Main and Maple. No such luck. I stopped for the red, tapping on the gas pedal as I waited for the light to change.

I looked in the mirror. I couldn't see David's face through the reflection on his windshield. That feeling of déjà vu crept over me. He was following me again. But this time I felt certain there was more at stake than a nylon strap hanging out of my trunk.

The light changed and I floored it. Deucey hovered in place while she gathered enough oomph to blaze ahead. I could almost picture David having to hit his brakes while my vehicle hesitated. I topped out at thirty, not wanting to attract attention from the authorities. Some car chase. I made it through the light at Rawlings Road and pulled into the strip mall.

David's car turned in behind me.

I gripped the steering wheel, angled into the space nearest the door, and bolted inside. Maybe David was heading over to Goodman's for groceries. He couldn't possibly be going to Sam's diner the same time I was.

I dove into a corner booth, as far from the door as I could get. In walked David, checking out the clientele. I scrunched down and pretended to look at the menu.

No good. He beelined for my booth.

"Hi," I said as he approached. I tried to keep my breathing normal but ended up sounding like an asthma sufferer.

"May I?" He gestured to the seat across from me.

I swallowed. "Sure. Of course. Why not?" Under the table, my foot started jiggling uncontrollably.

"Have you dined here before?" David asked, perusing the menu that had been tucked behind the silver napkin dispenser.

"One time," I said, wishing he'd quit stalling and get to the point.

"Any recommendations?" he asked.

"I'm having the Coney Deluxe with everything."

He nodded with eyebrows raised. "Really? I had you pegged for the Chef's Salad."

Both legs bounced. "I'm expanding my horizons."

"Good. That's very good." He caught my gaze and held it. "It's important to have an open mind."

I gulped, wide eyed.

"Hey, Tish." Samantha smiled at me as she walked up to the booth, order pad in hand. "David." She gave a terse nod in his direction. "What can I get for you?"

"Two Coney Deluxe and a chili fry." David smiled at me. "I'll split the fries with you."

Sam wrote down the order along with our drink requests and disappeared into the kitchen. Obviously, she missed my eye signals, pleading for help.

David crossed his hands on the table between us. "I think you've been avoiding me, Tish." His British accent took on a Transylvania twang.

"Avoiding you? Absolutely not. Just busy, busy, busy."

"I went to your house today."

"Did you? You know, I've been out campaigning for the open slot on the Historical Committee. I must have been gone when you came by."

"You were home for Brad Walters. And Rick Hershel."

"Who can explain it?" I tittered.

"Have you thought any more about my proposal?"

I paused, framing my answer with care. "Yes, I have. I'm honored and flattered that you would consider me wife material. But that's just not where I'm at right now. I'm sorry, the answer is no."

He shook his head. "That answer will only cause you grief later. You don't know enough about me to make the correct decision."

"I trust my instincts," I said.

His blue eyes held mine captive. "If you marry me, I will make all your dreams come true."

I squinted at him. How could he know what my dreams

318

were? I didn't even know. "Not sure that's possible. Thanks anyway."

"I'm serious, Tish. Whatever it is you want, just ask. I'll get it for you."

"Legally?"

"Just ask."

I sighed. "You're a really great guy, David. You're not the type that should have to bribe someone to marry him. Why does it have to be me? What about Tammy?"

He leaned forward and touched my hands. "It's you I love. Since the first day I saw you. I'm not bribing you. I just want to be with you."

Thankfully, I wasn't born yesterday. Had I been a notch more naive, I would have fallen into his arms, swooning. "Come on," I said. "I dumped my salad all over the vestibule that day. My hair was a mass of frizz. How could you have fallen in love with that?"

"You don't see yourself the way the rest of the world does, do you?"

"I don't?"

"You're everything beautiful and lovely and pure. There's not a blemish on your heart or in your soul. You're radiant. Vivacious. You're even quite funny. Believe me, you are like a fresh spring morning compared to what I've lived with."

"Wow. Thank you." I could take another forty years of compliments like that.

I snapped out of it as Sam arrived with the Coney dogs and drinks. She set them down without fanfare and left without a word.

I looked down at the hot dog mounded with chili and

cheese. Today it looked and smelled greasy, ruined by the stomach-twisting table conversation.

"Aren't you going to eat?" David asked, digging in without reservation.

"Mmm. Uh-huh." I picked at a bean with my fork.

"So what is it you want, Tish? What gets you out of bed in the morning?"

I twirled my fork and collected cheese and onions. "I guess the Victorian. Knowing all the stuff that has to be done before she's top-notch and ready for sale."

"What if I could help you get your asking price for the house? What if I could help you get all your inspections passed and a great appraisal too?"

"I just have to do the work, David. There's really no way around it."

"Open your mind, Tish. Imagine cashing out of that house with triple your investment. You could go back to college, or quit working altogether and have a family. You could start your own business or become a cable show host. What would you do?"

"I've never really given my life that much thought." I stirred my diet drink. "It's not as if I have a road map for the future. You know, first complete my current home, then move on to Such-and-Such City, then run for president. I have plans for the Victorian and that's it. Come May, I'll rent some furniture. Then I'll start looking for my next project."

It wasn't about personal goals and stepping up some ladder of life. It was about eating and having a roof over my head for the next year, without having to be a corporate slave or working with people who were perverts, or demeaning, or had no manners. Maybe I didn't think highly of myself in some areas. But I required dignity in my life. And the best way to accomplish that was to be alone. I never wanted to treat anyone the way my grandmother had treated Grandpa. And I never wanted to feel subhuman again. I couldn't control what anyone else did, but by golly, I could control myself and my actions.

"David, I don't want to marry you. That's just how it is." How could he misinterpret that?

David chewed and swallowed. "After your foray into my garage this morning, you need to reconsider that answer." He paused.

Not bribes, threats. I got the picture.

"We can be a team, Tish. As your husband, I can apply for citizenship. I can get out from under corporate sponsorship. And I can go after some of my dreams."

"Why didn't you do all that with Rebecca?"

"She divorced me before I was eligible to apply. Without a corporation backing my green card and an American wife, I have to leave the country. Don't make me go, Tish. We'll have a wonderful life together, I promise."

And if I didn't marry him? I shuddered, picturing a cold, damp grave next to Rebecca's.

I had to admit, however, that David made a convincing liar. If I hadn't stumbled across the documents on his desk and out in his garage, I'd have almost been persuaded that he did love me.

"Hello, Tish." I looked up to see Officer Brad standing next to our booth. My mind played the William Tell Overture. Salvation had arrived.

"Brad. Hi. Sit down. There's plenty of room." I scooted

over to the wall. Brad sank into the seat next to me, his broad form taking up most of my elbow space.

"I hope I'm not interrupting anything." Brad gave David a showdown stare.

"Not at all," David said, dabbing his lips with a white paper napkin.

"Great. So, Tish, how's the renovation coming?" Brad snared my eyes.

"Not as fast as I'd hoped," I said, forgetting everyone but Brad. "I'm working on the rec room idea again. I'm hoping to get around the system by filling the slot on the Historical Committee."

"Do you think that's a good idea before your trial?" Brad asked. "Kind of cements your motive for killing Dietz."

"For allegedly killing Dietz," I said.

"You know what I mean. A jury is going to see motive and opportunity. Whether or not a murder weapon is recovered, they'll put you away on circumstantial."

I flicked my eyes toward David, hoping Brad would get the hint that the killer was sitting in the booth across from us. "I'm working on that," I said. "I'm convinced the real murderer will be captured before I'm in danger of being convicted."

"Really," Brad said. "Do you think the person is going to step forward and admit guilt? Sounds a little too convenient. I don't think you understand the gravity of your position."

"Oh, believe me, I understand. I've been there and done that prison thing. And I don't intend to show up for a repeat performance." I glared at David.

David cleared his throat. "I agree with Brad," he said

322

softly from his place across the table. "You may not have a choice."

"I'm sure you'll do the right thing," Brad said, sliding out of the booth.

Don't go, I screamed in my mind. I reached out my hand, but he walked away without even a backward glance.

Now I was alone again with the man who held my life in his hands.

"Perhaps I can help you, Tish." David had a hint of a smile. "If I can make your murder charges go away, what would you give in exchange?"

Great. He'd figured out what made me tick. And he was right. I'd do practically anything to avoid prison again.

"I'm not guilty. I don't have to bargain with you."

"Tish." He slid his hand across the table and covered mine. "You're looking at me like I'm the enemy. I can help you. You get what you want, I get what I want, then we can get on with life . . . together."

I jerked my hand away. "You'll be getting on with your life, alright. Behind bars." I leaned across the table and bared my teeth at him. Drool dribbled down the side of my mouth. I wiped it with the back of my hand. "You can't get away with murder. As soon as I find Rebecca, you are going down."

"Just pray Rebecca doesn't find you first," David said with a smirk.

42

I strode out of the restaurant and into the parking lot. I slammed Deucey's door, steaming mad at myself for tipping my hand to David. I felt like a walking, talking dead woman.

"Stupid." I slammed my fists on the steering wheel. I didn't even own a gun. I didn't even believe in guns. But if I did, I'd probably sleep better. I couldn't imagine getting even one wink now.

I backed out and maneuvered my yacht out onto the main drag. I gunned it, hitting the speed limit right about the time the light changed to red.

I braked and rocked to a stop. What I'd give for a new vehicle.

"Sorry, Gram. I didn't mean it," I whispered toward the clouds.

A red car pulled to a stop behind me. I couldn't be sure, but it looked a lot like David's. The vehicle seemed to breathe as it hunched in the rearview mirror, waiting for the light to change.

I wasn't about to roll over and die so easily. I spun the wheel and pulled into the right turn lane, cutting in front of oncoming traffic. Tires screeched. Horns sounded.

In my rearview mirror, the red car drove straight through the intersection. I sighed in relief. Still, all I was doing was buying time. I'd have to go home sooner or later. And David knew it.

I accelerated, following the highway that led west of town. The commercial district disappeared, and the terrain changed to frost-covered rolling hills speckled with newer homes.

I drove another five minutes before deciding I made too easy a target. Who could miss my big blue boat amongst the newer, sleeker vehicles? A sign ahead announced the turn to Fish Lake State Park. I veered onto the two-lane, then took the first left.

The gravel road led between two guardrails flanked by swamp. Then came a slight rise, followed by hardwoods skulking twisted and bare in the bleak afternoon. The light dimmed as I drove into the timber. The path wound along the downside of a ridge that in the summer would have brought sighs of amazement. But now, with the landscape coated in the glum grays and browns of early winter, I could only think of the Haunted Forest.

The road narrowed. Deucey took up the entire space allotted for traffic. Hopefully I wouldn't meet someone coming the opposite way.

Just ahead, a two-track, blocked by an iron gate, led off to the right. Intrigued, I pulled the car off the road and shifted into park. The two halves of the gate met in the middle to form an ornate letter T. I strained to see out the passenger-side window, looking for a house beyond the fancy entry. The road wound through the trees, with no house in sight. For a moment I wished I'd be in Rawlings long enough to find out who lived down there. And maybe get a tour of the place.

It seemed like just my kind of home. Iron gates and miles of woods between me and the nearest neighbor.

No sense getting too excited. I popped the car back into drive and pressed the accelerator. Deucey stayed rooted in place. I pressed harder. The engine raced. My rear wheels spun. I felt the car sink.

I shoved the gearshift into park. I opened the driver's door and looked down. Mud everywhere. And I was stuck in it, miles from nowhere.

I patted my jacket pocket and blew a breath of relief. I had my cell phone with me.

I flipped it open, checking for a signal.

No bars appeared on the display.

"Come on." I tapped the phone against the dash. Still nothing.

Great.

At least I was parked in front of the only house for miles.

I stepped into the mud. My shoes made a sucking sound as I struggled around Deucey's front end and over to the gate.

I looked down at my sneakers. Definitely ruined.

I scaled the gate, using the letter T for a foothold. I made it to the other side and set a fast pace for the residence I could only pray was somewhere down the road.

If the sun were shining in my eyes and birds were chirping around me, I could almost imagine I was back at the lake house up north. Mom and I spent summers there on the Silvan Peninsula. It was only an hour's drive from our home in Escanaba. As soon as the snow melted, we'd drive out there and get the place ready for the season. Gram and Gramps had their own little cottage not too far away. We'd get together and do cookouts and swim in the bay.

But when Mom died, everything was sold. And Gram and Gramps bought the place in Walled Lake, about as far from the Silvan Peninsula as you could get. At least our new home had still been on the water. That helped make up for having to leave my friend Anne and my kitty Peanut Butter.

I crunched along the road, wishing I had a hat and scarf to guard against the chill. A gray, glassy surface shone through the trees ahead. I rounded a curve in the road and saw one of the many small lakes that dotted the area. On a bluff overlooking the shore sat a majestic log home. Leaves covered the path to the back door. Probably a sign that no one had been home for quite a while. I knocked anyway. Only the creak of trees answered. I checked the handle. Locked.

The clock on my cell phone read 1:50. I had plenty of time before dark. I could start walking home, and when my phone was back in range, I'd call for help. The temperature hovered right around thirty degrees these days, so I wasn't in danger of freezing. Not for a while, anyway.

I headed up the hill back toward my car. I saw its glossy teal through the gates. Pulled next to it was a silver sports car.

I ran toward the vehicles, waving my arms. As I got closer, I stopped dead in my tracks.

David's other car was a silver sports car.

I dove behind the nearest tree. I couldn't believe it. David had gone back to the house, switched cars, then came out looking for me.

I took in the desolate forest all around. And what better place to dispose of my body?

Crouching on the ground in utter fear didn't do much for my circulation. I started to shiver. I flipped open my cell phone again. Still no signal. And it looked like the battery wouldn't last much longer in this cold.

I headed off into the woods, staying low, scurrying from bush to bush until I couldn't see the cars anymore. Then I picked my way through the underbrush, hoping I was traveling somewhat parallel to the main road. I avoided the few patches of snow that lingered in the deep woods. All the exercise got my heart pumping. Everything but my ears felt toasty warm. I kept my hands in my jacket pockets along the way, playing with Rebecca's fingernail as a motivator to keep moving.

Fifteen minutes or so later, I checked my cell phone again.

No signal and no battery. Looked like I was walking the rest of the way home.

I stayed in the woods until I came to the swamp. I had no choice but to cross on the narrow road. And once I was over, there were mostly open fields for the next several miles back to Rawlings.

About forty-five minutes had passed since I'd seen the sports car up at the gate. David would have figured out that I was nowhere around and left by now.

Still, I listened for sounds of traffic. I heard only the brush of the breeze against tree limbs.

I ventured onto the causeway. Pebbles scattered as I scurried toward the other side. Then out of nowhere, I heard crunching gravel and a revving engine. My heart lurched.

I threw a glance over my shoulder. David's silver sports car was halted at the top of the rise, facing me and gunning its motor. And I was stuck on a ten-foot-wide strip of dirt surrounded by swamp.

Rocks flew behind the wheels as the vehicle blazed toward me.

I froze like a statue of a crazed gargoyle.

The car came at top speed. I could almost picture David smirking behind the tinted windshield.

Seconds before becoming roadkill, I flung myself over the wooden guard posts and into the swamp. The freezing water hit like a million needles piercing into my skin. I stood up in the knee-deep slime and gasped for breath.

I dragged my legs through the murky water toward the woods.

I glanced behind me. The sports car slid to a stop where the paved road began. The engine revved. Then the car sped off toward Rawlings.

43

My teeth chattered as I climbed out of the swamp and up the ridge. David didn't need to stick around to make sure my body was floating in the swamp. He figured with a bath like that, I was as good as dead. Some hunter would find me next year, curled into a ball under a tree somewhere. And with my car parked up the road at the T gate, no one would even be suspicious.

And David would go around humming "Another One Bites the Dust."

My body vibrated with cold. I could feel myself turning blue. I crossed the bridge again, safely this time, shivering in a slow jog. About a half mile south of the intersection, close to the road, sat a white farmhouse.

I set a goal to make it there alive.

Without trees to stop the wind, the cold cut through my clothes. I could barely feel my legs. They seemed to move by some power all their own. My clothing froze into a crusty shell. My lungs filled with molasses.

Not much farther. I was almost there. I couldn't give up.

"Grandma, wake up and take your medicine." I stood next to her bed at the Walled Lake house. Another morning, another round of pills. The woman would never die. I'd been caring for her two years already. The doctors had said six months at the most.

She groaned and opened her eyes. "Tisher, I don't feel so good today."

You haven't felt good for two years, Gram, I wanted to say. "I know," I said. "You'll feel better after you take your pills."

"I never feel better. I just want to die, Tishy."

Then do it, already.

"I know, Gram. It's hard." I held her head up while she swallowed her prescriptions with a sip of water.

"Give me some more of those." She pointed to her painkillers.

I moved the bottle behind a box of tissues on her bedside table. "Nope. It says one in the morning and one at night."

"Give me one more. Then I can go back to sleep."

"You're not going back to sleep. Sit up. I'll bring you a cup of coffee." I propped some pillows behind her and went to the kitchen to make a fresh pot. I held back the tears as I thought about the letter I'd gotten the day before, a friendly reminder from the MSU financial aid department that my scholarship award expired that coming September if it remained unused.

Gee. Thanks for the update.

I brought Gram her coffee along with the morning paper and sat in the chair next to her bed.

"What terrible things happened yesterday, Tish?" she asked.

I opened the paper. The front photo showed a collegian in a cap and gown. It was graduation time again. I folded the paper back up and set it on the nightstand. "Nothing too newsy today, Gram."

"Good. That's the way it should be." She sipped her coffee, spry as ever. "I have a hankering for some chicken paprikash tonight."

"Chicken paprikash it is, Gram." My life revolved around her appetite. I would give her a bath this morning, head to work at the Foodliner for the afternoon shift while a neighbor sat in, then come home with the fixings to make her special request.

And we'd do it all again tomorrow. I looked over at the paper. A corner of it showed a woman's smiling face under the black cap and tassel. It seemed that would never be me. Grandma was still kicking up her heels at life, no matter how bad she grumped about the way she felt. If I hadn't seen the x-rays of her lung cancer myself, I would have thought she was just throwing a hypochondriac tantrum so I wouldn't go back to college and leave her alone. Still, she'd made herself completely helpless. I had no choice but to stay home and care for her. How could I have done otherwise? She'd raised me when my mother died. I owed her everything. And if she wanted to die at home, surrounded by the only family she had left, then who was I to deny her?

I stumbled in a pothole. The ground in front of me came back into focus. I couldn't feel my body as I crawled up the farmhouse steps. I banged on the storm door. The rattle of glass hurt my ears.

A woman answered. Her gray hair was pulled back in a bun. She wore a starched shirtdress. Everything about her reminded me of Aunt Bea. I only hoped her heart ran along the same lines.

"Merciful heavens," she said. From the expression on her face, I knew I must look like Frosty the Snowman standing on her doorstep. She pulled me inside. Next thing I knew, I was in an old-fashioned farmhouse bathroom. The woman twisted the porcelain knobs of a claw-foot tub, then helped me out of my wet clothes.

"You just get yourself thawed out," she said, leaving me alone.

I soaked in hot water, filling the tub with more as the temperature cooled, until the tank was exhausted. Feeling like a boiled jellyfish, I eased up out of the tub. I toweled off and wrapped myself in the terry robe hanging on the back of the door.

I walked out of the bathroom to thank my rescuer. Next to dear Aunt Bea on the stuffy Victorian love seat sat Officer Brad, sipping a cup of tea.

"Mrs. Westerman called in with a report of a half-frozen woman on her porch," Brad said. "I never thought it would be you."

His teacup clinked on the saucer as he set it down. He came to me and put his hands on my shoulders. "Are you okay, Tish?"

My mouth wouldn't cooperate with my brain. My lips

flapped senselessly. Then I burst into tears. Brad held me as I cried. His chest was warm against my face. His hands rubbed my back. His cheek rested on the top of my head.

"It was awful," I said when I could speak. I looked up at him. "I got stuck up on the hill, then David tried to run me over. I jumped off the road and into the swamp so he wouldn't kill me."

Brad gave me a long look. "Tish. Where do you come up with this stuff? Just when I think you're someone who's got her life together, you pull something outrageous."

I stepped away from him, slack jawed. "You think I'm lying? You think I jumped in that swamp just for thrills?"

"When did you say this happened?" Brad asked.

I calculated backward. "A little over an hour ago."

He gave a condescending shake of his head. "David Ramsey couldn't have been chasing you. An officer radioed in his name for a traffic violation earlier today. David was most likely still pulled over during the time you're talking about."

"Maybe you're confused about the time. I know it was David. He was driving that silver hot-rod." I could still see the sports car hunched at the top of the hill, chrome and glass glinting, just before it barreled toward me. "Aren't you going to arrest him? I could have died today."

"I don't know what to tell you. What you're saying sounds a little crazy."

I poked a finger to his chest. "You're the one that's bonkers, here. David murdered Rebecca and buried her in my basement. I can prove it. And now he's trying to kill me." I stared at Brad. His brown eyes were filled with skepticism. "Aren't you going to do anything about it?"

He stood silent. I humphed and shook my head, betrayed. "I can see I'm on my own. Which is just the way I like it." I twirled and retreated to the bathroom.

I stuck my head out. "Mrs. Westerman? Could I have my clothes back, please?"

I locked the door and waited for my garments. In the meantime, I found a blow-dryer and took care of my hair. Brad certainly knew how to make me second-guess myself. I had been so sure the silver sports car had been the one from David's garage. But from what Brad said, it couldn't have been David.

But who else would try to kill me?

I found nail clippers in a drawer and did my toenails while I waited. Mrs. Westerman had tweezers too, so I attacked my eyebrows to pass time.

Fifteen minutes passed. Mrs. Westerman knocked on the door.

"Here are your clothes, dear," she said.

I took my things, still warm from the dryer, and put them on.

Presentable once more, I walked out into the living room.

"Mrs. Westerman, I don't know how to thank you for helping me today." I ignored Brad.

"Win that election, dear. That will be thanks enough," she said.

Brad leaned into my line of vision.

"I was telling Mrs. Westerman about your campaign plan," he said.

"I've always wanted to enclose my front porch," she said, "but the Historical Committee would never approve it. Officer Brad says you don't mind altering historic details in favor of modern living."

I thought about the magnificent front porch that made this farmhouse a classic beauty. I shuddered. I could never allow it to be marred with tacky screens and cheap storms.

"There are some projects that are certainly allowable in historic homes," I said. Removing my cistern was one of them. Enclosing her front porch was not.

"Wonderful. You can look forward to my vote come January." She shook my hand.

"Thank you, again, Mrs. Westerman."

"I'll drive you home, Tish," Brad said.

I clenched my jaw, holding back words that would strand me west of Rawlings.

I followed him outside. I got in the police cruiser and slammed the door. I tuned out the obnoxious chirp of the two-way radio. Brad started the vehicle and shifted into drive.

"Do you want to see where my car is stuck, at least?" I asked as we approached the gravel road that led into the woods.

"Is it up that road?" Brad asked.

I nodded.

"Let me get you home so you can rest. You've been through quite an ordeal. It'll be easier to check out your car and arrange for a tow truck once I know you're safe."

Safe at home. That was an oxymoron. But at least I'd have some time to work in the cistern. If I unearthed

Rebecca, Brad would have to arrest David. The police officer couldn't ignore concrete evidence forever.

Ten minutes later, Brad drove around the back of my place. He walked me up the porch.

"Stay warm. We don't need you getting sick." He touched my arm. "Call me if you have any problems."

I nodded, then went in the house.

I made sure the lights of Brad's squad car were out of sight before I headed down the basement steps.

44

I beat the chisel into the cement with heavy blows of the hammer. A sledge would have made the job easier, but with no car and no time to lose, my mini-version would have to suffice.

Pea-sized chunks of concrete flew toward my face. I blinked and kept pounding.

I was back. Back in Walled Lake. I scrubbed last night's supper off a fry pan and looked out the window at white sails bobbing on the water.

The heat of late July left the grass brown and withered. Still Grandma lived on. And so did I. The scholarship money would dry up in another month, and I faced spending eternity at the Foodliner.

"Tish." Grandma called to me from the bedroom. Her voice sounded weaker lately. "Help me, Tish."

I turned off the faucet and dried my hands.

"Coming, Gram," I said. It was almost time for medications, anyway.

In the bedroom, I bent and kissed her forehead.

She'd wasted away until she made barely a lump under the blankets.

"How are you feeling?" I asked.

Her skin had washed out to a pale gray. "Terrible. I just want to die."

"I know, Gram. It's hard."

"Tishy, give me some more of those pills." She pointed a crooked finger toward her painkillers on the night-stand.

I put the bottle behind the tissue box. "No, Gram, it says two in the morning and two at night." The dose had increased with the pain.

"I know, sweetie, but I hurt bad today."

I rubbed her arm. "I know, Gram. You'll be alright."

"No, Tishy. I don't have much longer. I don't want to feel this way. Just give me one more."

My fingers twitched. What could one more hurt? I hated to see her like this. I wished she could just slip away in her sleep instead of suffering on and on.

"Okay. One more. Just this once." I took out a pill and set it on her tongue. I held a glass of water to her lips and she swallowed the painkiller down.

"You're a good girl, Tisher. Just like your mama."

Wow. The nicest thing Grandmother had ever said to me.

"Thanks, Gram." I fluffed the pillows and smoothed her blanket, sorry that she felt cold even in this heat. Then I went back to my dishes, praying she'd die that night.

The hammer slipped and I hit the back of my thumb.

"Ow." My voice shattered the stillness of the basement.

339

I looked at my hand. A black blister formed under the skin. I sucked on it, waiting for the sting to go away.

After a minute, I grabbed my hammer and chisel and went back to work, picking away at a crack along the surface.

"Tish," Grandma called to me from the bedroom. "Help me, Tish."

"Coming, Gram." I grabbed the pile of whites from the floor and loaded it in the wash machine. I wiped the stifling humidity of late August from my brow. Five days left before classes started. I hadn't enrolled again this year. It was goodbye scholarships. Goodbye college degree. Hello life of menial labor.

I dumped in the laundry soap and turned the dial to start the cycle. I didn't want to go help Gram. I just wanted her to die.

"Tish," Gram called again.

I went into the bedroom. I fluffed her pillows without a word.

"I'm dying, Tish."

"I know, Gram." I swallowed a lump.

"I hurt, Tishy. I want to go home. Give me the rest of those pills."

I picked up the bottle of painkillers and clenched it in my fist. "You already took your pills this morning, Gram."

"Be a good girl, Tish. Open the bottle and give it to me."

"Gram." My voice came in a whisper.

"Tishy. I've lived too long. I hurt too much. Prove you love me and open the bottle." Her hand shook as she reached toward the pills. Her arm dropped exhausted across her chest.

A tear slid down my cheek. Gram had always been a strong woman. She'd handled everything life threw her way. It killed me to see her lying here so frail, so afraid.

I rolled the prescription bottle between my palms. The pills made a tiny *clickity-click* inside.

She lifted her head an inch off the pillow. "Open it and help me take the rest." She fell back, gasping for breath.

I squeezed my eyes shut. Grandma would be out of pain. I could go back to college. All I had to do was open the bottle of pills.

"Your mother would have helped me," she said.

I stared at her. Gram's eyes had lost their shine. Her skin was gray and loose. Her once coiffed hair hung in strings around her face. She couldn't walk, she couldn't use the bathroom by herself, and she couldn't eat without help. She couldn't feel anything but pain.

My mother was a good daughter. She would have been crushed to see Gram this way.

Mom would have twisted the cap and handed Grandma the bottle.

"Tish, don't leave me like this," she pleaded.

The cap turned beneath the pressure of my palm. "Here, Gram."

I set the open bottle in her loose grip.

She fumbled for the drugs. "Put a couple on my tongue, Tishy. Help me."

My fingers longed to obey. "Gram. Don't ask me to do that."

A pill fell out of the bottle and onto her chest. She scratched at her cotton gown with a nail until she could grip the pill between two fingers. She struggled to lift her hand. She set the pill on her tongue.

"Nnnn." Grandma pointed to her water glass.

I hesitated. One extra pill wouldn't hurt. I helped hold up her head. She took a sip.

She groped in the bottle for more pills.

"Stop, Gram. One's enough."

"Your mother wouldn't make me work like this. She'd help me." She shook out three pills at once and managed to get them into her mouth.

My heart wrenched.

Her finger angled toward the water glass. "Nnnn."

I helped her take a drink. A line of water drizzled down the side of her mouth. I wiped it with a corner of the sheet.

"I'm tired, Tish. Help me with the rest."

"Grandma." Tears poured down my cheeks.

"Think of yourself now. Go back to school. Get married. Have children." Her eyes watered. "Help me finish it."

My vision became hazy. The prescription bottle in my hand was all I saw.

I tapped out two tablets and set them on my grandmother's tongue. I held the water glass to her lips as she swallowed the pills down.

A peaceful look came over her face.

I felt a flash of relief, followed immediately by dread.

What had I done?

A minute passed. Grandma's look of serenity was replaced by one of agony. Her body thrashed as she gasped for air.

"Grandma!" I shook her, screaming her name over and over.

What had I done?

White foam dribbled out the side of her mouth. "Gram. Don't die, Gram. I'll get help."

I ran to the phone on the kitchen wall. I punched in 9-1-1.

The operator answered.

"Hurry. My grandmother is dying. She took the whole bottle of pills." My stomach heaved as I listened to Grandma wretch in the next room. "Please hurry. I wanted to stop her. Oh, Lord, I gave them to her. I helped her. I'm so sorry. I'm so sorry." I sobbed into the phone.

The operator said something about staying on the line.

I peeked around the doorframe and watched Grandma. Her legs quivered and her head lolled from side to side.

I covered my mouth in horror. "Grandma, don't die," I whispered. "Please don't die."

The paramedics arrived and hovered around her for ten minutes or so. I heard the words "massive cardiac arrest."

They moved her to a stretcher. One man looked up at me from his place at Grandma's side. He shook his head, then pulled the sheet over Gram's face.

A sound like a wounded animal formed in my throat

and filled the house as the medics carried her body past me and out to a waiting ambulance.

I crouched, sobbing, on the hard concrete of the cistern. I shook my head back and forth and pounded a fist on the ground. "No. No."

But nothing could change what I'd done. I'd thought I was saving my life, getting out from under a burden. But all I'd done was put my life on hold while I paid the price for my impatience. I recalled the looks of disgust on the faces of the jurors as the prosecution played a segment of the 9-1-1 tape again and again. And no matter how many times and ways my attorney asked the question, I couldn't deny that I'd set pills on her tongue and held the water glass to her lips.

Yes. I'd killed my grandmother.

The flashlight dimmed. I looked up at the adjacent window. Night had fallen while I'd been digging up the past. The walls of the cistern were barely visible in the fading light.

I squinted at the job in front of me. I'd made a hole in one section about half a cantaloupe in size.

I picked up my hammer and started chiseling at a loose piece.

It was December by the time everything had been decided. Four months of attorneys and questions and courts. Then came the word that felt like a defibrillator against my chest. "Guilty."

Demonstrators marched outside the courthouse on the day of my sentencing. Posters on long sticks bobbed among the protesters as the cops led me up the marble steps. "Life for a Life," screamed the death penalty proponents. "Grandma-Killer," accused the right-to-lifers.

Maybe they'd been right. Maybe my life was worthless. What had it mattered that the judge had said, "Three years," and slammed down his gavel? I'd given myself a life sentence anyway.

Streaks of dirty white striped my dust-covered fists where tears had fallen. Bloodstained hands. I'd always be guilty of murder. Nothing could make it go away.

Would I ever have the courage to do what Dorothy had suggested? "Get it right with God. Then get on with life," she'd said.

Brad went to church. I could ask him how to get it right with God. Because more than anything, I wanted to get on with my life.

I wanted to live for my grandmother's sake, because she couldn't anymore. Live for my mother's sake, because she missed so much of life herself. And live for my own sake, because even if the dead couldn't be brought back to life, I had to believe that the living could.

I gave the hammer a powerful swing. The head crashed against the chisel and tore up a chunk of concrete the size of a potato.

I moved the piece aside. A faint odor of rotten eggs and old tuna fish wafted from the hole I'd made. I jumped away from the smell, knowing in my gut what it must mean. I crawled for the flashlight, skirting the crevice. I shone the weak beam into the gap. Bile rose in my throat at the sight of raw, white knuckle bones protruding from the hole. Remains of flesh covered the far ends of three visible fingers. And on the third was a ring with a large center diamond surrounded by mini stones.

"Rebecca," I whispered. An electric charge rushed through my body at the sound of her name.

45

My flashlight went out.

No matter. I'd found enough evidence to clear myself of Dietz's murder. With a paper trail just two garages over and a dead body to boot, David would spend the rest of his life behind bars. He certainly couldn't claim a mercy killing in his case.

I heard a creak. I froze in place, listening.

The steps groaned under the weight of an intruder.

My hands turned cold with fear. I crept backward and pressed against the side of the cistern, afraid to be discovered by whoever was now in the cellar with me. Faint shadows shifted on the wall above the cistern as someone passed beneath bare lightbulbs.

Beads of sweat dotted my skin despite the cold stones and frigid air around me. An ache worked its way across my shoulders and down into my legs. Chills shook me. I knew a fever when I felt one. Perhaps my plunge into the swamp earlier today shouldn't have been topped off with a dip in the cistern.

I only hoped the visitor couldn't hear my teeth chattering.

Upstairs, the back door opened and slammed shut.

Feet scuffed against concrete as the basement intruder headed toward the opposite end near the furnace.

Thumps sounded above me and moved across the kitchen floor. The steps creaked as the newcomer joined our basement party. The latest arrival stopped at the bottom of the stairs, perhaps listening.

I tried to hold my breath, but it came in gulps of fear. I squeezed against the cistern. Cold stone jutted into my frame and sucked the last bit of warmth from me. I huddled, shivering.

Footsteps approached my corner.

I wanted to escape, but there was nowhere to run.

I heard breathing. Just beyond the cistern wall.

A shoe took a foothold somewhere on the opposite side. A shadow appeared above the ledge, then the silhouette of a man's head.

I gasped.

The man jerked his head in my direction. It was David.

"Tish?"

My heart fired cannons in my ears. I'd hoped to be invisible despite the pale wash of lightbulbs.

"What are you doing in there?" His proper British accent made him seem so harmless.

"Don't come any closer." My voice came out machine gun fashion as I battled the chills.

"My word. Are you all right?" he asked.

What a pretender. What a liar. What a greedy, murderous jerk. I couldn't believe I'd actually fallen for him. Talk about a poor judge of character.

"I found her, David. I found Rebecca."

He mumbled an oath under his breath. "How bad are you hurt? Here, give me your hand. I'll help you."

He reached toward me.

I shrank back. "Don't come any closer."

"Hurry, Tish. Let me help you out of there before she comes back."

"Before who comes back?"

"Rebecca. You said you found her."

"I did. She's buried in here. As if you didn't know." I spat the words at him.

He glanced around the blackness of the cistern.

"Unless you're a magician, I'm quite certain Rebecca is not buried in there. As much as I wish she were. Now give me your hand, or I'll have to come in and get you."

"Don't you smell that?" The foul odor permeated the bottom of the cistern. "You think I don't know who that is? You buried her with her wedding ring on, you heartless creep."

His hand reached toward me once more.

"Don't touch me." I tried to back away, but my muscles felt like rigor mortis had set in.

"I'm here to help you, Tish. Give me your hand."

I couldn't see his face with the only light in the basement coming from behind him. He sounded sincere, but I had to admit, he was an excellent liar. Rebecca lay dead beneath my feet. And the only way David could get me to trust him was to pretend she was still alive.

I wasn't about to fall for it. "I don't believe you."

"Tish, please. We're running out of time. You know a little more about her business than she's willing to tolerate. I can't say what she'll do to you when she comes back."

"If you care so much about helping me, how come you tried to kill me this afternoon?"

Silence.

His voice sounded too smooth to be trusted. "I had no idea. What happened?"

A round of chills shook me. "You tried running me over with your flashy sports car, and I jumped in the swamp. Duh."

He looked off to one side. "Rebecca." David's voice took on a pleading tone. "I've got enough guilt that you're involved in the whole mess as it is. Don't make it harder on me. Give me your hand so we can get out of here."

My hammer was more than arm's reach away somewhere in dark. I couldn't make a grab for it without putting David on the alert. And for all I knew, he was holding a gun. My best hope was to negotiate my way out of the cistern.

"Leave town, David. Just go away. I promise I won't tell about Rebecca. I'll cover for you." I tried to keep my voice calm and steady, but it didn't take a polygraph to tell I was lying.

"I wish I could take your advice," he said. "But I'm turning over a new leaf. After everything you know about me, I'm sure it's hard to imagine that I really love you, but I do." He paused, hanging his head. "But timing was off by about five years and one marriage. And by trying to force things to go my way, I created a monster.

"As soon as Rebecca got wind of the divorce papers, she was back in Michigan, staying at the house, threatening to turn me over to the authorities if I didn't withdraw my petition. My crimes add up to twenty-five years or more. She loves to hold that over my head."

I thought of the twenty-five red roses David had given me, and the morbid card I'd found to go with them. David didn't seem deranged enough to create such an elaborate charade. And yet, if he were capable of murder . . .

"I'm sorry, Tish," David said. "I know I led you to believe Rebecca was the one to file for the divorce."

"Why didn't Rebecca want a divorce? She's been gone a year, hasn't she?" I asked, hoping to shed light on his diabolical thought patterns.

"As long as we're married, she figures she can control me, even from across the country. But Michigan is a no-fault state. She can't stop the divorce process once it's started. Only I can. I'd risk prison, deportation, and even death to be free of her."

So, David had filed for divorce and pretended Rebecca had been the one to file. Probably hoping I'd be a sucker for his puppy-dog eyes.

I'd fallen right into his net.

"Rebecca really can't turn me in to the authorities without implicating herself," he said. "And the penalty for her crimes adds up to far more than twenty-five years."

There was a shuffle and a shadow behind David. Then from nowhere, an object hit the side of his head with a sickening crunch.

46

I screamed.

David's silhouette disappeared from above the ledge. I heard muffled thumps as his body settled against the floor on the other side of the cistern wall.

Then came hard breathing. But not from David. Some shriller quality to the sound made me think of a woman.

"Tish," a voice said in barely a whisper.

Chills attacked me.

The sound of scuffing on stones. A face appeared above the cistern. Wisps of blonde hair shone golden in the pale light.

"Tish is what they call you, isn't it?" The alluring voice was unfamiliar.

I squinted to see the face, but couldn't make it out in the dim light.

"We haven't met," the speaker said, "but we're practically neighbors. I used to live around here."

I thought about Jack's insistence that the woman who used to live here entered the house with Dietz the night of his murder. Perhaps this was the woman he'd been thinking of.

And from the confident toss of her head and the evil dripping in her voice, I could only conclude that she was the illustrious Rebecca Ramsey.

But if Rebecca really was still alive, then who was buried at my feet?

"Sorry you had to see that." Rebecca hefted a spade and laid it along the top ledge. She set a flashlight next to it.

I squeezed back a bout of guilt. David had tried to warn me about his power-hungry wife. Now he was dead because I hadn't believed him. The fatalities that could be in some way attributed to me had grown to outrageous proportions.

But I'd have time to wallow in self-pity later. Figuring out how to escape the cistern alive was the immediate issue.

I rubbed my arms in an attempt to thaw my muscles. If I could move, I could reach the hammer. Then I'd have a fighting chance against this lunatic.

Rebecca hoisted herself onto the ledge and sat there. Her legs dangled into the cistern. She rested one hand on the shovel. With the other, she picked up her flashlight and shone it in my face.

I squinted and held up a hand against the light.

"My, my," she said. "You really do look like Sandra Jones. How ironic."

She flashed the light at the bottom of the cistern. The exposed diamond cast glimmering beams on the stones of the tomb. I glimpsed the hammer, close to the cistern wall, between my captor and me.

"I see you and Sandra have already met." Rebecca pointed the light back in my direction. "How did you know she was under there?"

I shrugged. "A hunch, I guess." No sense giving away my own shaky sanity. It was all my imagination, wasn't it, brought on by a guilty conscience, finally cleansed?

Rebecca kicked her legs casually against the cistern wall. "Too bad David had to end up pulling a 'Sandra.' Guess religion does that to people."

"I don't know what you mean." My body vibrated with cold.

"Sandra was my right-hand woman. You could almost say she made me what I am today. She taught me everything I know about schmoozing the system. And with David's help manipulating computer records and manufacturing endorsements, I built a dream life for myself. You should see my penthouse in L.A. And if you think that silver Corvette is something, you'd love my new Jaguar."

"Sounds like you didn't have much to do with your own success." I made a show of sitting on my bottom, nonchalantly extending both legs toward the hammer.

"Behind every great woman there are a few dead bodies. It's the only way past the glass ceiling." Rebecca let go of the spade and flipped her hair back. "I wish it didn't have to be that way. But when people know your intimate secrets, they have to be able to keep them for life. That holy roller stuff doesn't have a place in the real world. You want to suddenly get a social conscience, then you better be ready to die for it."

Rebecca directed the light across Sandra's grave. "Anyway, she asked for it. I warned her not to ruin my life. I worked hard to get where I am, and no backbiting wench gets in the way of my plans." She laid the flashlight across the ledge and gripped the shovel. Her knuckles shone white. "It was her choice. She could have just played along. But she had to try breaking it off. Then she threatened to turn me in."

With a leap, Rebecca was in the cistern. She crouched low and threatening. The handle of the spade twirled in her hands. Metal flashed in the light.

"If Sandra could have kept her mouth shut a little longer, maybe she could have had a proper funeral, instead of being buried under cement in a hole in the basement."

Rebecca lifted the shovel over her head and smashed it on the concrete. Sparks flew from the impact.

I screamed and jumped, imagining Sandra's head directly beneath the blade. My ears rang in advance when I thought about that shovel against my own head. I felt the hammer beneath my shoe. I inched it toward my hands, all while cowering in utter fear.

"Casey was smart. She kept quiet about everything Sandra told her, so she got the nice, quiet death. Martin wasn't so smart. Not to mention my idiot husband."

"How did Martin cross you?" I might as well keep her occupied while I planned my attack.

"Greed was Martin's tragic flaw. He tried to blackmail me. So I simply said I knew where Sandra's diamonds were. I led him down here, and the rest is history."

"And you poisoned Casey?"

"It was easy. I injected small doses of arsenic right into her jugs of supposedly pure water. It's in your water now too. I thought I'd be nice and let you go just as quietly. Too bad you couldn't mind your own business."

My fingers touched cold metal. I gripped the hammer in my hand.

With a shriek, Rebecca took a step and swung the spade. I leaped forward and slashed at her shin with the hammer. Her shovel hit the rocks where my head had been, echoing through the basement along with her cries of pain.

Rebecca fell backward. She leaned against the shovel and stood. I twirled, wound up, and threw the hammer at her face. She dodged the weak throw and bad aim with hardly any effort. I reached for the abandoned chisel next to me and clenched it in my hand.

Rebecca came at me. Her shovel looked like a spear aimed at my heart. I rolled to the side. The blade hit the wall, driving the handle into Rebecca's stomach.

She grunted and came at me again. I spun away at the last second, avoiding her crashing blow.

The cistern grew foggy. The fever took its toll. I didn't know how long I could avoid the inevitable. It would be so easy just to give up and let her finish things. What did it matter, anyway? No one would even miss me.

On instinct, I jerked to the left. My ears rang from the sound of metal on cement. That one had been close. I dug deep for the strength to keep fighting.

Rebecca lifted the shovel. While it hung in the air, I attacked. Momentum took us both to the ground. I heard a dull *thunk* as I landed on top of her on the hard concrete. I scrambled to pin her arms beneath my knees, a move I'd learned in prison. I held the chisel over her head, ready to plunge it into her neck if necessary.

But Rebecca never moved. A wet patch formed beneath her head.

I gulped in deep breaths, half crying, half laughing. The cistern grew gray with fog. I slid off Rebecca and onto the concrete floor. I curled into a ball and thanked God I was still alive.

47

I woke in my cot with a pounding headache. Winter sun poured gray into my meager master suite. I must have passed out in the cellar. Apparently someone found me and put me to bed.

I sat up. Throbbing blasted my ears. My cell phone danced on the wood planks as if it had a life of its own. The whole house vibrated. At first I thought the din came from an approaching train. But as the cobwebs cleared, I realized a jackhammer pummeled the concrete one floor below.

I rolled over and covered my head. They were digging up Sandra.

Memories of the night in the cellar engulfed me. I didn't yet have the strength to look back. Pain knifed through me at even a vague recollection.

The knot in my throat gave way to tears.

I must have cried myself back to sleep. The next time I woke up, I felt refreshed. The reverberation of the jackhammer was gone from both the basement and my mind.

Off in the kitchen, a spoon clanked against a pan. I

smiled. My neighbor Dorothy must be fixing me break-fast. My stomach gurgled at the thought of food. I couldn't wait to get some nutrients into my system. The fever had left me weak and groggy. It would probably be a day or two before I was back to myself.

I sighed. A day or two before I could get back to the business at hand, renovating the Victorian.

I thought about the months of work ahead of me, and waited for that swell of anticipation I always got midway through a project. The feeling never came.

Today something inside me felt different. Did it really matter if I gave the house a total facelift? It was kind of homey just the way it was. Maybe there didn't have to be a master suite on the first floor with a whirlpool tub and walk-in closet. Maybe the bedrooms and bathroom upstairs were sufficient for some mom, dad, and kids. And as far as a rec room in the basement went, why not let someone who actually planned on living here decide what to do? Maybe a new owner would rather have storage down in the basement. I'd gotten a good start fixing this old place up. Someone else could take it from here. I definitely needed some time off. I needed a place to heal. Not Cancun, but someplace that felt more like home.

I swung my legs over the edge of the cot. I was wearing my oversized tee-and-shorts pajamas. I must have been pretty dead to the world if I couldn't even remember changing my clothes.

I stood up, shaky and light-headed. I slipped a sweat-shirt and sweatpants over my sleeping gear and walked to the kitchen.

I leaned against the doorway and shook my head in surprise. Brad stood in front of the stove, stirring some concoction. He bent over the pot in concentration. A red-and-white checked apron protected his jeans and heather sweatshirt.

"No, you don't," he said to the contents. The brew sizzled over onto the burner and sent up a cloud of steam accompanied by the salty smell of burnt chicken broth.

I giggled to see the oversized man hunkered over the rebellious blend.

Brad turned my way and straightened. "Welcome back, Sleeping Beauty."

"Hey, thanks. What's cooking? I'm starved."

"I bet you are. I've got some homemade chicken noodle soup for you."

"Did you make it, or did Dorothy?"

"I'm insulted. It's my own recipe."

"Is it safe to eat or should I have my Tums on standby?" I asked.

"I see you're back to your old self." He tapped his spoon on the edge of the pan.

"You're right. I'm sorry." I hung my head. "I'm trying to turn over a new leaf." Those were the same words David had used . . .

I pictured the spade meeting the side of his head, the sickening clunk at contact, and the thud of his body landing on concrete. I bent over double, sick from the vision.

Brad raced to my side. "What's wrong? Here, sit down." He helped me to the floor.

Sobs wracked my body as I let the memories come. Brad sat alongside me and let me use his shoulder for a Kleenex. He smoothed my hair, calming me. After a few minutes, I caught my breath. Then I asked the question I'd been dreading.

"Is David dead?"

Brad rested his hands on his lap. "He's got a nasty concussion, but he's still kicking."

I nodded my head, relieved.

Brad tapped his thumbs together and continued. "David's looking at deportation after he serves a reduced sentence for helping convict Rebecca. He can place her at the scene of the crime the night of Sandra's murder. He even kept the shirt Rebecca was wearing when she killed Sandra. Fished it out of the trash for a time like this. With bloodstains and dried concrete all over the fabric, I'd say Rebecca is going to spend a long time behind bars."

I remembered the dark puddle beneath Rebecca's head in the cistern. "So Rebecca's going to be okay?"

He leaned his head back against the cabinet. "She's in custody at St. Joe's Hospital. Cracked her skull pretty good, but she'll recover."

I guess I was glad she was still alive. She'd have gotten off the hook too easily if she had died. This way, she'd have lots of time to think about her crimes.

But that would be years of reform and reflection down the road. I should know.

I caught Brad's eyes. "I guess I passed out. Who found me?"

"Jack. He was prowling around the basement window

again. He saw you and Rebecca going at it with a shovel, and he ran to get me." He nudged my shoulder with his. "And it's a good thing he did. If you'd have laid there on the concrete much longer, you'd have been dead from fever."

"Yeah." I felt my forehead. "It cleared up pretty quick, though. I feel great today."

"You've been zoning in and out of sleep for nearly three days. No wonder you feel better."

"I was out for three days?"

"Completely zonked. Dorothy, Tammy, and I took turns keeping watch over you."

I grabbed his arm. "How's Tammy doing? Last time I saw her, she was on the verge of making a big mistake."

"Everything's okay. She's back on track. And she's giving you credit for helping her figure things out. David thanks you as well. You're a bigger influence around here than you realize."

It was nice to imagine I could be an influence of any kind, especially a good one.

Still, Brad's words brought a tweak of sadness. I knew I couldn't stay in Rawlings. Things hadn't gone according to plan. But more than that, I felt a restlessness.

My cue to move on.

"And Sandra?" I asked.

"She's tucked in safe down at Lakeside Cemetery. There's a memorial service for her tomorrow, if you're up for it."

"Yeah. I wouldn't miss it." I paused, thinking. "Hey. Do you happen to know if she was wearing both shoes when they found her?"

"As a matter of fact, she was only wearing one. They found the other shoe, along with the murder weapon, behind the museum garage. How did you know about the shoe?"

I shrugged. "Would you believe me if I said x-ray vision? Anyway, I'm just glad Sandra will have a proper burial."

I owed Sandra a huge debt. I felt free for the first time in my life. Free of my past, free of guilt, free to accept God's love. I was only sorry it took her death to bring about something that should have been obvious all along. I snuggled against Brad's shoulder, recording the moment for future reflection. My heart would have a rough time letting go of his always-there-for-me brand of friendship. And I knew I could lean on Tammy and Dorothy too, as I mopped up my latest mess. Loving David had certainly taken its toll. I'd put my heart on the line and ended up getting soaked. Only time could wring out my disappointment.

I angled my head toward Brad's cheek. "How about taking me to church with you Sunday? I'm up for a new adventure."

Brad drew in a deep breath. His arm looped across the back of my neck. "Tish. I'm so glad you're safe." His mouth nuzzled my hair. "You know I love you, don't you?"

His words burned.

I pivoted until I was facing him on the floor. I looked into his eyes. They crinkled in the corners when he smiled. But he wasn't smiling now.

I swallowed. "Brad. I'm sorry. I just . . . you know,

now just isn't a good time." My voice died for lack of better words.

He pulled me close until my head rested against his chest. "Well, even if you don't love me, you can't stop me from loving you."

I smiled into the warmth of his body. "Love me if you must. But I can't give anything back right now."

"I know." He took me by the arms and held me where he could see me. "But I'll be waiting for the day you can. After all, you're the first woman to accept my invitation."

That Sunday I walked through the door of the Rawlings Community Church. No thunder rumbled. No lightning bolted across the sky. Instead I felt a sense of belonging as hands reached out in greeting.

Sam Walters dashed from her place in the band and almost knocked me over with her hug. "Tish! I'm so glad to see you!"

I laughed with pure joy over her exuberant greeting. "Your brother finally broke me down. So here I am."

I squeezed into a soft-cushioned pew next to Brad. At least a hundred lively people, many with children, filled the sanctuary. It certainly differed from the stiff, formal church of my upbringing. The pastor even gave a children's sermon.

"When you've done something wrong, what do you want to do?" the pastor asked.

"Hide," said a young boy.

The congregation chuckled.

The pastor continued, smiling. "You want to hide because you are afraid of getting punished. And because your parents love you, they put you in time-out. It's your mom and dad's job to make sure you learn right from wrong. But God's job isn't to punish you. His job is to love you. Never be afraid to go to God and tell Him what you did. He will help you do the right thing the next time because you were brave and came to Him. Remember that God always loves you no matter what."

I struggled for self-control. Wasn't that my story? I'd done wrong and was afraid to tell God. The court had been my parent and given me time-out. But God had never stopped loving me through any of it. Sadly, I'd only punished myself more by pushing Him away in shame. But He'd always loved me. He still loved me, no matter what.

Through watering eyes, I could barely make out little-kid bodies going back to their seats. I put a hand to my temple, pretending to rub at a headache, and coughed to disguise my sniffles.

After the service, Sam's band buddies joined Brad and me for a Coney Deluxe. I laughed more than I had in years. But behind the smile was an ache. Rawlings would never be more than a pit stop as I ambled through life.

February arrived before I got all my loose ends tied up and was ready to pass the keys to the Victorian back to Rick Hershel. Feeling something like reverse déjà vu, I signed the seller's papers, putting the Victorian back in Rick's hands. I hated to contribute to his obsession, but with the profit from the sale, combined with my returned bail money, I had enough for a hefty down payment on my next place. He'd made a good offer for the Victorian, considering the improvements I hadn't gotten around to making. Guess he loved the house more than anything. But I wasn't about to mention that to his new wife, who'd forked over 50 percent of the down payment.

From what Dorothy told me, Rick's ex had moved back to her hometown in Ohio. She was happily living in her maintenance-free condo on the golf course, and glad to be back from her yearlong trip to Uganda. She'd apologized for not writing sooner, but she couldn't find the time with all the demands placed on the medical team she'd headed up in Africa.

Twenty-four hours after signing the papers, I was packed and ready to depart. I looked at the clock on the dash of my new SUV. Time to go if I was going to make it to my destination today.

I put the Explorer in reverse and backed out of the garage. Over my shoulder, I took my last look at the rear of the Victorian. The siding had never gotten that paint job I'd envisioned. The house still looked as haunted as it had the day I'd arrived in Rawlings.

But I knew the inside had been cleaned and painted. I'd left a blank slate, the perfect canvas for all the great ideas the new owners could come up with.

A fist pounded on the hood. I turned to look ahead. Brad stood in front of the Explorer, hands on hips, as if daring me to run him over.

I rolled down the window. "What are you doing?"

He came around my side of the car. "Tish. Don't leave. Give it another day."

I stared at him. Tears threatened to roll. I blinked them back.

"Hey." I touched his cheek with my finger. "I want to get there tonight."

"C'mon. You know what the forecast says. Wait until tomorrow." Maybe his eyes gleamed brighter than usual, but not from tears. Couldn't be from tears.

"Brad." His name came out a whisper. "I'm going. Don't try to talk me out of it."

He held my eyes captive for a moment. Then he leaned in the window and touched his lips to mine. I closed my eyes. I treasured the warmth of his breath, the softness of his skin. Maybe I could stay in Rawlings. Brad and I could work things out. I didn't have to go digging up the past anymore. I could let it lie, embrace the future, never look back . . .

Brad pulled away, his eyes searching mine.

"I have to go," I said. Off in the distance came the sound of a whistle. I put the car in drive, hoping to beat the train.

I steered past a classic teal Buick, parked at the museum next door. The old curator waved to me from the front porch. I stopped and rolled down the passenger window.

"Take good care of Deucey or Grandmother will haunt you," I said with a smile.

"I've been looking for a new girlfriend. Your grandmother still available?"

I laughed and waved.

I turned left onto Main Street.

I crossed the railroad ties with barely a tremor.

"Goodbye, Rawlings," I whispered as I accelerated and headed north, toward the Upper Peninsula, my childhood home. There I'd rest and relax and recover from the months and years of tragedy that had bombarded my life. No more bodies in the basement. No more power-hungry, murderous ex-wives. Just peace and quiet and fresh air.

And maybe, after a while, I'd even forget the brown-eyed man who loved me.

Acknowledgments

Thank you:

To the women of ACFW Critique Group 15 for your honesty and encouragement.

To Janet Kobobel Grant for choosing my entry for "Kill Me If You Can" as Best of Show at the 2004 ACFW Conference. What a blessing that has become!

To family and friends who encouraged my writing habit and stood by me through tough years.

and

To God who makes all things possible.

A Sneak Peek

BOOK 2
Kill Me If You Can

A PATRICIA AMBLE MYSTERY

1

Who said you can never go home again?

What a bunch of hooey.

I was home. Again.

And while perhaps not a single soul that passed me tonight on the frozen highway would recognize me, I still knew where to find home: Number 3 Valentine's Lane, a dilapidated log cabin in the middle of a cedar woodland squashed between the creek and the bay.

Yeah. I knew where I was going.

Now I just had to figure out where I came from.

I squinted through swirling snowflakes and squeaking wipers to see the turn ahead. I barely missed the bank of white made by the plow as I maneuvered my Explorer onto the narrow two-track that led a half mile down to the house.

Around the final curve, the porch light blazed a welcome through the storm. The realtor must have left it on for me. She'd hated to hear I was driving up in the worst blizzard of the year, but obviously had faith enough that I'd arrive safely.

I pulled into the driveway, which already had several

inches of new snow since the plow had last been here, and turned off the engine.

Silence. A balm to my nerves.

My boots crunched in the drifts as I walked around to unload my suitcase and sleeping bag. How many times had I done this very same thing in the past? Pull up to the new home, take out the suitcase, bring in the sleeping bag and cot . . .

I did a quick calculation. This would be my fifth renovation project. The last one had just about ended my career. The spooky old Victorian had been home to a body buried in the basement. Finding the corpse had almost been too much for me. But God knew not to give me more than I could handle, and I finished the project unscathed—physically and mentally, at least.

But as for my heart . . .

I slammed the hatch closed. It didn't merit a trip down memory lane.

Better to keep my mind here in the present, down Valentine's Lane, and the project ahead of me.

And if the front porch were any indication, I'd have plenty of work come spring. The boards bounced as I walked to the door. The thin layer of ice covering them crackled into spidery veins.

The realtor had warned me not to buy anything sight unseen. But I had seen it—twenty-six years ago. How much could it have changed? It still felt like yesterday that I'd run around in these woods and swam at the sandy beach out front. I knew when I called Northern Realty a few months back and found out this very cottage was for sale, the one I'd spent my summers in as a kid, that

God had made it all possible. I knew He meant for me to come here. To come home.

I put my hand on the doorknob and paused, hoping the agent hadn't let me down. When I'd asked her how I'd get in the house tonight, she'd laughed.

"Nobody up here locks their doors. I'll leave the keys on the table for you, if you think you'll need them."

"Up here" was the Silvan Peninsula, a stretch of land that stuck down into Lake Michigan in the state's dislocated top half. On one side of the narrow strip were the unpredictable waters of the big lake; on the other, the calm, sheltered shores of Nocquette Bay. I'd survived the cities and towns of lower Michigan, now I'd discover if I could hack the wintry weather and isolation of Michigan's Upper Peninsula, or the U.P. as the natives called it.

The door swung open into the kitchen and I flicked on the overhead light. The room looked so . . . small. I hadn't realized how a place could shrink in a little over two decades. But, I guess I wasn't a scrawny seven-year-old anymore. Tonight, the red-and-gold-speckled '50s countertops reached my hips instead of my chin. And if I put my hand up, I could almost touch the white asbestos ceiling tiles. Back then, I'd had to climb on a stool piled with books to retrieve my stuck gum.

Still, everything was as I remembered: tacky beyond compare.

I dropped my gear by the door and walked through to the great room. I hit the switch, but nothing happened, the fault of either ancient wiring or burned-out bulbs.

The light from the kitchen spilled onto the fireplace against the far wall. The massive limestone chimney would probably still be standing long after the rest of the house collapsed around it.

A few pieces of furniture were scattered around the room, left by the previous owners. I sat on a tatty green sofa, and gave a test bounce. The spring beneath me gave a twang. My eyes misted. It was the very couch I'd jumped on as a kid.

Boing, boing, boing . . .

"Patricia Louise Amble," my mother had yelled from the kitchen, "get off that sofa!"

I smiled at the memory and leaned back.

Mom died young and beautiful. While I only remember the smiles and fun, there were apparently dark times that she kept from me. I was later told that when my father left her, Mom changed. Gone were the carefree days of youth. She was single and had a child to support. She was alone and afraid. And without a church upbringing, she had no Jesus. No one on whom to lay her burdens.

Before the summer of my eighth year, she was dead, entangled with the metal of her Ford pickup at the bottom of Mead Quarry. A cry for help that was never heard, until it was too late.

I wiped at a tear that trickled down one cheek. I used to be angry when I thought how Mom abandoned me. I considered suicide to be an act of pure selfishness. Then time passed, and suddenly the tables were turned as I found myself recovering from another act of suicide, but this one done out of selfless love.

Either way, whether from being a martyr to oneself or to others, suicide made a cruel tonic for those left behind.

Now that I was thirty-three, six years older than my mother had been when she'd killed herself, I had a little more understanding of the trials of life. How they can beat you down and poison you. How they can make you weary and fill you with despair. The little twists and turns I encountered on my narrow road often threatened to plunge me into my own abyss of hopelessness. It gave me compassion for my mother. It made me yearn to travel back in time and tell her of my one salvation, my one hope.

I stood up and headed back to the kitchen. The past had drifted up and captured me again. But wasn't that what I was here for? To discover my past? To discover my mother? Her loves, her hates, her favorite color, her shoe size?

Only after the death of my grandmother, who'd raised me from the age of eight, could I even entertain the thought of looking into the past. As long as Grandmother had been alive, she'd discouraged probing questions. It must have been like a knife in her heart the night she'd gotten the call that my mother was dead. Even years later, she couldn't talk about Mom except with vague descriptions and scattered details that left an incomplete picture of the woman who'd birthed me.

I might be off to a late start, but I wanted to know my mother. I wanted to know everything about her. Her life held the key to crates of unanswered questions that cluttered my mind and kept me locked in limbo. How could I love someone else, commit to someone else, if I didn't know diddly about myself or my heritage?

I grabbed my gear and climbed the staircase to the second-story balcony. From here I could look down into the great room. Tomorrow, I'd be able to gaze out the high picture windows and see across the bay to the silo-like tower over in Nahma. But tonight, the blackness was broken only by an occasional swirl of snow against the glass.

I set down my things and leaned against the rail. I almost gave a contented sigh, but I knew better than to alert some watching demon of my inner happiness. Next thing I'd know, all chaos would break out in my life.

Though I held my pensive pose, I was still thanking God in my mind. I couldn't believe I was actually here. As a kid, I'd promised myself that when I grew up, I'd buy this cottage and live in it, and bake pies for the Fourth of July celebration down in Port Silvan, and make lemonade for all the children that would come to swim on Saturdays.

I'd never baked a pie, but I could probably figure out the lemonade. Would I be breaking my promise if I drank it alone?

A yawn, punctuated by a squeak in my throat, sent my thoughts in the direction of bed. Ghosts of the snowflakes I'd battled on the road the past eight hours danced before my eyes. Time for some sleep.

I dragged my stuff into my old bedroom and set it by the door. I flicked on the light and stood in numb surprise. It looked like I wouldn't need my cot after all.

The room was furnished with a twin bed, a table, and a chair. A puffy patchwork quilt was turned back to reveal crisp white sheets and a plush pillow.

Who would have taken time to make up a bed for me? As nice as the realtor was, I couldn't imagine that she'd done it.

A piece of paper was angled on the pillow. Perhaps it was a note from my fairy godmother. I stepped across a braided rug and reached for the page.

My hand jerked back as if slapped. It wasn't a note—it was a photograph. Of my mother. Her high school graduation picture lay torn in two pieces on the pillowcase.

Written in thick black script across her smiling face were the words "DON'T ASK WHY."

Nicole Young resides on the shores of Lake Michigan with her children, cats, and tiny Yorkie. Home renovation is a way of life for the author, whose first project was converting a Victorian in lower Michigan into a thriving bed & breakfast. She returned to Michigan's Upper Peninsula in 2001, where she owns and upkeeps vacation rental homes. Nicole plays fiddle and sings with two local bands, and enjoys horseback riding on the beautiful Garden Peninsula.